P9-DIW-540

ES
SE
NCE

ALSO BY
KIMBERLY DERTING

THE PLEDGE

THE ESSENCE

KIMBERLY DERTING

MARGARET K. McELDERRY BOOKS
NEW YORK LONDON TORONTO SYDNEY NEW DELHI

MARGARET K. McELDERRY BOOKS
An imprint of Simon & Schuster Children's Publishing Division
1230 Avenue of the Americas, New York, New York 10020
This book is a work of fiction. Any references to historical events, real people, or real locales are used fictitiously. Other names, characters, places, and incidents are products of the author's imagination, and any resemblance to actual events or locales or persons, living or dead, is entirely coincidental.

For information about special discounts for bulk purchases, please contact Simon & Schuster Special Sales at 1-866-506-1949 or business@simonandschuster.com.
The Simon & Schuster Speakers Bureau can bring authors to your live event. For more information or to book an event, contact the Simon & Schuster Speakers Bureau at 1-866-248-3049 or visit our website at www.simonspeakers.com.
The text for this book is set in Avenir.
Manufactured in the United States of America
2 4 6 8 10 9 7 5 3 1
Library of Congress Cataloging-in-Publication Data
Derting, Kimberly.
The essence : a Pledge novel / Kimberly Derting.—1st ed.
p. cm.
Summary: Seventeen-year-old Charlaina "Charlie" Hart has defeated the tyrant Queen Sabara and taken control of Ludania, only to have Sabara's soul fuse itself with her own.
ISBN 978-1-4424-4559-8
ISBN 978-1-4424-4561-1 (eBook)
[1. Fantasy. 2. Kings, queens, rulers, etc.—Fiction. 3. Soul—Fiction. 4. Language and languages—Fiction. 5. Social classes—Fiction. 6. Ability—Fiction.] I. Title.
PZ7.D4468Ess 2013
[Fic]—dc23
2012012656

To my Granny, who taught me
that no woman needs to be
what's expected of her. I miss you.

ACKNOWLEDGMENTS

It makes sense to start with the person who gave me my first big break, so I have to thank my agent, Laura Rennert. I've said it before and I'll say it again: You are amazing! And to Taryn Fagerness as well, for being such a brilliant negotiator on foreign soil . . . thank you for taking *The Pledge* to so many countries I've never been.

Closer to home, I'm so fortunate to have such an incredible team at Simon & Schuster, starting with my amazing editor, Ruta Rimas, who, given the chance, would probably have edited this sentence to make it better. Thank you not only for your expert advice, but for being such a great supporter of my books! I'd also like to thank Anna McKean and Chrissy Noh for all their publicity and marketing mojo, and Justin Chanda for allowing me to be a part of the S&S family.

For my incredible covers, I have to thank Ugla Hauksdóttir, whose photography is amazing, and who, fortunately, posted some of her images online for my cover designer to find. To the gorgeous Anna Þóra Alfredsdóttir who makes "Charlie" look not only stunning but fierce on this cover. And to the brilliant Michael McCartney, I can't thank you enough for finding Ugla's images in the first place, and then turning them into the most amazing covers!

I'm also incredibly grateful to Carrie Ryan and Margaret Stohl for their support of *The Pledge*. It means a lot to have the respect of your peers, but it means even more when you can count those people among your friends.

To the Debs, who've continued to be there through the ups and the downs of publication. To Erin Gross for all the work you do on both *The Pledge* and the Body Finder novels' fan sites . . . you rock! To Shelli Johannes Wells for letting me lean on you—and call you almost daily—to vent, brainstorm, and critique my (sketchy) first drafts. To Tammy Everton for helping me with names, even when I need them to be . . . unusual. And to Madeline and Molly, just because I thought it would be fun to put your names in my book.

To all of my friends and neighbors who've come out to support me again and again and again . . . I feel blessed to have you all in my life!

Lastly, I couldn't do any of this without my amazing family. Thank you for being flexible, supportive, loving, and patient. A writer's life can be crazy and unpredictable, and without you, I couldn't do any of it.

PART I

PROLOGUE

He approached respectfully, cautiously. Warily.

She'd always been capricious, his queen. But of late, she was nothing less than unpredictable.

He knew why, of course: the new queen of Ludania.

He waited twenty paces from the throne, as was customary. She would speak first. Until then, his lips remained tightly sealed.

When at last he heard her voice—like the chords of a song, lovely and melodious—he knew her mood. Tolerant. Magnanimous.

Yet he couldn't suppress the trepidation that always quivered in his belly during these brief encounters.

"Come closer," she coaxed, and he found himself drawn toward her in the same way that some animals were drawn toward their brightly colored predators. "I can barely see you all the way back there. And I want so badly to see your face."

He stepped closer, counting his paces in his head so as not to overstep that invisible barrier between respect and indiscretion, all the while allowing himself to fall prey to her seductive tone. "Yes, Your Majesty." When he reached her, he had to quell the urge to bow, a habit he'd only recently developed. One that had been browbeaten into him in his new post.

Here, though, it wasn't an action that would be tolerated.

Forcing himself to remain upright, he waited for her to explain why she'd summoned him.

"I hear she's managed to take the throne fairly effortlessly."

It wasn't a question, and his mind grappled for the appropriate response, knowing full well he had best not answer incorrectly. "Not so effortlessly, Your Majesty. She still struggles with decorum and with balancing the new freedoms of her subjects. Not all are pleased by the changes she's making."

She considered his words and he could practically feel her mood easing. A knot unraveled within his own chest.

"I hear she has many who stand by her side, including Sabara's own grandsons."

His lips ticked up. He answered without hesitation, "They are male, Your Majesty. What does it matter if they support her reign?"

She smiled back at him, and he felt a surge of promise at having known the right response so quickly. He wasn't stupid; he had only to trust his instincts.

"I hear," the queen continued in her lilting voice, "that she is beautiful."

At that he faltered. He knew what she wanted to be told, but to lie was unforgivable. He conjured an image of Queen Charlaina in his mind—her pale blond hair and shimmering blue eyes and skin that glowed even when she didn't realize it was so. He tried to find some fault he could relay to his queen—something that wouldn't reveal his forgery. Instead he lowered his voice to a whisper, hoping she wouldn't notice the apprehension hidden there. "Not half as beautiful as you, Your Majesty."

That, at least, was not untrue. His queen was nothing if not striking.

And heartless, he realized, as she spoke her next words.

"I want her dead." There was no change in her inflection; it was that same conversational banter. As if she were simply searching for information, prying for news, as she would with any good spy.

Yet even he knew this was no ordinary request.

He cocked his head, unsure what the proper reaction was now. "Dead," he stated flatly, careful not to question the command.

Her lips bowed, ever so perfectly, making her look more like she was ordering dessert than an assassination. "Dead," she said again. "You can handle that, can't you?"

He took another step forward, no longer concerned with decorum. "And how do you propose I do that, Your Majesty? How do I get her away from her guards and her family and the contingent of soldiers who follow her every move? Are you expecting a suicide mission from me?"

"I thought you might ask that." She raised her hand, a quick signal, and the door was opened. A young woman with tangled braids and dirt-covered clothing shoved her way inside. She was younger than the queen and himself, yet she carried herself with more confidence than both of them combined. She didn't count her steps or wait for the queen to speak first.

She grinned when she saw him standing there. "Didn't expect to find you here." He couldn't help noting that she sounded even less like their queen than the last time he'd seen her.

He bit his lip against the urge to tangle his hands around her braids and drag her up against him, yet he said nothing.

"The summit is approaching," the queen responded, ignoring the brazen girl who stood insouciantly before her. "It's been many decades since an invitation's been extended to a queen of Ludania." Her lips pursed, as if she were holding back a secret. "This year's going to be different, however. This year the Vendor queen is to be summoned. And this year, she'll have to leave the safety of her palace fortress to travel north." She looked at each of them in turn. "I expect the two of you to find a way to stop her from reaching her destination. Understood?"

He didn't dare hesitate, and he didn't have any qualms about what he was being asked to do. It was an order, after all. "Of course, Your Majesty. Anything else?"

The queen's gaze narrowed when she answered. "Keep her safe," she explained, casting a quick glance at the girl with smudges on her face. "She might not want the part, but she's still my sister, and a princess of this realm."

The girl drew a razor-edged knife from her boot and flashed her teeth at the queen. "Don't worry about me. I'm not the one who'll need protecting."

I

In the privacy of my dreams, I'm a warrior.

I'm still me, of course, just a tougher version of me. More valiant and fearless.

I've always loved those dreams, the ones in which I can wield a weapon without breaking a sweat, or cut a man's throat without blinking an eyelash. In them, my body is honed and fine-tuned. My mind is as focused as any Canshai master of lore's, and I, too, can move objects simply through my powers of concentration. My spirit is dogged.

No one can stop me. I am invincible.

I tried to summon those feelings now, as I lay facedown in the mud, blinking furiously against the grit blinding me, and spitting out mouthfuls of pond scum. Unsteadily, I wobbled as I rose to my feet, moving entirely too slowly, my legs trembling beneath me.

I am fierce, I tried again to convince myself, but that unblinking resolve I so desperately craved had been seriously shaken.

My weapon had disappeared somewhere in the slimy pit

I had just pulled myself from, so it was only me . . . and my opponent. I needed to think quickly. I knew he wouldn't wait long before striking again.

Staggering to my full height, which unfortunately was not nearly as impressive as his, I struggled to find any weakness in his defenses. He was both massive and armed, and, as if reading my mind, he lifted his steel blade to his forehead in a mock salute, his lips twisting into a sneer.

"Your Majesty." His voice rumbled—a sound like thunder coming from deep inside his chest. "It seems you find yourself in a most precarious position." His eyes narrowed as he closed the gap between us, and my heart stuttered. "Whatever shall you do?"

He lunged then, thrusting his sword toward me, the sharpened edge glinting as it sliced through the air. Fortunately, I recognized its trajectory and was able to react in time, dodging left at the very moment the blade arced right.

I felt the air ripple at my earlobe. Too near a miss.

But even as relief uncoiled in my chest, I felt my foot slide in the slick mud. I lost my balance and careened backward, falling hard once more. My breath rushed out in a painful *whoosh* as my spine connected with a sharp stone beneath me. My mind was still scrambled, trying to beckon my inner soldier, trying to conjure that fierceness within . . . to overlook the pain.

Warriors do not cry, I admonished myself silently. And then I dared a quick glance at his feet, which were still coming for me. *He is a true soldier.*

I swung my leg. It caught him right behind the ankles, hooking them, and I dragged as hard as I could, trying to sweep his feet from beneath him. My fingers clawed at the soil beneath me as I struggled against his massive weight, but I refused to surrender.

And then I felt him give. I felt him buckling above me, and he, too, was falling.

The moment he was on the ground, at the same level I was, I raised both my booted feet, my knees cocked and my thick heels aimed directly at his head. The blow could be deadly if delivered correctly. In the temple, just as I'd been taught.

I hesitated, staring into my attacker's hard brown eyes. He'd had no qualms about hitting, kicking, pushing, and nearly stabbing me. I knew because I bore the bruises to prove it.

"What are you waiting for?" he jeered, his white teeth flashing, reminding me that *he* didn't have mud in *his* mouth. "Finish it."

I wanted to. I wanted to be the girl from my dreams. Tough like Brooklynn, or determined like Xander. Willing to kill if necessary.

But I wasn't. And I couldn't.

Sighing, I dropped my feet as I turned to roll onto my stomach so I could push myself up from the ground.

And then I froze as my numbed mind recalled the first rule of battle: Never turn your back on your opponent.

Before I could reconcile my mistake, he was on top of me. I never even heard him. He was stealthy, like a tiger. And I was at the receiving end of his claws.

The knife at my neck seemed to have materialized from nowhere, and there was a moment when my blood turned to ice as he dragged its blade along the base of my throat until its point converged with my hammering pulse.

"That's what happens if you break rule number one," he growled against my ear, his breath like fire. Then he withdrew his blade, shoving me back to the ground. And again, I found myself eating dirt.

"Dammit, Zafir," I complained, getting to my already battered and bruised knees. "You knew I'd given up, there was no need to attack again."

Zafir held out his hand, both as a gesture of submission and as a genuine attempt to help me up. I took it, but only because my back was still throbbing where the rock had jabbed me. "There's always need for attack. Remember that."

"I'll never be a skilled combatant, will I?'

"No," he stated flatly, gripping my hand and yanking me to my feet as if I weighed less than nothing.

I swayed slightly and glared at him, but kept my mouth shut. He was right, of course. I was inadequate.

I waited while he waded up to his ankles in the shallow pond to retrieve my sword—*his sword*, actually—and wipe it clean. Bending over, I stifled a groan as I hefted the one he'd been using from the ground where it had fallen. It weighed at least five times what mine did and had intricate carvings, not just around the hilt but continuing along the length of its curved blade. To anyone else, the carvings would appear to be gibberish.

To me, the girl who could understand all languages, they were poetic: *Danii, a weapon forged of steel and blood.*

I grinned over the fact that Zafir's sword bore its own name.

And that whoever had crafted his steel had lovingly engraved a message declaring not only its name but also its origin. I'd asked him about it once—about the origin of the weapon and the language engraved into its blade. He'd told me only that he wasn't born in Ludania, and that the weapon had been an ancestral gift.

"We'd best get back before Sebastian tells your father what you've been up to."

"*We,*" I corrected, trading him weapons so that I didn't have to drag his through the silt, and wishing, once more, that I were stronger. "What *we've* been up to, you mean."

Zafir glared down at me. "I wanted no part of this. I'm a reluctant participant."

"But a participant nonetheless," I maintained, lifting a brow. "And maybe if you were a better instructor . . ." I trailed off, trying not to let my disappointment come through in my voice.

"It's not my instruction that's lacking." His pointed gaze found me. "Your Majesty." He added my title as if it were an afterthought, even though we both knew it wasn't.

"Whatever. I might as well be spending all my time in riding lessons considering how little my fighting's improved. At least then the horse might do what I want her to."

"I believe those were my exact words. You need riding lessons, not fighting lessons. You're a queen, not a soldier." And then he added it again, this time his lip twitching ever so slightly. "Your Majesty."

We reached the stand of spark willows, beneath the largest of which we'd tethered our horses. During the day, the drooping branches' tips, which nearly brushed the ground, were extinguished and the trees served as the perfect shelter for the enormous animals we'd ridden, shielding them from view. At night, however, the nibbed ends of each branch would burn bright in shades of blues or reds or white, depending on the blossoms. A million tiny buds of light would flicker and flash, casting this entire sector of the forest in an ethereal glow in which nothing—and no one—could hide.

Something I understood all too well, I thought as I glanced down at my hands, where light flickered just beneath my skin.

Zafir slipped through the curtain of wilting boughs and, after a moment, returned holding the reins of two magnificent mares. Magnificent, that was, to those who appreciated horses.

Unlike me.

It was unnatural for humans to be riding animals. Or at least that was what my aching body insisted, even before I readied to take the saddle once more.

I wasn't like Brooklynn. I seemed incapable of learning that natural rhythm required to master horseback riding, that same rhythm she possessed when sitting astride her stallion. The easy way her body moved and rocked, not just in sync with the horse, but almost as if she'd become an extension of it. Like part of a single fluid wave in which they seemed to become one.

I, however, remained separate from my animal, remaining stiff, and bouncing and lurching uncomfortably. My body fought the motions of the beast beneath me, resistant to its gait.

In truth, they terrified me, the horses. All of them. They were large and unpredictable and far too powerful.

Yet another reason I could never truly be warrior. What kind of soldier couldn't manage her own steed?

Stretching my back and preparing for the ride home, I reached up to the saddle's horn and balanced one foot in the stirrup as I hauled myself up, throwing my other leg over the smooth leather seat. Once I was settled, Zafir handed me the reins, and as he did, my stomach tightened. I hated this part. I hated that it was in my hands to command this beast.

A country, sure. An animal larger than my royal guard, no thank you.

When we returned, Sebastian was already waiting for us in front of the stables. He rushed out to take the reins from me, and held the mare steady while I dismounted.

I glanced around, searching for Brooklynn. "Is she here yet? She promised she'd be here when I got back." I hated the edge I heard in my own voice. "She's late, isn't she?"

Zafir took great care to stifle a yawn.

Sebastian frowned and bowed low, clutching the leather reins in his hands. I stared down at the top of his head, envious that any man could be blessed with such lustrous curls. They were the color of polished mahogany, matching his eyes to perfection. It was unfair, considering that I'd been born with hair and skin so fair they were nearly transparent, not a single curl in sight.

"Your Majesty. I'm sure she's just running . . ."—he lifted his head and scowled upward at the sky, noting the sun's location, completely unable to mask his worry about the time—". . . behind schedule." His last two words sounded less than convinced, and I fought the urge to giggle at his attempt to assuage me.

Zafir was less composed, and his laughter boomed like a thunderclap across the meadows, making the poor stable master jump. "Knowing Brooklynn, she's probably off causing trouble. Probably getting you into a war, if I had to wager."

I cast a warning glare in Zafir's direction; Sebastian didn't deserve to be laughed at. "Don't worry, Sebastian, I don't blame you for Brook's absence." I sighed heavily, not wanting to do this alone, and unwilling to admit why. "I suppose we can start without her," I muttered.

Sebastian perked up at the idea, and I was reminded that this was his true passion. This was why he'd been made stable master after barely reaching the age of legal consent. At eighteen, he was the youngest stable master the palace had ever had. No one knew his way around a horse the way Sebastian did.

Plus, he was patient—assuring me I would grow more comfortable, that my skills would improve. That time would give me the confidence I so desperately needed.

But Sebastian was serious about his instruction, and training with him was as physically exhausting as my fighting lessons with Zafir. It wasn't simply about sitting in a saddle—anyone could do that, he'd repeated time and time again. He wanted me to learn the finer points of horsemanship: riding bareback, emergency dismounts, jumping, and groundwork. He worked both the horse and me until we were unable to work a moment longer.

"You won't be sorry, Your Majesty," Sebastian vowed, pulling his red bandana from his back pocket and tying it around his head, something he always did before my lessons. "With a little more practice . . ." He hesitated, as if trying to convince himself and not me. "With a little more practice, you'll be riding like a champion."

I bit the inside of my cheek at the thought of me as a champion rider. "That sounds . . ." My lip quivered ever so slightly. ". . . wonderful."

Sebastian's face lit into a huge, triumphant grin as he dipped his head once quickly before straightening and spinning on his heel, his shoulders high.

"Oh, and Sebastian?"

He stopped and turned back around. "Yes, Your Majesty?"

"Will you please just call me Charlie?"

Sebastian's brows crumpled, uncertainty clear in every feature.

But it was Zafir who answered. "No." His voice was like iron. Unyielding. And then he looked down on me from his horse, and his gaze was equally obstinate. "He will not, *Your Majesty*."

BROOKLYNN

Brooklynn stood on the street, staring up at the scarred sign that hung above the door. She hated the pang that coursed through her, the ache of nostalgia that betrayed her as she questioned whether being here was wise or not.

Still, wise wasn't her reason for coming. And neither was nostalgia.

She had a job to do. An important one. Longing had no place in her world. . . . Not today, anyway.

She tamped down the emotions and shoved her way through the battered wooden door. Even the weathered brass of the door handle beneath her fingertips was entirely too well-known to her.

Inside, she scowled at the man behind the counter. He looked older now than she remembered, more haggard. The skin around his eyes was lined and leathered, as if he were a man accustomed to a life of hard labor. As if he'd spent years working in the fields rather than inside the walls of a butcher's shop. She watched as he rubbed his grizzled beard, graying in places it surely hadn't been before.

It was his eyes, though, that held her attention as he noticed her standing there—they were as sharp and focused as ever, and filled with spite. She'd always hated that physical similarity between them: the dark brown of their eyes.

He wiped his hands on his stained apron, and Brook was reminded why she'd never been bothered by the sight of blood. She'd grown up with it.

"I need a minute," he grumbled in Englaise to the older man behind the counter with him.

"I'm almost off work," the man responded in a firm voice, as if he was accustomed to having this conversation. "Five minutes. And then I leave, whether you're finished or not."

Brook watched as her father's face drained of all color. She could tell that he wanted to scream, that his rage was bubbling so close to the surface that even she was cringing inside as she waited for the explosion that was surely coming. But when he answered, his words were quiet. Controlled. "It's *my* store, Anson. Do I need to remind you again? *You* work for *me*." The muscle at his jaw flexed, jumping spastically. "*I* make the rules here."

Anson just shook his head, as if the notion was absurd. "But I shouldn't have to remind you that I have rights now." And then he repeated, "Five minutes."

Her father untied his apron and threw it on the floor as he stormed into the backroom, leaving Brook to either wait or follow.

She was comfortable with neither, but she was already here,

and they had only five minutes. She might as well get this over with.

Casting an apologetic look at the older man, she slipped behind the counter and went through the doorway that led to the chilled room where her father was holding a cleaver and slicing—pointlessly—into the remains of a carcass that had clearly already been carved, its usable meat already packaged.

"Can you believe him? Six months ago he was mopping blood off the floors and discarding entrails. He wasn't even permitted to speak to me. Now I have to pay him a wage he doesn't deserve and allow him to interact with my customers. Now, he thinks *he* can tell *me* what to do." He hacked into a section of rib cage and pieces of bone and flesh sprayed outward. "This is your fault. You and your queen!"

Brooklynn walked toward the familiar carving-block work surface and ran her fingertip over a section in which she'd carved her name when she was just a girl, back when she still made all of her B's backward. The wood had been new then, shiny and polished, yet her father hadn't chastised her for marring it. He'd simply marveled at her handiwork, boasting that his daughter might have a future as a woodworker or an artist.

He'd never imagined she'd become a soldier.

Or that she'd turn against him.

"You need to tell them to back off. What you're doing is foolish," she insisted, ignoring his complaints about the New Equality. "All you can hope to accomplish is to get yourselves killed." She glanced up to watch his reaction.

His face twisted into a sneer. *"Is that what your queen tells you? That we can't gain enough power to overthrow her?"* He took a step closer, still clutching the bloodstained cleaver in his fist, and Brook recognized that both his language—the all-too-familiar guttural intonations of Parshon—and his stance were meant to intimidate her. *"If I recall correctly, we wouldn't be the first to challenge a queen . . . and win."*

Brooklynn's eyes narrowed at the close-minded coward who stood before her. She drew her fingers away from her childhood carving, disgusted that she'd allowed herself to remember the man he'd once been. It was hard to imagine why she'd so desperately yearned for his approval for so many years, why she'd craved his notice.

Because he's your father, she silently chided herself. Of course she'd wanted his approval; she'd been a little girl without a mother and he was all she'd had.

Maybe if he'd spent more time with her after her mother had died, made her feel like something other than a housekeeper, she wouldn't have found a home with Xander's rebel army. Maybe she wouldn't be a commander in the queen's army now.

"You can't win, is all I'm saying," she spat back at him, speaking only in Englaise—the voice of the people—and knowing that it galled him that she did so. He preferred the old ways: a class system in which he was better, by birth, than nearly half the country. But what he conveniently forgot was that, by that same system, he was classified as a Vendor, and there'd been those who'd looked down on him, in the same way he looked down on Anson.

Brook, however, would never forget what the class system

had meant: a lack of free will. "How many supporters can you possibly have? Three, maybe four hundred? To do what, go backward? To undo the good Queen Charlaina is trying to do? To give up the freedoms her reign has offered? Are they willing to give their lives for your cause?" She gave him a look that said exactly what she thought of his cause: *not much*. Then she glanced down casually at her fingers, examining a hangnail. "Besides," she explained, "we'd crush you in a matter of seconds." Her lips parted slowly, spreading into a grin as she glanced up again. It was daring, filled with intentional defiance as she baited the man before her, watching as the color rose in his face.

His lips tightened and his jaw flexed. Not a flattering look for him, she noted.

"You don't know the half of whose support we have. What would you say if I told you that you're outnumbered? That I could stop you from leaving here today if I gave the order? That me and my little insignificant band of protesters have the queen's best friend at their mercy?" The meaning of his words was crystal clear. He would sacrifice his own daughter to send a message to the queen.

Fortunately for her, Brooklynn didn't back down that easily. "What if I reminded you that you *don't* have the queen's best friend at your mercy, but rather the commander of the First Division of the Royal Armed Forces? What if I were to tell you that to harm me would be considered treason, and that the mere threat that just passed your vile lips could send you to stand in front of a firing squad? Or worse, get you sent to the Scablands?" She took a step toward him, closing the slim gap that remained between them, until they stood—father and daughter—nose to nose.

"You don't have the authority," he challenged in Parshon.

There wasn't a trace of tolerance in her hardened expression. "Try me."

He studied her for a long moment. He laughed then, a tight sound. Brook could taste the foul flavor of tobacco on his breath, lingering with the rancor inside him. The skin around his eyes wrinkled, like crumpled paper, but the eyes themselves remained flat. Emotionless.

"I was only jesting, dear daughter. You know I'd never harm you." And suddenly he was the father who'd bragged of Brooklynn's wood-carving skills. The same man who'd held her up on his shoulders to watch street performances and had given her sugar-covered fruits and sweets when her mother wasn't looking. He reached out to stroke her cheek. Brook jerked away when his fingers—so cold they felt as if they belonged on a corpse—grazed her. "We're flesh and blood, you and I," he cooed. "If we can't depend on each other, who can we count on?"

II

I crept as silently as I could into the kitchens, which weren't nearly as quiet as I'd hoped they'd be. It was hard enough to sneak around with a giant by my side, and it only became harder with everyone bowing to me and whispering words of respect, and then whispering some more when I passed. Gossip mostly.

This was one of the hardest things to get used to: people noticing me. I'd spent my entire life trying to go unobserved.

Funny, though, how convention tried to dictate my actions now, when once it was simply convenience. I'd merely worn the clothing available to any girl of my status—the Vendor class—and never thought to complain. Now that I could wear whatever I wanted, now that class was no longer an issue, I hated being told what was—and wasn't—proper for someone of my *stature*.

And pants most certainly were not considered queenly.

I ignored the strange looks I received for my attire—gapes and stares whenever I donned trousers. But it made no sense to try to sit sideways on a horse when I could gain much better balance by sitting astride, something a skirt would never allow me to do.

Plus, the fighting lessons. I couldn't possibly fight in a dress, could I? Not with any amount of decorum, anyway.

Of course, my father could never know that. He didn't approve of me doing anything that put me in harm's way . . . and hand-to-hand combat would most certainly fall under that category, lessons or not.

The rest of it, taking my place on the throne, hadn't been nearly as hard as I'd imagined. I'd adjusted quickly, or at least I'd adjusted quickly by my standards. Considering that I hadn't wanted the position in the first place, I thought I was doing pretty well.

In fact, there were things I actually liked about my new role.

Like seeing my country released from the tyrannical rule of an oppressive queen and her antiquated notions. Hearing the words of Englaise spoken everywhere I went, while never having to pretend I couldn't understand what was being said. And the fact that my parents no longer had to work from sunup to sundown to provide for us.

I grinned as I caught a glimpse of my father, his arms buried all the way to his elbows in a thick pillow of bread dough as he concentrated on kneading and pulling and twisting the mass, forcing it to conform beneath his insistent hands. Some things, it seemed, would never change.

A woman in the kitchen staff caught me standing in the doorway and dropped into a curtsy. "Your Majesty."

My father glanced up from his task. "Spying now, are we?"

I stepped all the way into the immense kitchens, Zafir remaining silent by my side.

The palace kitchens were a far cry from the kitchen my father had once worked in—the one in our family restaurant. Here, he had seventeen ovens, five enormous sinks, and an endless stretch of counter space on which to work.

Yet even though he refused to stop working in the kitchens, he had acclimated to this life much faster than I had. He looked younger, healthier, happier than he had in years. Maybe ever. Even the callouses on his hands had grown less coarse during the weeks since he'd stopped toiling at our family restaurant.

I smiled. "Just wondering why you can't find something else to fill your time. A hobby or something. Maybe you should take up horseback riding. We could take lessons together."

Wiping his hands on the well-worn towel that draped from his belt, he met me in the center of the polished marble floor, finer than any of the stone tiling found in the vendors' part of town. "Yes, I can see that's working out so well for you." He reached out and plucked a leaf from my hair as he examined me with a worried expression, surely inspecting the bruise on my cheek that had nothing at all to do with riding. "Are you certain this is something you should be doing?"

I shrugged. It's not as if I enjoyed the lessons. "That's what I'm told. If I ever plan to leave this realm, the train lines only extend so far, and until we can establish trade with the other queendoms—those with access to fuel—we don't have a lot of other options. Sabara's resistance to technology and change has left us stunted." Her name tasted like bile on my tongue, leaving a bitter aftertaste that turned my stomach. "Ludania *will* progress if I have any say in the matter. Even if it means I have to learn to ride a horse. . . ." I shrugged again.

He laid his hand on the side of my face, pressing it to my cheek like he had when I was just a girl. "Well, be careful. It's admirable that you feel such a strong desire to tend to your country, but you need to take care of yourself as well." He glared at Zafir, not caring that the guard stood several heads above him. "Your country needs its queen."

"I'm fine," I said, and I wondered which of us, exactly, I was trying to convince. "Besides, I think I'm getting better at it. The horse is starting to like me."

Beside me, Zafir chuckled beneath his breath.

I turned to scowl at him. "What? You don't know. You weren't even there."

Riding lessons were one of the rare occasions Zafir left me in someone else's hands, mostly, I assumed, because he didn't care for the horses and only rode when absolutely necessary. Each and every time, though, he told Sebastian that he was under the threat of dismemberment should any harm fall upon me. And although I was sure Zafir was only joking with the boy about injuring him, Sebastian took the giant guard at his word, keeping close watch over me during those lessons.

"I hear things," Zafir answered. "And the things I hear sound nothing like the things you just said. If it's possible, I hear you're actually getting worse."

My mouth opened to argue, but my father spoke first. "You are supposed to be with her at all times. You are never to leave her unattended."

Zafir shifted uncomfortably. It would have been almost

laughable to see the giant squirm, but just as a smirk found its way to my lips, my father turned on me. "Is that how you're running things around here? Exposing yourself to danger by roaming about without protection? You put us all in danger by behaving that way, Charlaina. Angelina's not yet ready to take your place should something happen to you."

It was impossible not to notice that everyone around us had stopped what they were doing and were listening as my father scolded me. I felt like a child, and my shoulders fell as I dropped my head. He was right, of course. But it wasn't entirely my fault.

I tried to remind myself that I was the queen, that I was the one who gave orders. This was my queendom. But it didn't matter. *He* was still my father.

I shot a scathing look at Zafir. "I wasn't alone," I finally answered, but my voice carried no real weight, and even I knew it was a pathetic excuse.

"Really?" If I hadn't known better, I would've sworn my father was enjoying this, letting me know that no matter what my position, I was still his daughter. Honestly, though, I think he was really just worried. "Who was with you? Claude?" he asked, naming another one of the royal guards. "Xander or Max? Because I'm sure it was none of them; I've seen them around the palace today. *All of them.*" He emphasized the last words, making certain I wouldn't try to lie to him, to appease his fears.

"Sebastian," I admitted, almost in a whisper.

I knew even before he responded what was coming. *"Sebastian?"* he said, practically choking. "The stable boy?"

This time I lifted my head to meet his gaze. "He's the stable master."

"He's just a boy!"

Inwardly, I rolled my eyes. Outwardly, I tried to be reasonable. "Dad, he's not. He's of age, and he's the best instructor there is. Besides, nothing happened."

My father's eyes raked over me, taking in my mussed hair, my dirty face, and my ripped trousers. He knew *something* had happened, but he didn't need to know I was training to fight as well. He'd never forgive Zafir if I told him that part.

"Fine," I finally said, hating his scrutiny and knowing he wouldn't relent. "Next time I'll take Zafir." I could feel Zafir stiffen beside me, and I had to squelch the urge to smirk. That's what he got for mocking my riding skills . . . or lack thereof. "Will that satisfy you?"

And just like *that* my father was smiling at me, as if he'd never been worried or angry in the first place. But there was a triumphant gleam in his eyes that hadn't been there before. "That would make me more than satisfied, Charlaina. That would make me positively overjoyed." And then he winked at me. "Now you should go get cleaned up."

I was learning that a palace dinner was as choreographed as any intricate dance production. The courses were served at predetermined intervals, and the kitchen and serving staffs were masterful, understanding the nuances—the subtlety of the meal's progression—in ways that made it seem effortless. They would appear with new offerings before I'd even realized that the last plates had been removed from before me.

Dinner was one of the rare moments I had with my family,

as a daughter and a sister, and, as my time became stretched thinner and thinner, I frequently found myself looking forward to our evening meals.

Yet another adjustment to life on the throne.

Spread before us now was a succulent roasted goose drizzled with a honeyed citrus glaze, peppered parsnips drenched in a rich cream sauce, and asparagus tips coated with herbed butter. My father's breads—served hot and fresh from the ovens, with a crisp brown crust—were placed at even spaces across the table. I closed my eyes as I caught a whiff of the warm loaves, remembering the days when *I was* the serving staff. I reached for a slice as I listened with growing interest to the discussion around me.

"Preparations for your visit are coming together nicely," Xander explained, looking pointedly in my direction. "The question is: Are you?"

I traced my fingertip around the carved pattern on the cup sitting on the table before me. It was a seal that had once been outlawed in my own country: the Di Heyse family crest. "I think so," I answered, trying to sound more confident than I felt, and ignoring the flutter in my belly whenever the subject of my upcoming visit to the Capitol was broached. "I'm not sure what more I can do to prepare. I don't think it's whether I'm ready or not at this point, I think it's whether the people are ready for me."

I didn't say what was really on my mind. I didn't remind them of the last time I tried to go out in public.

I didn't have to.

"It'll be fine. Everything's been prepared. Word has been spread. No one will be surprised this time," Xander explained, his mouth curving playfully. "They're as ready as they can be for a queen whose skin glows."

I grimaced at the reminder, my eyes dropping to my hands in my lap. Sometimes I could almost forget what everyone else saw when they looked at me . . . the light dancing just beneath the surface of my skin. "It's starting to fade," I answered pathetically. "It's nearly gone now."

At that, all eyes were on me, and I felt my skin burning anew. I knew they could see the lie in my words. . . . every place they looked.

My lips tightened into a hard line. "It's faded," I insisted, this time with more conviction. "And it will be full daylight when I venture out. Surely it will be less . . . less . . ." I struggled for the right word. "Noticeable."

Max reached beneath the table and squeezed my hand. "It'll be fine," he said in the same reassuring tone Xander had used. And then, because I needed it, he leaned closer, his voice dropping. "They'll love you. Just like everyone else does. They'll know that you are the one responsible for making things better, and that you have their best interests in mind. No one's ever worked so hard to make their lives better." A slow smile tugged at his lips, and my concentration slipped.

It was Xander who brought me crashing back to the present. "And yet despite all of your hard work," he interjected with a laugh, his voice ringing down the length of the table, "I wonder how many other queens are eating dinner with their fingers." He winked conspiratorially at Eden—standing guard at my sister's back. Eden, who pretended not to notice his every move. It was almost easy to forget that she and Xander had once worked together so closely, that she had been his right hand as he'd led the revolutionary movement that fought to overthrow his grandmother's cruel regime. It was almost impossible not to notice how Eden's moods shifted whenever Xander entered the room, how the very air around her became lighter. More hopeful. Yet her expression remained vigilant, her duty never forgotten.

My gaze slipped to the slab of buttered bread I held half-way to my mouth. How was I supposed to eat it if not with my hands? I wondered silently, refusing to give them the satisfaction of thinking I cared at all. With a fork and knife? I dropped the half-eaten bread onto my plate.

"What makes you think it won't be just as awful this time?" I argued, turning the conversation away from my table manners. I hadn't forgotten the gasps of surprise during my official coronation, when my cape had been removed and those in attendance had gotten their first real glimpse of my skin.

"That was then, Charlaina," my father said, reaching across the table to push more bread my way. Bread, to him, was always the solution. "Surely they can have no qualms now. Not after these past months. Not after all the positive changes you've made."

I weighed my father's words, along with the fact that my glow was no longer a secret. I couldn't stay locked inside my palace forever. I'd been training for this job for months now, learning the proper way to be the queen of Ludania. It was time for me to meet my people.

I stood alone in my bedchamber, wishing I could find peace the way everyone else did. Only when the hour ticked far past midnight did Zafir ever leave me. When there was nothing to do but sleep. The guards posted outside my door never moved, but I often wondered if they knew about the secret doors, the hidden passageways behind the walls that tunneled like a labyrinth, connecting one room to the next.

I stared into the mirror, pondering my own image and wondering if Xander and Max were right when they'd said I could do this. I wondered if I was the right girl to be sitting on the throne and ruling Ludania.

I understood the reasons it had to be me, of course, yet at times I still felt like a fraud. Like a girl playing dress up . . . donning a paper crown decorated with only glitter and glue.

Clumsily, I reached to unclasp the delicate necklace I still wore as it glinted at my throat. My fingers were shaking, and frustration welled as I struggled, fumbling with the clasp.

Then I heard it. A voice

I can help you. The voice was hushed, almost far away as if it were coming from down a long, hollow tunnel, but I knew who was speaking. I knew who whispered inside my head.

Sabara.

Sabara who should have died months ago. Sabara upon whose throne I now sat, whose queendom I now ruled.

She was still here. Living inside my body.

Taunting me.

I dropped my hands as I gaped at my image—*my* image—staring back at me from the mirror. "Leave me alone." I whispered, wondering how I'd sound to anyone who came upon me now, standing in the empty chamber of my bedroom. Talking to myself.

The mad queen.

That's what I'd become, I thought as I stood there, waiting for something to happen. Silence stretched like an endless cord that tugged at my gut, making me realize I was all alone, that she hadn't heard me.

That maybe she wasn't really there at all.

My shoulders fell.

I was tired, so very tired, and I had to be up early in the morning.

My bare feet crept along the carpet to my bed, the covers rumpled from when I'd tried once already to sleep. I prayed fervently that this time I'd find what I so desperately needed. Rest. Peace.

I curled into a ball, wrapping my arms around myself and felt my eyelids fluttering, growing heavier and heavier. . . .

And just as they closed, I heard the faintest voice coming from deep within me.

Let me help you, Charlaina.

III

I tiptoed through the darkened palace hallways, wishing it didn't have to be this way, wishing I had another choice. But I didn't. Not now.

There were times, during the deepest part of night, when I could almost forget who I was. Almost forget the responsibilities that weighed on my shoulders, forget the future I was expected to forge, and the lives I held in my hands. At least until I passed the occasional sentry and saw them start suddenly with recognition, bowing their heads low and shattering the silence with their reverent: "Your Majestys". In the spaces in between the night watchmen, in the shadowed stretches where no one else dwelled, I could almost believe I was still the same girl. The same Charlie I'd always been.

Except that Sabara was with me . . . even when I was awake.

I approached the guard standing outside the heavy wooden door at the end of the hallway. Here sconces that had not so long ago held candles and oil lamps were now outfitted with electricity, and a small bulb cast him in a bowl of pale light. Like all the others, his eyes widened as he realized who it was that approached.

I lifted my finger to my lips before he could utter the all too familiar, all-too-formal phrase as I stepped past him. He didn't try to stop me, despite the fact that the person he guarded slept soundly on the other side of that door.

I eased it open, grateful that the hinges were well oiled so it didn't creak, the way many of the palace doors still did. Inside the darkened bedchamber, the newly appointed royal guard glared at me. My lips curved as her black eyes burrowed into me, lancing me with suspicion.

I was above reproach and she knew that, but her overprotective nature was one of the things I admired most about Eden—one of the reasons I'd accepted her as my sister's guardian. She trusted no one.

But I was her queen. She had no business second-guessing my reason for being here. Even if it was the dead of night.

I nodded at the woman now sworn to protect Angelina with her life.

Leave us, I mouthed, and saw the flicker of hesitance cross Eden's face before acceptance loosened her stance. She sighed from between clenched teeth, her only audible answer. Yet the air around her remained charged, as it was wont to do in her presence. Her moods were palpable, and I could feel her dissatisfaction with my request. Yet she obeyed silently, slipping from the room.

As I caught sight of my little sister, a tiny angelic form buried beneath layers of delicate silk and finely woven damask, my breath hitched. I hated to see her sleeping alone. I hated that we no longer shared a bed.

It won't work, the voice whispered in my ear, and I closed my eyes, ignoring it as I crept closer on bare feet. I didn't wish to wake Angelina; the last thing I wanted to do was frighten her. But I needed her now.

I stood beside the bed for a moment, wondering at the luxuries we were now afforded, and realizing that they changed nothing. We still needed each other. And we still had secrets.

I lifted the heavy covers and slipped beneath them, letting them fall around us once more, blanketing us, shielding us from all else. Instinctively, my feet reached across the downy mattress we lay upon, seeking out my sister's warmth, just like I used to do before I was a queen. . . . and she a princess. When we were just sisters, sharing a bed.

I'd planned to wake her slowly, before asking for her help. But the instant my skin touched hers, I felt her body spasm—her eyes shot wide, and her expression glazed as she gaped at me, startled. "What are you doing here?" I felt her shift farther from me, distancing herself. "Can't you just leave us alone?"

I frowned. "It's me, Angelina. Charlie." My skin flushed, and I could both feel and see the glow coming off it now. A glow that had all but vanished over the past several weeks. Now intensified by Angelina's presence.

Her blue eyes squeezed tightly shut as she blinked at me. When they reopened her gaze was clear again, focused. "What—what are you doing here, Charlie?" she asked again, sounding confused and small, unaware of her initial reaction to me.

I relaxed. *She hadn't realized it was me,* I told myself. *I'd merely surprised her.* "I need you," I practically begged, afraid I already knew what her response would be. "Please. Just try again."

In the light shimmering from my skin, I could see the tears in her lucent blue eyes. If only it would stay that way. If only it wasn't losing its strength. Then I wouldn't be here right now, begging my little sister for help.

The glow, I believed, was what held Sabara at bay . . . and only Angelina could bring it back.

"I already tried, Charlie. It didn't work," she whimpered, and I was reminded that she was not even five years old yet. Too young to be burdened with my problems.

I reached across the sheets and gripped her hands tightly in mine. This time she didn't flinch away, and I squeezed her small fists, relishing the feel of the potential I knew she held. The power she wielded, not yet fully realized. I didn't want her to know how badly I needed this. I couldn't tell her why it was so important, although I feared she already knew. *"Please, Angelina. For me."* Parshon slipped from my mouth, feeling strange on my tongue, but I was desperate.

She sighed, her narrow shoulders sagging with the weight of my request. I could see her reluctance, but she pulled her hands from mine and gingerly laid a small palm on each one of my cheeks. She inhaled and closed her eyes, a look of peace settling over her beautiful little face. *I shouldn't be asking this of her,* I reprimanded myself.

Healing, that was what I needed from Angelina. I needed her to fix me. I needed her to make everything right. To make me better.

Heat surged from Angelina's fingertips. I jerked back, recoiling from the very thing I sought. But she held on, staying with me, her touch insistent and warm and healing all at the same time.

My arms locked stiffly at my sides, as a ripple of revulsion flared within me. I struggled with myself not to strike my sister's hands away from me, not to break the bond she'd forged between us. Shrieks unleashed within me—not my own—like wails carried on a ferocious, icy wind. They scratched at my insides, panicking as they tried to find their way out. But I bit my tongue, tasting blood. My blood. From *my* body.

I struggled to hang on. I refused to give up.

The entire room lit up. I could see Angelina clearly; she burned as brightly as I now did. At least on the outside. From within, my vision blurred and I clenched my jaw as blackness swelled, growing like a tidal wave, threatening to drown me.

And then Angelina's hands left me and I gasped, falling in a boneless heap on the feathery pillows of her bed. I was sweating from head to toe, and my chest ached. This time when Angelina's fingertips grazed my face, skimming my jaw, there was no magic in her touch. Just the tender concern of a sister.

"How do you feel?" she asked softly, her voice brimming with anticipation. Hope.

I didn't have to glance at my skin to see the flickering glow I'd been so desperate for. Still, I sighed. "Tired, Angelina. I'm so tired."

She just lay down beside me, settling her head against my chest as if she were listening to the unsteady thrum of my heart, assuring herself I was still alive. That I was still me.

I wished I knew the answer to that question myself.

Her arm fell across my stomach, such a familiar gesture, and I knew she was sleepy, that I'd probably worn her out. Guilt suffocated me at having awakened her.

I listened to the sounds of Angelina's breathing, while at the same time I searched within myself, hoping and praying I was all alone now, that Sabara was gone. Once and for all.

I don't know how long we stayed like that, wrapped around each other in the dancing light emanating from my skin, but I was certain that Angelina, first princess of Ludania, had at last drifted off to sleep.

It surprised me, then, when I heard her voice, so young, so quiet, fill the air around us. "It didn't work, did it?"

I squeezed my eyes shut, not wanting to hear her words. She was wrong, she had to be. But I gave her the only answer I could, the truth. "I don't know," I whispered back to her.

Angelina nodded. "I wish she'd leave us alone."

Surely, from where she lay, she could hear my heart's ache. "Me too," I said, my voice barely audible now. "Me too."

I stumbled from Angelina's room, my legs quivering, moving through the passageways of the palace and casting light wherever I went. There was no escape, no place I could be alone.

I knew, even before I'd left Angelina's room, even as I'd bent over her sleeping form to give her one final good-night kiss, watching her lids flutter, her eyes flitting back and forth beneath them as she finally succumbed to her exhaustion, that it hadn't worked.

She can't help you. She's not strong enough to keep me at bay. Sabara was still with me.

I reached out to steady myself against the wall, and an armed guard—one of the night sentries—turned his curious gaze in my direction. But I glared at him until he turned away once more. The affairs of the queen were not his concern, unless there was a matter of security at hand. And at the moment I knew I appeared safe, despite the fact that I was anything but.

Black coils of invisible smoke enveloped me, twisting and spiraling through and around me, until they were all I could see or hear or even breathe. I was suffocating in Sabara's insidious grasp.

"No!" I insisted, pounding my fist against the wall and gritting my teeth. I didn't care if I drew the guard's attention again. He wasn't my problem. Sabara was trying to push me out.

Laughter erupted, echoing ominously and grating against my ears, rasping along each and every nerve fiber of my body. *Poor child. Poor, wretched child. You have no idea what you're up against. No idea how to stop me, do you?*

I gasped as I fell to the ground, sickened by how close to the truth her words had hit. My heart shuddered violently within the dwindling space of my chest.

I didn't know how to make her go away. I hadn't figured out how to make her leave me alone.

The sight of me curled in a ball on the thick carpet must

have raised alarm because I heard the guard's voice coming from somewhere outside of me. "Are—are you okay, Your Majesty? Do you need help?"

I didn't answer. I couldn't. I concentrated instead, focusing everything I had on smothering Sabara. On quelling her treacherous voice, the one that tempted me with its malice. That whispered evil and deceit.

She isn't me. Not yet. I am still in control, I reminded myself, again and again and again.

I dropped my head, forcing myself to draw in one breath, followed by another, and another. The remaining darkness was deluged by a shower of glittering sparks as my flesh torched. I called up every ounce of reserve energy I had, clutching my hands into fists as I wrapped my arms protectively around myself.

"Go away," I told her in a shaky voice. And then louder, more resolved. "Leave me alone!"

The only sound I heard was the whisper of booted footsteps, the guard's steady gait as he rushed away from me. Surely, he'd assumed I was speaking to him.

But I heard—and felt—nothing from within. I stayed there for what seemed like an eternity, waiting to see if she'd return, if she'd come back to torment me. The oily black smoke that had just moments earlier choked me, seemed to have vanished, evaporated into oblivion, and now I could breathe again. Clearly. Freely.

It wasn't until I felt someone reaching for me, and I heard the familiar voice against my ear, that I dared to open my eyes at last. "You have to stop doing this, Charlie." Max's words scolded me, but his soft voice—and his fathomless gray eyes—were gentle and filled with unspoken reassurances. "You're scaring the guards." He picked me up from the ground, lifting me and clutching me to his chest. I let my head fall heavily against him as I listened to his heart beating an unsteady rhythm, and I knew the real truth of his statement.

It wasn't the guards I was scaring. It was him.

IV

When I heard the knock at my door, I closed my eyes, staving off the headache I'd been fighting all day. "Tell him to go away," I told Zafir, unable to even get off the bed where I was sprawled with my fists crushed against my throbbing temples. "No more lessons today. I can't take any more."

It had been a rough day, and Baxter, Sabara's former adviser who was now in charge of tutoring me in the finer points of palace life, had been patient, doing his best to pull me out of my foul mood and placate me when my tolerance grew thin. But patience wasn't what I needed now, and the idea of facing Baxter for yet another lesson made my head pound even more violently.

What I really needed was sleep. And peace and quiet inside my own head. Neither of which I'd gotten the night before.

Max had carried me back to my rooms and gently put me back to bed. He'd even waited there with me until long after he thought I'd fallen to sleep. But sleep had been tenuous and hard to hold. Like so many threads of light carried on the dawn.

Eventually, after he'd gone to his own chambers, I'd given up on it, choosing instead to concentrate on my schoolwork. Funny how I'd once thought that being queen would mean no more studies. Now, it seemed, studying was *all* I did.

Zafir's voice interrupted my thoughts. "It's Brook, Your Majesty."

At his words, I bolted up. "Let her in." I jumped off the bed and was already halfway to the door when Brook came inside. "Where've you been? You missed our lesson yesterday."

She dropped low before me, preparing to greet me formally, but before she could say the words, I stopped her. "Please don't, Brook. It's only me, and we're all alone." I glanced at Zafir, daring him to argue as Brooklynn rose to her full height once more.

"*Our* lesson, Charlie?" she answered, peering over her shoulder to Zafir. "I'm not the one who needs lessons. I'm not the one afraid of horses." As she turned back to face me, I could see that her skin was flushed and her eyes glittered feverishly. "I'm to tell you we have company for dinner, an emissary from the Third Realm." She grinned then, looking so much like the little girl I'd once played with—rather than the commander of an army—that I was taken aback for a moment. "Your father says to dress for dinner."

"Dressing for dinner" meant actually wearing a dress. A proper one . . . not one of the comfortable cotton shifts that allowed me to run and move freely, to play with Angelina in the woods, or to wade through the ponds with bare feet. All things I'd also been told were not queenly activities.

Sometimes the rules were unsettling.

I took in Brooklynn's attire, ignoring the dull ache behind my eyes. To anyone else I'm certain she looked intimidating in her sleek ebony uniform. I'd let her design it herself when I'd made her a commander in my armed forces, and I'm sure that was exactly what she'd intended—to be the picture of intimidation. She was dressed entirely in black, with even the buttons fashioned from polished onyx. I'm certain her choice had nothing at all to do with how the color complemented her subtly bronzed skin, or the way her dark curls glistened against the midnight field of leather.

To me, however, she still looked like Brook.

Beautiful. And damaged.

"I need to talk to you." Brook's voice was quiet as she drew me away from Zafir.

I gave him the almost imperceptible signal to turn away so I could change, and then whispered back to her, "What is it?"

Brook sighed, settling onto the edge of my bed as I unbuttoned the front of my blouse and tossed it in a crumpled heap on the floor before unzipping my trousers. "I went to see my father yesterday, in preparation for your visit to the Capitol," she explained, her words tumbling together. "Xander was right, he's definitely up to no good."

I winced, I knew how hard seeing him must have been for Brook. Her dad wasn't like mine. He would never have kept her safe if she'd had a secret to keep. He would never have killed for her. "Did he give you any idea what he's planning?"

"Not yet. But he made threats against me. And against you . . ."

I stopped tugging the gown, which was only halfway to my

hips. "Did he say anything specific? Do you think he plans to try something?"

She shook her head, anticipating my thoughts. "I don't think he's in any position to be a serious danger. Not yet anyway," she explained. "Besides, I told him what would happen if he didn't back down." She exhaled loudly. "I'm not sure he'll actually listen, but he heard my warning clear enough."

I tugged the black velvet dress the rest of the way up, past my hips and over my bare chest. I turned my back to Brooklynn, lifting my hair out of the way and leaving the matter of the threats alone for the moment. "How was it for you? Seeing him again?" The zipper glided smoothly, and I held my breath, letting it find its way along my spine.

When she didn't answer right away, I turned to look at her. I saw something flash behind her eyes, and I knew that the real Brook—the girl who had once been only my friend and not the commander in my army—was aching.

"Fine," she answered when she realized I was watching her. "Serious or not, I think you should tell Max and Xander about his threats. I think you should reschedule your tour through the city."

I was shaking my head even before she'd finished speaking. "No," I insisted, equally quiet but adamant, leaving no room for her to argue.

Her back stiffened and I could feel her withdrawing from me, even though she remained where she was. It wasn't the first time I'd felt this, a growing distance between us. Although Brook was now a soldier in my service, I wasn't sure she had grown accustomed to the shift in power between us. I'm not sure either of us had.

I hated the seemingly cavernous fissure that had spread, cracking our friendship.

I walked over to my mirror and closed my eyes. "I'd like a moment alone, please," I whispered. "Do you two mind waiting outside? I'll only be a minute."

Even without looking, I could sense the charged silence between them, and I knew they'd exchanged a look—deciding whether to acquiesce to my request or not. Then I heard the door, and I was alone at last.

Behind my eyes, my head continued to ache. Sometimes I wondered if this was too much for one person: the lessons and the rules, the meetings and the responsibility that sometimes felt as if they were crushing me.

The solitude.

I opened my eyes, blinking at my reflection as I studied the gown I wore. The black fabric fell in cascading waves, hugging my body in all the right places. I still couldn't get used to the trappings of my position and wondered if I'd ever stop preferring darker colors—blacks and grays and the deepest shades of russet, colors that didn't stain—despite the dressmaker's best efforts to persuade me otherwise. I was still a vendor at heart.

I ignored the fact that that same dressmaker had disregarded my preferences and had sewed in intricate gold beading along the waist and hemline.

And then there were the other doubts, the ones that had nothing to do with me at all. The ones that came from *her*.

Listen to your friend, Charlaina. Not everyone can accept change. Not everyone wants the kinds of freedom you've offered them.

Sabara's voice filled my head like liquefied hatred. Loathsome and wretched. It seeped through my veins like bile and I braced myself against the mirrored vanity, leaning closer and trying to see past my own eyes—to see *through* myself—to get a glimpse of her. I wanted to know if she was in there, somehow watching me from the other side of the looking glass.

But it was just me. I was the same girl I'd always been, except that now I looked tired, drawn; my eyes were bleary.

I decided to prod her, hoping I sounded stronger than I felt. Hoping she couldn't read my thoughts as well as my emotions.

"Say what you will, Sabara," I ground out on a hushed breath, feeling somewhat foolish. "But I'm not the one trapped. I'm not the one entombed in a body that's not my own." To make my point, I curtsied to the likeness that stared back at me and stood again sharply. My actions were jerky, like my limbs were being pulled by a puppeteer's hands. But it was only me. I was the one pulling the strings. "I'm the one in control here, not you."

The door opened then, and Brooklynn peeked inside. "Did you need something? I thought I heard you," she asked, scrutinizing me, and I wondered what she saw as I slowly stood again, letting my arms fall to my sides.

I shook my head, staring at her, still not ready to trust my voice.

"Well, come on then." She reached out her hand and I

stepped toward her. "Look at you, all fancy and queenly." She grinned, holding out her arm for me, acting as if she were my date for the evening. Acting as if nothing had changed between us . . . as if we were the same old Charlie and Brook.

I smiled sheepishly, looking down at my black dress. "We match," I said, because I could think of nothing else.

Brooklynn laughed at me, leaning her head against mine as Zafir held the door for the two of us. "Oh, Charlie, when will you realize: We've never matched. It's what makes us perfect for each other."

Something electric filled the air the moment I entered the dining hall. At first I thought it was Eden. It was typical to feel her emotions, even when her face was completely blank.

As if she could ever manage that, I thought, smiling inwardly. She wore expressions like accessories, jewelry to match her stormy moods. I noted her usual suspicious glare as she stood protectively behind my little sister, who was already seated at the dining table. Eden's coal-black eyes took in every minute detail of the room.

But it wasn't her that I sensed; I was certain of that. I recognized her mood instantly. Watchful and wary. A hawk guarding a sparrow.

No, it was something else that had the tiny hairs at the nape of my neck standing up in warning.

And then I saw them on the other side of the room, near the windows that overlooked the gardens. The cluster of people spoke among themselves, and I could see only their backs. They were too far away for me to get a good look, but it was hard to imagine that any of them was the emissary Brook had told me about—an ambassador who'd been dispatched to be the face of their nation. Even from here, they all appeared too rough and uncivilized to be suitable.

Besides, emissaries were almost always women. Unlike me, most queens tended to prefer other women in their highest counsel positions. Or so I'd been told.

Max stepped forward then, with Claude shadowing him. Unlike Zafir, who had once been one of Max's royal guards, Claude had decided to remain with Max. It hadn't mattered to Claude that Max no longer held a royal title after his grandmother's death.

I was the queen now.

But they didn't know what I knew about Sabara. That she'd somehow survived. That she'd found a way to be heard in the deepest recesses of my mind.

Even I knew it sounded like madness.

I grinned as Max met me at the doorway, blocking most of my view of the room and all thoughts of Sabara. He was dressed in full ambassadorial regalia. In his official role he was my chief adviser, the person who kept me apprised of policies both foreign and domestic. Unofficially, he was the person I most counted on in this world. He protected me. Not me the queen. Just me, Charlaina. Charlie.

"You look beautiful," I whispered, letting him take my arm.

"I was supposed to say that."

"That you look beautiful? Be my guest, but I think it sounds better if I say it."

A ghost of a smile pulled at his lips as he drew me closer to his side than any adviser should. "Our guest is anxious to meet you."

Already my father was sitting beside my little sister and my mother at the long dining table set with polished silver and gleaming china. His pale blue eyes, so much like my own and Angelina's, sparkled approvingly as he took in my appearance.

Smiling back at him, I tried to ignore the other sensation that plagued me. The one that warned me that something was . . . *off*.

"Where is she?" I forced my gaze to Max.

"He," Max corrected me. "The ambassador is a he." And when I flashed him a curious look, he grinned down at me. "I know. What is it with these progressive queens and the men in their lives? His name is Niko Bartolo. He's the *adviser* . . ." He raised his eyebrows meaningfully as he glanced down at me, intentionally reminding me that he, himself, was more than just my adviser. I felt myself blushing. ". . . . to Queen Vespaire of the Third Realm."

The Third Realm was at least two days—and one full queendom—from Ludania by train. Six by horse. These visitors were far from home.

"Do you know why Queen Vespaire has sent him?" I asked, pretending everything was as it should be. That the tension knotting my stomach was simply the result of nerves.

"Are you all right, Charlie? You don't look well." Max frowned, scrutinizing me.

But it wouldn't have mattered what my answer had been, because the moment Max moved, just the barest amount, I found myself standing in front of the congregation of men who'd just moments earlier been contemplating the view of the gardens. It was hard to imagine that this particular group had any appreciation for flowers or statues or ornate fountains. I imagined they'd much prefer armories and taverns and brothels.

There were five of them in all, I counted quickly, trying to appraise the situation . . . to evaluate my uneasy feelings. Not one of them appeared to have washed or changed after their long journey, and their worn riding pants and coats were still covered in dust and grime from the road. Beneath their clothing, their skin was equally weathered and sunbaked.

Four of the men stepped forward as Max and I approached, aware of my presence at once. And all four of them dropped low before me.

"Niko Bartolo," Max said, his voice slipping into a cadence far more formal than his usual bantering tone. "I give you Charlaina di Heyse. Queen of Ludania."

The fifth man, standing just behind the others, eased forward then, bending as if to follow the lead of his men at the very moment his eyes lifted to mine. Eyes so amber they were very nearly molten. Eyes that both unsettled and comforted me, and found their way straight to my core, piercing me like a steel-tipped arrow. I stood frozen on wobbly legs, mutely acknowledging that *he* was the reason my skin itched. He was the cause of the ache in my gut. This perfect stranger who now held my gaze.

My grip on Max's arm tightened, and I immediately hoped he hadn't noticed, although I was certain he must have. Yet if this ambassador—this Niko Bartolo—felt even a fraction of what I was feeling, he gave no indication. He dropped into a flawlessly executed bow just as his men had done, until I found myself staring—wordlessly—at the golden halo of his hair.

Inside, my stomach twisted.

Or was it something else that roiled, straining to be noticed?

Max tugged at my arm, reminding me that five men were at my feet, waiting for permission to rise.

"It—it's a pleasure." My voice barely registered, but it was all I could manage.

Niko stood once more, doing everything the way he should. It was I who was faltering. I who struggled to understand my uncertain reaction.

He held out his hand to me and I stared at it, my mind struggling to unravel each simple action. Beside me, I felt Max nudge me, slight but perceptible. Just enough to get me moving again.

It was strange to watch my hand settle into this stranger's, almost as if it were someone else's hand I watched. Niko lifted my fingers to his lips, kissing the back of them reverently. "Your Majesty," he intoned, his voice perfectly calm. Perfectly innocent. And then he lowered his voice, and made a sound, an almost indistinguishable gravelly noise that came up from the back of his throat.

Except that it wasn't just a noise. It was a word, spoken in a foreign tongue, one I'd never heard before. Yet I understood its meaning.

"You," he'd said.

I jerked back and watched him through wide eyes, trying to tamp down my curiosity but failing miserably. The longer I stood beside him, the more conflicted I felt. The more intrigued as well.

You? Was that really what he'd said? What could he have meant by that?

I pulled my hand away, suddenly anxious to have it back. Away from his grip.

Xander interrupted then, making an exuberant entrance as he and Aron came tumbling through the open doors, wrestling and shoving each other. They seemed not to notice it wasn't just the two of them in the enormous dining hall.

"Get off me, you wag!" Aron grunted as Xander caught him in a headlock and pulled him all the way down so he was very nearly kissing the floor.

Officially, Aron held no title or official role in my administration, but he was invaluable to me all the same. Maybe what I'd really needed was another friendly face around as I adjusted to my new position.

It was Xander, however, who'd taken Aron under his wing, making it his task to teach Aron the finer points of combat and weaponry.

And horseplay, it seemed.

Beside me, Max's breathy chuckle drew my attention away from the golden-eyed ambassador. It wasn't a stretch to imagine Max jumping into the rambunctious fray of flying elbows and knees.

"Admit that I won," Xander insisted, laughter clear in his voice. "Tell me I'm a superior marksman."

Neither *boy* was even aware of the audience they'd drawn. At least until Angelina giggled from her seat at the table.

Simultaneously, I watched both of their heads snap up. And almost equally synchronized, each of them jerked to attention as Xander released Aron from his grip.

Xander, as usual, was the first to recover, standing tall and handsome and looking unruffled, as if they'd just strolled in casually to join our assemblage. As if they hadn't forgotten it was dinnertime altogether.

Aron's eyes, however, were still sparkling with recalcitrance, his gaze directed solely at Xander. "It was his fault," he muttered, shoving Xander with his shoulder in a last-ditch effort to win whatever quarrel they'd been having.

Xander ignored the dig from Aron as he dropped his head and uttered, "Your Majesty."

I forced a glare for them both, warning them each in turn to behave . . . and knowing that neither would listen unless he chose to. Then I allowed Max to show me to my place at the table.

As I did, I passed Angelina, who looked tired, bruised circles outlining the nearly translucent skin beneath her eyes. Guilt coursed through me.

Guilt and that other thing. That sensation I had yet to identify.

It took a moment for her to meet my gaze fully, for her eyes to stop fluttering nervously away from mine. But when she did, when I had her attention at last, my face fell into a remorseful frown.

I'm sorry, I mouthed. I desperately hoped she understood me.

It took a moment, but the sliver of a smile that dusted her lips made my heart flutter.

Of course she'd understood me. Angelina always understood me.

Xander and Max were already waiting for me in the library after dinner. I'd gone up to Angelina's bedchamber with my mother to put my little sister to bed, where I'd whispered silent assurances to Angelina that I wouldn't be waking her again. I couldn't bear to see the dark smudges of strain on my sister's face.

But it was more than just that. I needed to get away from Niko Bartolo too, from the strange buzzing I felt whenever I'd looked his way. The strange tingling, just beneath the surface of my skin, whenever my mind wandered to thoughts of touching him.

I was glad he'd be leaving in the morning. Glad I wouldn't have to see him again until the summit.

Assuming I could convince Max the invitation was a good idea.

"It's a great opportunity," Xander said, looking up as Zafir and I entered the room. Then he turned pointedly back to Max, "For her *and* for Ludania."

"I disagree," Max said through gritted teeth. "She's not ready. She's only just begun learning what her role entails within the boundaries of Ludania. Sending her to the summit now would be like setting her loose in a den of lions. They'd eat her alive."

I wandered to the sofa and, instead of sitting down, leaned against the arm. "*She* is right here," I reminded them, crossing my arms. "Besides, Xander's right, this could be the opportunity we need, Max. My chance to appeal to the other queens, to reestablish the trade Sabara had abolished. We could use their assistance. Ludania needs access to new technologies and medicines. We need access to energy sources. Maybe I can reestablish fuel trade, or bargain for electric power. I don't want to miss this opportunity."

"You don't understand, Charlie," Max said, dropping onto the sofa beside where I was perched. He sighed, leaning forward, his elbows on his knees. "It's not just about duty. You're talking about trying to go toe to toe with women who were born into their positions, bred to wear their crowns. These women were groomed as queens. They live and breathe the rules of decorum. They were raised learning the etiquette and protocols of each and every queendom they might ever come into contact with."

"I have to agree. You'd have a lot to learn if you were to go," Xander interjected, with a laugh. "And we all know how much you love your lessons." He winked at me, and I wondered if Baxter had told him how difficult I'd been that day.

I wondered too what he'd say if I told him it was Sabara's fault.

Inwardly I sagged, but I couldn't give up that easily. If what Niko Bartolo had said was true, then Sabara had been turning down invitations from the other queens to attend the summit for more than a century . . . since long before she'd inhabited her last body.

I envisioned Sabara's reluctance to attend, confused by her reluctance to see her country progress and evolve. That would have meant that she'd have had to evolve too, to acquiesce to the fact that there are better ways than the old ones, I supposed. Something Sabara still refused to do.

I couldn't let my people be left behind simply because I was afraid to face the challenge ahead. "But they're still people," I argued. "Surely they'll understand our plight. Surely they'll understand that I can't know the things that they do, that my situation is . . ." I searched for the right word, but there was only one. "Unique."

Max reached for me then, no longer caring about convention and rules now that we were alone—just he and Xander and Zafir and I. He pulled me onto his lap and let his lips rest against the top of my head. "Ludania is only just getting to know you, Charlie. Are you sure you should be leaving so soon? After everything you've worked so hard on? One class? One language?" His mouth moved down, brushing my cheek now and I no longer cared that every eye must surely be upon us. His lips were soft and enticing and begged for me to pay attention to them. "Do you really want to leave now?"

Zafir, still standing near the door, cleared his throat, reminding me that Max and I weren't alone. I jerked back, bumping into the sofa arm behind me, and Xander laughed. "You know your duty ends at guarding her, don't you, Zafir? You act more and more like her father every day."

"There's nothing wrong with decorum," Zafir responded, unruffled by Xander's ribbing.

I glanced sheepishly at Zafir. He was right, of course, I

hadn't meant to get distracted. There were more important matters than Max's lips. "Who would rule in my absence?" I asked them, not really sure of the protocol.

Xander answered first. "Someone will have to stay, and since Max knows the realm better than anyone else, he's the obvious choice. Of course"—his silver eyes flashed, glinting wickedly—"I'm happy to stay in his place. I've always wanted to sit on the throne."

My stomach felt as if it were filled with rocks. . . . a million sharp, pointy-edged rocks. "He could," I suggested hopefully to Max. "Stay here, I mean. You could tell him everything he needs to know before we leave. He knows the palace, and since at least a third of the forces come from the men he brought with him, they'll listen to him if the need arises. Plus, he understands the importance of maintaining peace." I squeezed Max's fingers in mine, trying to convey my desire for him to agree. And then I asked the question I was afraid to ask, even after the past months. "You trust him, don't you?"

For years Max and Xander had been at odds. They'd been estranged, each serving on a different side of the conflict. When Xander had turned his back on his grandmother, taking up arms against her, he'd deserted a much younger Max, leaving him under the palace roof with a woman who'd despised him. By the time he'd come of age, Max had rebuffed his royal upbringing in an entirely different way: by joining the military. It was something no royal had done in decades, possibly centuries. He was a disgrace in his grandmother's eyes.

But, ultimately, being on opposite sides of a revolution had been what put Max and Xander in front of each other again. It was when they found me that they'd been forced, for the first time in years, to communicate. To cooperate.

And now, just months later, here they were, living under the same roof once more. Living in their boyhood home, and forging a new future for the country they both loved.

But did either of them trust the other?

Max's gaze met Xander's with more certainty than I'd expected, although his voice didn't sound quite as sure. "Of course I do," he said. And then, he added, "He's my brother."

Neither of them was as certain as they should have been. It was clear that they were both still deciding what, exactly, their relationship was, and would be. They were brothers, certainly, but that didn't guarantee love. It wasn't the promise of a bond.

I knew because I'd seen too many family members forsake their own. I thought of Aron and Brook, both of whom were nothing more than chattel to their fathers.

I was glad to see Xander and Max work toward repairing those frayed family ties, even if it made them both squirm to do so. I had never promised them comfort if I sat upon the throne.

I was never promised comfort either.

"Tell Niko Bartolo I'll be attending the summit," I told Xander at last.

Summer had given way to the harvest season, but the nighttime temperatures rarely dipped lower than the daytime ones. It was unseasonably warm for this time of year, but neither Max nor I complained as we lay stretched out on our backs, staring up at the spectral clouds—apparitions suspended in the black sky above us, allowing the moon only the briefest glimpses of the earth below.

Even though the light from my skin was fading, my encounter with Angelina the night before made me the brightest thing out here.

But at least in the gardens I could hide myself. The space within the hedged walls was quite possibly the most peaceful place in the world, and the two of us found ourselves existing among the shrubbery and flowers and fountains and pathways more often than not, whispering secrets of what was and what would be, and of all the things we wished for. Yet more and more often, I found my mind wandering to other things, even when—like now—I watched Max's lips moving.

Things like Sabara, and what she wanted from me.

Max stopped talking and shifted onto his side, propping up on one elbow as he stared down at me. His eyes were nearly as dark as the midnight sky and just as cloudy. "Did you hear anything I just said, Charlie?"

I turned my attention to him, shaking away thoughts of the dead queen as I rolled in the soft grass beneath us and leaned up so we were eye to eye. My mouth curved devilishly, yet I shrugged as guilelessly as I could manage. I knew exactly what I was doing. "No, but I'm sure it was eloquent and well thought-out. Bordering on brilliant, I'd wager."

The corner of his mouth ticked up, ever so slightly. "I don't suppose it would do any good to repeat myself, would it?"

"Probably not." I looked away from him, staring up at the sky once more. The clouds had shifted, parting to create a vaporous tunnel through which the full moon shone, throwing dazzling threads of light along the clouds' edges.

"You can't avoid the topic forever, Charlie. You'll tire before I do," he argued. A point he'd tried to make a thousand times before. One I had no problem rebuking.

"Of course I can. I'll just keep pretending I didn't hear you."

Silver splinters flickered in Max's charcoal eyes, similar to the silver of his brother's eyes. His hand shot out to brace the back of my neck and his teeth flashed white in the pale light of the moon as he leaned closer. I could feel his breath before I realized his lips were brushing mine. Not kissing, just feathering over them. Reminding my body—and everyone with eyes—what Max was capable of doing to me.

Beneath my skin, light exploded. Tiny bursts that fragmented the darkness around us, igniting like lightning storms. Inside, the same things were happening to me, only no one could see those detonations, the ones that curled my toes and made my breath catch in the back of my throat.

"Eventually you'll hear me," Max whispered against my mouth, in answer to my intentional snub. "And eventually you'll agree to be my wife."

My voice hitched against the obstruction in my throat as tiny fireflies of light danced over my skin. "Don't fool yourself. . . . Eventually *you* will agree to be my king. But," I persisted, "only when I'm ready. And not a moment sooner." No longer able to resist the enticement, I pressed my lips all the way against his with a frustrated sigh.

Max smiled as he kissed me, and I knew he felt he'd won a minor victory.

Even though he'd never actually said the words, I knew he loved me. He'd proven himself time and time again: putting himself in harm's way, challenging his grandmother on my behalf, showing his willingness to sacrifice himself, and pledging to keep me safe. But that didn't mean we were ready to be married. I might be capable of ruling a country—or maybe I wasn't, and Ludania would suffer simply because of the fact that I was born with royal blood in my veins—but I certainly wasn't ready to be anyone's wife. I wasn't ready to claim a husband to rule by my side, even one that I could easily imagine spending the rest of my life with.

This wasn't a decision to be made lightly, and queen or not, I wasn't even of age yet. I hadn't even finished school, something no one but me seemed concerned about.

Max knew my reasons, and I was sure he understood them. But it didn't stop him from reminding me time and time again that he planned to outlast my obstinate rebuffs. That he would one day be my husband.

Although as far as I was concerned, he already belonged to me.

I pushed him down so I was leaning over him as he lay on his back once more. When my lips finally left his, they were tingling, stung by the currents that crossed between us. The curtain of my silver-blond hair fell over his much shorter, much darker hair as I cocked my head to the side and studied him. He was far more handsome than any man I'd ever dreamed of kissing as a girl, and more honorable than anyone I'd ever known, save my father. And when he looked at me the way he did now, I could almost believe I was as beautiful as he assured me I was—again and again. Something that seemed impossible when I didn't see myself through his eyes.

"Are you sure I can do this?" I asked, when I trusted my voice not to falter.

His lazy smile grew. "Kiss? I'm certain of it. In fact, you're rather skilled. Should I be worried about your mastery?"

I shoved him, and then I toppled forward, collapsing onto him so I could feel his heart beating beneath my cheek. "You know what I mean. The summit. Are you sure the other rulers will take me seriously? That I won't make a fool of myself?"

"Oh, I'm positive you'll make a fool of yourself." His words were mocking, but his tone was serious and laced with tenderness.

I lifted my head to stare at him, and his knuckles reached up to graze my jawline thoughtfully. "But that shouldn't stop you. And knowing you, it won't. You were right, Charlie, Ludania needs this. I didn't want you to go, but not because you can't handle it, not because you're not ready to face every queen on this planet. My own reasons are far more selfish." He shrugged beneath me. "What can I say? I'm afraid. If I had my way you'd never leave the safety of the palace walls where I can at least guard against those who might try to harm you." His mouth quirked upward, the shadow of a smile tugging at his lips. "But that's not you, is it? You'll go, and you'll face those queens, and damned if you won't win them over and convince them to do whatever you want them to in the process. You'll have them eating out of your hands, I swear you will."

Fueled by his unnecessary praise, I could feel my cheeks glowing. . . . in every sense of the word. His fervent support was both sweet and humbling.

"And if I don't?"

He lifted his head, his forehead resting against mine, his gray eyes luminescent in the light coming off me. "Then it'll be an adventure, won't it? Either way, I plan to be there, watching over your every step."

I sagged, letting the panic that had been weighing on me slip away. "You're coming then?"

"I wouldn't miss it."

NIKO

Pacing seemed to quiet his mind, but there was nothing he could do about the fire that ripped through him.

He hadn't felt that kind of heat in more years than he cared to count.

It was her. It was most definitely her. He'd recognized it the moment he'd come face to face with her, the moment he'd nearly forgotten to bow before a queen.

Yet it wasn't *who* she was he cared about, it was that flare of something within him he'd believed was long dead. That unnamable something that sparked to life the instant she looked at him with those pale blue eyes.

It was good to be alive again, he thought before he could quell the notion. But why the hell did she have to be this young queen? Why here? Why now?

Maybe it would have been better if that part of him had stayed buried, dead, after all.

Maybe ignorance truly was bliss.

It was too late now, though. The thoughts had been stirred, the feelings ignited. He wouldn't be able to tell himself just to forget about her. She was here.

She was close.

V

The ambassador had left early the morning after his arrival, carrying with him my acceptance to attend the summit. I was both terrified and exhilarated. Now, besides preparations for my visit into the city, I had to cram in a lifetime of foreign decorum training into the two weeks before it was time to depart for the summit.

In my lessons, I discovered that greeting another queen with a friendly hello, or even a stately—and in my opinion, respectful—bow was completely unacceptable in many countries. Instead, I was forced to memorize the customary greetings for each nation whose queen would be in attendance at the conference. Or more important, which greeting would be considered offensive to which monarch. Queens, apparently, were a testy lot—something I not only needed to understand, but was expected to emulate in some people's opinion.

I even learned that there was a customary greeting for me, as ruler of Ludania.

It was ridiculous of course; any greeting would be fine.

Although I was glad to have been warned that in one queendom it was considered polite to spit at the queen's feet, I supposed I'd have been taken aback if someone had spit at me without warning.

Still, there were lessons for every conceivable convention I'd need to follow at the summit, from table manners to how I sat in my chair—including the position of my hands on my lap—to the order in which we were permitted to enter and exit a room.

None of it mattered to me. Not really. Except in the sense that it might get me what I wanted, and that not knowing these things might stand in the way of the goods and services I hoped to barter for my country. The alliances I hoped to forge in the event I might ever need to call upon another country for help.

In that sense, these were some of the most important lessons I'd ever learned. Some of the most valuable tools at my disposal.

Even better than my ability to decipher languages.

To make matters worse—and they had most definitely gotten worse than the never-ending tutorials—there were dozens of fittings to stand still for, something I hated almost as much as the daily riding lessons I was now subjected to.

I also knew that the train lines went only so far, and many of those, even within the borders of Ludania, were still under repair after years of revolutionary battles and sieges. Many a train line had been cut in order to tighten the rebels' stranglehold on Sabara.

Which meant there would be times when our journey would

be on horseback . . . an idea that made my skin prickle with gooseflesh.

The only things I could no longer manage were my fighting lessons with Zafir. My dreams of being a valiant warrior had gone up in smoke.

Now, even as I stood stock-still in front of the wide windows of the library, listening while Xander listed the queens I had the best chance of collaborating with, the ones with whom I had the most in common, every muscle in my body ached from the punishing lessons Sebastian had been subjecting me to.

Brook, whom I'd badgered into riding with me, seemed to feel none of what I did. In fact, I would have wagered she was enjoying herself.

I swear she liked the beasts.

It was so unfair.

"Charlie? Were you listening?" Xander's tone was scolding, like one of the schoolteachers from the vendors' school Brook and I had been forced to attend throughout our childhood, where Parshon was the only language we'd been permitted to speak.

"Of course I'm listening. You think I'm not paying attention? I know this is important."

Challenge flashed in his eyes. "Then what did I say?"

Searching my memory, I struggled to recall some of the words I might have heard even after I'd stopped letting them register. "You said"—I stalled, thinking I couldn't be too far off if I guessed it was something about a queen. Everything was about queens these days—"that Queen Langdon prefers the company of dogs over people." I tried not to make it sound like a question, but there was no real conviction behind my words. Even Xander could hear that.

He smiled, and I felt a surge of pride. I wondered how in the world I'd managed to get it right when I'd barely heard him talking.

"I did say that," he said slowly. Too slowly. He moved closer to me, circling like a predator about to go for the throat. I followed him with only my eyes, trying to keep my stiff neck in one place. "In fact, I believe it was *yesterday* that I said that," he clarified, narrowing his gaze as he disappeared behind me, to where I could no longer see his derisive expression. When he came back around, back into my line of sight, he added, "And about Queen Hestia . . . not Langdon." He sighed then. "Charlaina, please, this is serious."

"Fine. I wasn't listening. There's too much; I'll never learn it all in time." I dropped my aching shoulders, tired of pretending. "I want Baxter back," I whined. "At least he doesn't yell at me when I get . . . tired." I sagged bonelessly into one of the tapestry-upholstered chairs that was worth more than our entire home had been—probably more than our entire city block—when we'd lived in the west side of the Capitol, where most vendors dwelled. Or at least where they dwelled when the classes were still divided. Now they could live in any home, in any part of the city they chose. Their children were free to attend any school and make their own decisions about the clothing they wore, what they studied, and what they wanted to be when they grew up.

The possibilities for the people of Ludania were endless. It's how I'd always wanted to live.

There was a rap on the door, and Zafir stepped inside.

"I'm sorry to barge in, Your Majesty. Word just came from the Capitol of another protest against the New Equality."

I rose from my chair, exchanging a quick glance with Xander. Protesting wasn't unusual, or even unlawful, under my rule. There had been several since the announcement that the class system was being abolished. "Was it violent?" I asked, wondering why Zafir felt the need to interrupt.

"Not particularly. But there were effigies burned during the gathering."

"Effigies?" Xander asked, his eyes narrowing. "In whose likeness?"

But we both knew the answer to his question, even before Zafir's voice came, filling the taut silence. "In yours, Your Majesty."

Inwardly, I recoiled, but somehow managed to nod, turning my back to the two of them, so they couldn't see the strain on my face.

Fear and confusion I could understand. Change was frightening for everyone. The integrations were tricky. Former Counsel people didn't want those who'd been born of the Vendor class living next door to them, didn't want their children going to the same schools. And Vendors didn't want to live among servants.

I didn't know how to make them understand that class no longer mattered. That everyone was equal. People living with people. Children attending school with children.

It still astounded me that anyone would want to go back to the old ways. To curfews and segregation and being told where, when, and what they could speak. To live in fear of being sent to the gallows for miscalculating a simple glance.

"Maybe Max was right, maybe Ludania needs me here. Maybe I'm not ready for such a"—I closed my eyes, having a hard time forming the words—"such an important task."

Xander's reaction was not at all what I'd expected. I thought he might give me a pep talk, assure me that, of course, I was ready. Say something—anything—to allay my concerns, the way Max had done.

But Xander wasn't Max. Xander was hard. He was steely and determined, and rarely minced words. He'd turned his back on his family because he wanted a different kind of life. He'd led his friends and comrades into battle, watching some of them die for his cause. And he had the scars to prove it.

Literally, I thought as he came to stand in front of me, and I noticed, for the first time in a very long time, the scar that slashed across his face. Normally, I didn't even see it. It had become invisible to me.

Today, it was all I could look at.

"We don't have time for you to be 'tired.'" His voice was low, but firm. "You're a queen, not a child. Start acting like one."

Zafir took a warning step toward Xander, but I raised my hand to stop him. I didn't need his help. I lifted my chin. Fire beat through my veins now.

"I'm *your* queen, in case you've forgotten. You can't speak to me like that, Xander. Not now. Not ever." I met his gaze directly now, daring him to challenge me. I hated saying the words and my throat constricted around them even as they spilled from my lips, a harsh admonition.

Xander grinned then, a wide, self-satisfied grin that made the scar across his cheek pucker like a shiny smirk.

I crossed my arms, trying to maintain my anger, but too baffled by his reaction. One minute he was yelling at me, the next he was smiling like a fool.

"My apologies, Your Majesty," he stated crisply, succinctly. "But that's exactly the kind of queen you need to be when you go to the summit."

My frown deepened.

Xander reached for my hand, and even without looking I could feel Zafir stiffening. His protective nature was rivaled only by Eden's. Xander's fingers felt like the coarse polishing cloths used by cabinetmakers to buff wooden edges until they were smooth and ready to be finished. Hands that had toiled and warred.

His voice was softer now, and for a moment I understood the reason that Eden's moods shifted whenever Xander was near. I wondered if he spoke to her like this. If, when they were alone, he ever used the persuasive tone he was using on me. "A queen needs to be strong and resolute. She can't let others push her around, Your Majesty." The inflection he put behind those two words—words I generally despised—gave them a whole new meaning. They sounded fresh and new, like a breaking dawn might sound. Like a pledge. Goose bumps shivered over my arms, but I didn't move to rub them away. I held his gaze. "You," he said, bowing all the way to the ground before me, "are becoming a true queen."

VI

The vehicle came to a sudden stop in front of the large, polished school building and my fingers edged up to the glass that separated me from the real world. I told myself I could do this, even as my hands trembled.

"I never thought I'd be here again," I said breathlessly, more to myself than to anyone else. I was surprised, standing there now, to realize that so little had changed in the past months, despite the fact that *everything* was different now. The school looked exactly as it had before. Even the name was the same: the Academy.

Except that starting today there were no more restrictions on who could attend. Everyone would be allowed. Children born of all classes, who'd once been segregated by birthright, now clustered and converged on the smooth marbled steps, making their way toward the entrance.

I'd gazed upon this particular building so many times before, and even though it had once conjured feelings of disgust and envy in me, a sudden, inexplicable wave of nostalgia flashed through me as I stared out at it.

Crowds were already gathered in front, squeezed together on the sprawling lawns and spilling out into the streets, body against body as far as I could see. I knew they weren't here to see the doors of the school opened. They were all awaiting their first glimpse of their queen.

"You're ready," Brooklynn assured me, her fingers finding my shoulder. I ignored the quiver in her voice and wondered if she felt what I had, the same sense that we still didn't belong here.

I simply nodded and reaching down to release the door. Zafir was already on the other side of it, waiting to shield me as much as to escort me up the steps.

Brooklynn remained behind me. I suddenly wished I hadn't insisted that Max stay behind with Xander to work on preparations for the summit. I wished, too, that my parents were here just to hold my hand and comfort me.

"Stay close, Your Majesty. Not everyone is happy about what's happening," Zafir insisted as he leaned down to help me out, slipping his arm protectively through mine.

I stood slowly. All around me everything went still. Silent.

Every person there was watching me. I could feel their eyes boring into me, through me.

And then I reached up and pulled back my hood.

The first gasp was nearby, followed immediately by another and another, and still another, until it was one unified sound.

I waited, lifting my chin and staring straight ahead, too afraid to focus on anyone or anything. Too afraid to breathe.

Only when the initial shock had worn off, when the people in attendance had grown accustomed to my appearance, and conversations had started—murmurs that rippled through the crowd—did I allow myself to look around. I nodded at one of the soldiers, a woman who stood beside us. Her uniform was similar to Brook's, and she held a military rifle across her chest. There were other soldiers positioned at similar intervals lining the pathway ahead of us that led up to the steps of the Academy, and presumably surrounding the entire building. There was nothing discreet about their presence.

"Charlie!" A girl's voice came from just ahead of us, and I caught a glimpse of a golden-blond girl with flushed cheeks waving frantically. "Over here!"

"Look, it's Sydney!" I called over my shoulder to Brooklynn. "Sydney!" I shouted just as eagerly as she had, signaling for her to join us. Then I turned to the soldiers who were keeping the crowd at bay. "Let her through."

Zafir scowled as he stepped closer to me, just as Sydney was squeezing through the onlookers. "You shouldn't let people address you like that, it's . . . it's improper."

"Oh!" Sydney exclaimed, coming to a stop in front of us. Her mouth opened in surprise. "I—I'm sorry," she stammered. "I meant Your Majesty, of course."

She looked like she was about to drop into some sort of ridiculous curtsy or bow, so I reached for her, wrapping my arms around her in a fierce hug, grateful to see at least one friendly face among the crowd. "Ignore him," I said, grinning at her.

The last time I'd seen Sydney, she was with Brooklynn and

the rest of Xander's rebel troops, just after they'd seized the palace. From the pinched expression on Brook's face, I didn't get the impression she was as thrilled to see Sydney as I was.

I hugged her again. "He's just nervous around crowds. You can call me whatever you want." I wrinkled my nose. "Except 'Your Majesty.'"

"Really?" Sydney questioned uncertainly. "I think he might be right about this." She eyed Zafir nervously, chewing her pink lips as her eyes traveled the length of him, taking in his full height. "I think it *is* disrespectful if I call you Charlie."

"So then call her Queen Charlaina or 'my queen' or something equally stuffy," Brook offered irritably, adjusting her rifle and doing her best to look intimidating. And then she turned to me. "Really, Charlie, if you actually plan on doing this, we probably should get up there. You have a school to inaugurate."

I let Brook lead me toward the steps, dragging me by the hand just like in the old days when we were simply vendors' daughters attending School 33. It probably wasn't protocol for a queen to be led by one of her soldiers—even if that soldier was a commander—but I didn't care. She was holding my hand, and I needed that at the moment.

I reached for Sydney's hand too, clutching it and hauling her along with us, not wanting to leave her behind. Whether Brook liked it or not, the three of us had just become a trio.

Standing at the top of the steps, the gravity of what I was about to do, of the changes I was asking of my people, stole my breath. I took a moment to absorb the meaning of the phrase "my people" as I looked down upon them, the faces of those who'd gathered to watch me, to support me. And those who didn't.

There were dissenters among the crowd, that much I knew. I'd heard their calls of malcontent—boos and hisses and shouts of indignation—as I'd made my way past them. Yet they couldn't deter me. I couldn't help feeling good about what I was doing. I now ruled a country where such opposition was permitted. Openly and freely.

Unlike Sabara, I would never send someone to the gallows for harboring an opinion, much less for sharing it.

This was a new dawn in Ludania—a New Equality for all. It couldn't be helped that not all agreed.

A podium awaited me, and I hesitated as I approached it. I was about to give my first public statement, short though it might be.

Sydney stepped to the side, and Zafir and Brook fell back.

I took my place as, below me, a military transport came to a stop on the street.

They were here.

"Good morning," I declared, drawing all eyes to me as I began to speak. "Today, I stand before you, not as your queen or as a vendor's daughter, but as a citizen of Ludania."

I cleared my throat, determined not to sound timid or frightened, grateful no one knew how my palms perspired. "For some, times of change can be trying. But these times can also present great opportunity, a chance for us to show what we're made of, to show our dignity and fortitude. A chance for us to grow."

My gaze roamed over the expectant faces that stared back at me, and my confidence swelled. "This is one of those opportunities. This is our moment to show the world that we don't have to be burdened by the limitations of a class system that no longer works. That we *can* work together as citizens of one country . . . as one people . . . with one language." I gripped the sides of the wooden stand. "I'm not asking you to forsake your heritage, to turn your back on the traditions you've grown up with. What I'm asking is that we, as citizens of Ludania, learn to use language not as a divider, but rather to unite us. To make us whole.

"On this momentous day, we will continue the process of abolishing the laws that have divided our people for centuries. The students of this school—and schools across our nation—will no longer look upon one another as vendors, servants, counsel, or outcasts, but instead as classmates." I raised my fist in the air. "This is my pledge to you."

For a moment there was silence, and I wondered if I should say something more, if it wasn't enough of a statement. My heart replaced the words in my throat, choking me with uncertainty and regret.

Then a rumble went up, moving through the crowd with a life of its own, as cheers and shouts rose to a thunderous roar. Colorful bits of torn paper were thrown, tossed high into the air, and looked very much like feathers as they were carried on the breeze. My heart soared with them, those tiny scraps, and I was certain my skin glowed brighter and burned hotter as I stood there, watching it all.

As the cries died down, the door to the vehicle opened on

the street below, releasing the first of the children who'd been transported for their first day at the Academy. That was when the cries of opposition began.

Almost louder, it seemed, than the cheers of hope. And they came in every flavor of language: Termani, Parshon, Englaise.

"Go back to your own schools. . . ."

"Servants don't belong here. . . ."

"You're not our kind. . . ."

"Death to the queen!"

I held my breath, bracing for trouble as I scanned the crowds. I searched face after face, not sure what I expected to find. I could feel both Zafir and Brook right at my back now, as if they too, sensed danger.

Then I saw the first boy, small and timid-looking, making his way down the sidewalk toward the school. Toward me.

I moved away from the podium and hovered at the top step. I went down one and then another.

Brook stopped me. "What are you doing? You can't go down there now," she hissed under her breath.

"It's okay. He's afraid." I met him halfway down the steps, and by the time I did, there were a dozen more children behind him, all wearing varied expressions of eagerness, reticence, hopefulness, and fear. This was all new to them, all frightening and exciting at the same time.

I knew how they felt.

I leaned down to the little boy who'd been brave enough to go first. "What's your name?" I asked, staring into his wide, brown eyes.

He ducked his head, keeping his gaze averted, and I was reminded once more how things used to be.

"It's okay," I told him. "You're safe here."

Slowly he lifted his chin, until he was eye to eye with me. His voice was just as small as his stature. "Phoenix, Your Majesty. My name's Phoenix."

I rose, and held out my hand for him. "Welcome to the Academy, Phoenix. Glad you could make it."

The Academy was only my initial stop, but it was the longest of my tour through the city. My day had been rigidly planned, and each stop timed carefully. I would stay here throughout the morning classes so I could assess how the changes were being implemented, and then I would be escorted to Capitol Hall, so I could see how the New Equality was being handled by the city's officials.

The first thing I was aware of as I walked through the hallways, was that other than the fact that it was a school, the Academy was nothing like School 33.

Here, the students were assigned individual storage lockers, a place where they could store their books—books that were new, the pages undamaged and held together by unbroken bindings—rather than lugging them in their overstuffed book bags from class to class. They had supplies like paper, pens, ink, paints, and canvases. They had instruments for their music units, and all manner of equipment for games and sport. The desks, too, were unmarred by years of use and disrepair, and all were perfectly matched and aligned in neat rows. The walls were freshly painted, clean and pristine.

Everything sparkled. Everything shone as if it were new. As if the school had been fashioned from the very wallets of prosperity.

But the greatest difference of all had nothing to do with the building or the trappings of wealth, it had to do with time—the changes made since Sabara no longer ruled.

Now, there was no daily pledge. No formal recitation made to honor the queen.

To honor me.

It was strange, the void its absence created at the beginning of the school day, and we all—even the instructor of the class I sat in on—awkwardly traversed that space as if, at any moment, the city's loudspeakers might crackle to life once more, filling the hallways and the streets outside with the ominously familiar words. I could feel the students' curious eyes falling upon me more times than I could count. I tried to pretend I didn't notice, but it was impossible to ignore entirely. It weighed on me, and I hoped that soon the strangeness of it would pass. That soon the people would find that normalcy I so wanted for them.

I turned my gaze to Sydney, whose class this was, and I smiled.

It will be okay, I told myself, acting as if I didn't see Zafir looming in my periphery. As if I didn't know Brook was right behind me, guarding my back rather than taking notes as other kids her age were.

I'd expected to be swarmed the moment I'd stepped into the Academy, to be overwhelmed by questions and eager admiration, even if I didn't necessarily want that sort of attention. So it had been sort of strange, the bubble that formed around us instead. Either because of who I was, or because of Zafir's intimidating scowl, most of the students made an effort to steer clear of us, giving us an unnecessarily wide berth. Even going so far as to avoid making eye-contact with me altogether.

I was something of a pariah. Like an exile who'd been banished to her own personal version of the Scablands.

But there were a few students who went out of their way to try to make me feel welcome, to make me feel . . . special. In particular, one determined girl called Delta, younger than me by only a year or two. She'd been assigned to escort my entourage between each class hour, asking if we needed anything, if I knew where I was to go next, if I was enjoying myself.

Zafir jumped a little each time she appeared, as if startled by her enthusiasm. I wasn't sure I'd ever seen him so unnerved.

"I don't trust her," he warned between clenched teeth when she scurried away through the lunchtime crowd to get me an apple I'd never actually requested. I'd simply commented that hers looked delicious. I was certain she would have offered it to me if she hadn't already taken a bite.

"She's harmless, Zafir. Just trying to be helpful. It's sweet, really."

"Don't confuse sweet with cloying. The latter can be difficult to swallow."

Brook sat down beside me, carrying a tray overfilled with two bowls of stew and a plate of steamed potatoes. Since Zafir and I already had our food, I assumed it was all for her. She skewered one of the potatoes with her fork and dunked it into the stew. "The girl?" she asked. When Zafir nodded, she said, "I don't trust her," she announced, right before stuffing the entire potato in her mouth.

Sydney joined us then, her own plate filled with fresh vegetables and a strip of herbed whitefish. That was another thing different about the Academy; they served food here, prepared to order.

Brook curled her lip at Sydney's light fare but held her comments, probably because her mouth was too full.

"So? How do you think it's going?" Sydney breathed in a hopeful tone. I almost hated to answer her question . . . especially in front of Brook and Zafir.

I was grateful to see the new system working. To see kids who'd once been divided, schooled under the same roof, and those born to parents of the Serving class attending school at all.

To hear Englaise spoken everywhere.

But I wondered how long the protesters would remain out front. I wondered how long they'd remain peaceful.

I shrugged. "It's fine," I answered. "It'll be . . . an adjustment."

"What's it like?" Sydney asked, smiling reticently. "Living in the palace, I mean. Being the queen."

It was an interesting question, and I thought about it as I pushed my fork through my bowl. "It's . . . an adjustment," I said again, smiling self-consciously.

Brook nudged me, winking conspiratorially. "Yeah, an

adjustment," she repeated, as if it were some sort of inside joke. It wasn't, and she was the only one at the table grinning.

Sydney frowned at her, and I wondered if she thought Brook was somehow unhinged. I was starting to wonder myself.

"It's weird," I went on. "There are parts I like, things that are easier . . . especially for my family. Others . . ." I lifted a piece of seasoned beef from my stew and thought of my riding lessons. "Others I can do without. But I like what I'm able to do, the changes I can make." I tasted the meat, savoring the flavor, simpler than the foods we had at the palace, closer to those my parents had prepared in their restaurant. "What are people saying? About me? About the way things have changed?"

Brook leaned closer now, and the color in Sydney's cheeks bloomed. Her shoulders lifted as I held my breath, worried about what she had to say. "Mostly, it's good," she finally replied. "Mostly, they're relieved not to have to carry their Passports wherever they go, or to live in fear of lifting their eyes at the wrong moment. The gallows were torn down during the last lunar cycle, and the Central Square is now a place of music and dance, where street performers gather." Her gaze dropped to her plate then. "Surely you know that others aren't as pleased with the new order of things. My mother says their reach is marginal. But she says that even marginal can be damaging when strategically placed."

I thought about that, about Brook's father, and his small band of followers. Marginal was probably a good way to describe them.

Strategic was probably better.

Delta came back, carrying a crisp, red apple in both of her hands, holding it out to me as if bearing a gift. Her smile was so infectious, I nearly giggled as I took it.

"Please, Your Majesty, if there's anything else I can get you, anything at all . . ." Her offer dangled between us.

"You really don't have to" was all I said, not wanting to be waited on here, of all places. "And, please," I insisted. "Call me Charlie."

"Pssh," she scoffed, waving her hand at me. "I could never." And then she skipped away, a satisfied smiled on her face.

Inwardly, I sighed. I would be glad to get back to the palace, to the life I was becoming familiar with. To my routine and my family.

Zafir reached down and snatched the apple that I held halfway to my mouth. I turned in time to see him chucking it into the trash. "Sorry, Your Majesty. You can't be too careful."

I hadn't meant to slip away from Zafir and the others.

Or maybe I had. Probably, I had.

All I'd really wanted was to have a few moments of peace before leaving for Capitol Hall. . . . A few moments during which I could collect myself and gather my thoughts. It didn't really matter, though, I supposed as I stood in front of the washroom mirror examining my reflection: my silvered hair, my wide blue eyes, my skin—so pale and luminous, casting a light of its own. I doubted I'd have long before they realized where I'd gone to.

I could remember, when I was little, staring at my reflection for hours and wishing I looked like Brooklynn. Wishing I had her dark hair and dark eyes. Wishing that *my* skin was the color of baked honey rather than colorless milk.

She could never be you, I heard a dusky voice whisper. *She could never contain the kind of power you contain.*

My fingers gripped the edge of the sink "Not now, not now, not now . . ." I dropped my head, repeating the words as I willed Sabara away.

Closing my eyes, I counted.

One. I took a breath and held it, trying to find the strength to crush her.

Two. I imagined shoving her, pushing until she was buried deep inside of me once more.

Three. I let the air out slowly and opened my eyes again, blinking against the harsh overhead light.

But the face staring back at me from the mirror was no longer my own. It belonged to a woman with wild red hair and red-hot eyes. Her skin was the only likeness between us: white as alabaster.

I startled, my hands—and hers—flying to cover my face.

But before I could breathe, or even blink, she was gone. It was me again, staring back from the other side of the glass.

Only me.

I trembled, no longer sure I could trust myself. No longer certain my eyes hadn't deceived me.

And then I heard her voice again. *Trust me. Trust . . . us.*

There is no us, I insisted silently, biting my lip until it bled between my teeth. I felt frustration uncoil, and this time I knew it was my own.

That couldn't have been her. That couldn't have been Sabara in the mirror staring back at me.

Sabara was dead.

"You're dead!" I shouted, my voice determined and angry, daring my reflection to shift once more. Daring my eyes to see her.

I don't know what I thought would happen in that moment, but what I didn't expect was for the world around me to disintegrate into utter pandemonium.

It was the blast that came first, rumbling the floor beneath me and splintering the mirror into a million tiny shards until my reflection was unrecognizable, even to myself. Instinctively, my arm shot up to cover my face as I crouched low. My fingertips clawed the edge of the porcelain sink for support. Above me, the electric lights flickered and blinked.

For the briefest moment, as my heart hammered painfully, I thought the worst of it had passed with that single explosion, and I allowed hope to fill me as I breathed again.

But then a second blast ripped the air, and everything around me went black, the power failing at last. From above, I was showered with broken ceiling tiles, sharp and unforgiving. I ducked beneath the lip of the sink, squeezing my eyes closed against the dust that choked me as I tasted my own stomach acid rising in the back of my throat.

Over the ringing in my ears, I heard screams and shouts, cries for help that filled the hallways beyond the closed door, reverberating in frantic discord.

My eyes widened as I was suddenly aware that the bathroom wasn't completely cloaked in blackness, not in the way it should be.

Pale light sparked from my skin, turning me into a beacon of sorts . . . A living, breathing beacon. I searched the rubble around me, trying to gain my bearings, and realized that there was a second source of light, faint but visible, coming from just beneath the closed door.

Scrambling toward it on my hands and knees, I moved recklessly over fallen debris, razor-edged pieces that nicked and abraded my palms. I dropped onto my stomach as a third explosion shook the ground like an earthquake, and this time I heard something else as well: the unmistakable sounds of gunfire.

I couldn't stop myself from wondering whose weapons those were. Who was firing upon whom.

The door, when I finally reached it, was warm . . . hot, even. And I worried about what that might mean, about what I would be walking into if I tried to go out there. But I couldn't stay here, cowering in the washroom. It might end up being my tomb if I didn't at least try to escape.

More screams found their way to my side of the door, piercing me, and I held my breath, bracing myself as I decided to go for it. I had to.

I used the handle to drag myself up, and I eased the door open. Outside, the hallways were blanketed in gloom, and the acrid taste of smoke choked me and singed the hairs inside my nose. I tugged at the hem of my shirt, lifting it to cover my mouth. But I couldn't stop moving; I had to get out of there.

Students rushed past, pushing me out of their way, and I

heard more shouting and more shots fired. I kept my head low, but I stayed on my feet and kept moving, trying not to trip over the debris in my path. The only thing I could see was myself, my own skin, and even the light that came from within me couldn't penetrate the thick, black clouds that billowed everywhere. It reflected off the smoke, making the smoke look as if it were coming from me, as if *I* was the source of all this destruction.

"Zafir!" My voice rasped, but it was lost in a tide of shrieks and chaos.

I reached a door and I slid my hands over it as I slowed to peer inside the broken pane where a window had once been. The classroom beyond was choked with the same dense smoke that filled the hallways. But some light filtered in through the third-floor window on the other side of the room.

Beneath the teacher's desk, I could see three younger students, barely older than Angelina, huddled together. Hiding. I recognized the small black-haired boy who was coughing so hard I worried he'd swallowed too much of the roiling smoke—there seemed no more room in his lungs for real air.

It was the first boy off the bus that morning: Phoenix.

But it was the body of the instructor lying on the floor beside them, her eyes large and unblinking, that made me realize I couldn't just leave them there. Half of her skull had been caved in from a fallen chunk of ceiling plaster.

Just as I was opening the door between us—or what was left of it—another detonation jarred me, knocking me all the way to my knees. As I fell, my chin clipped the opening left by the broken window, and jagged glass, like teeth, dug into my skin. Something warm dribbled down my throat, into my collar, and I knew it was blood. But none of that mattered. Not now. Not yet.

"What happened?" I heard a girl's voice shout from somewhere beyond the billowing haze behind me, and instinctively I stilled. "It wasn't supposed to happen here. Orders were to wait till she reached Capitol Hall—"

"Orders changed," a male voice interrupted her. "The timeline had to be moved up."

"So where is she? Who has eyes on her?"

There was a moment of silence, and in that moment I was certain what it was they were saying. Me. They were talking about me. I was the reason for the attack.

I tried to take a step backward, away from them. I needed to find Brook or Zafir, to warn them. To find help.

But my reprieve was brief, and either because I'd moved or because the smoke around me had cleared, I heard the girl again and knew I was no longer cloaked by the thick clouds.

"I see her!" It was the girl again, but now her words were hushed as I tried to place her voice. "Over here!" she whispered again. "She's here."

That was when I realized where I'd heard her voice before: It was Delta.

When she reached me, relief swelled inside my chest as I told myself I must have misunderstood the meaning behind her words. Clearly, *she* couldn't be responsible for the attack, she was a student here—my liaison for the day. She'd been looking for me because she wanted to help me. I lifted the back of my hand to swipe self-consciously at my oozing chin. She reached down, her fingers gripping my arm as she dragged me to my feet. "Come on," she said, and she was right, of course—we needed to keep moving.

"The children," I blurted out. "There are children in there." I turned back toward the door, but her grip on my arm tightened. Too tight.

The crunch of footsteps drew my attention as an older boy, tall with long legs, came running toward us then—stumbling, really—through the churning mass of fumes. His face was streaked with ash and sweat, and his haunted eyes were filled with unspoken horror.

"You can't go that way!" he warned, begging us to listen. "They've got guns! They're shooting the teachers, and even some of the students."

I held my hand out to him, trying to formulate the right words so I could tell him it would be all right, that we'd find a way out of the school, that we'd be okay.

And then Delta raised her hand too. But hers wasn't empty, and the gun she held looked cold and menacing. Just like her eyes. Cold. And menacing.

She fired once, and then once more, and the boy's body stiffened, his eyes going wide with disbelief. Nearly as wide as my own.

It wasn't until he fell forward, his mouth gaping slackly, that I could move again. I lurched toward him, my fingers digging into the back of his shirt. But I knew it was too late for him when I felt his body convulse with finality beneath my fingertips.

"What are you doing?" I shrieked up at Delta, but I already

knew that, too. Zafir had been right about her. She wasn't to be trusted.

I scrambled toward her, not really thinking clearly, only wanting to stop her before she could do anything like that again. Before she could kill someone else. I reached for her gun, *my* hands clumsily clawing at *her* hands. Yet despite the fact that she was younger than me, and somewhat smaller, she was strong, and she seemed to know what I planned to do even before I did. I clutched at her wrist, meaning to twist her arm, the way Zafir had taught me to do. But she easily deflected me, jerking the other way and grabbing my arm. She rotated it until I was the one whose wrist was cocked at an unnatural angle. Until I was the one who gasped. She released me then, shoving me to the ground.

Suddenly I understood what Zafir had been trying to explain to me all those weeks we'd been training: Technique conquers power.

Delta had technique on her side.

That, and a sleek metal weapon that was pointed right between my eyes. The light from my skin reflected off its polished surface.

It was then that a man came to stand beside her, seeming to materialize from the very smoke itself like a wraith.

"In there," she ordered in Termani, jerking her head toward the door where the children had been cowering. *"She said there are children hiding inside."*

"We were told not to harm the Counsel children," the man countered, but Delta stopped him.

Her lip lifted into a snarl, her eyes never leaving mine.

"Then check to see if they're Counsel or not. If not, then they don't belong here," she spat. *"Get rid of them."*

"No!" I shouted, even as the man spun away, obeying her order. "Why are you doing this? What do you want?"

She stared down at me, and I wondered if she even realized that I'd understood her words, that I'd understood what she'd said as she pressed the steel barrel to my forehead. *"We want the Vendor queen, of course."*

And then a gunshot split the air.

VII

Blood. Everywhere there was blood.

I blinked, using both hands to wipe it away, ignoring the other bits that clung to my skin and wincing as my stomach recoiled.

Blinking again, I struggled to find my voice. "H-how did you find me?" I managed at last.

Brooklynn cocked her head, stepping over Delta's limp body without a second glance as she kicked the gun out of her way. She sidestepped the blood that was pooling on the floor, coming from the wound in Delta's forehead. "You're kidding, right? You know you glow, don't you? You're pretty much the only thing I *could* see."

I glanced down at myself. Of course. The glow.

She pushed past me, keeping me at her back as she held her own gun—one I hadn't even realized she'd been carrying—at the ready. "I saw someone else." She tipped her head toward the classroom door. "Did he go in there?" she asked, and when I nodded mutely, she nudged the door open with the toe of her boot.

I felt like I should do something. Instead I just stood there, helpless. Immobile.

"Drop it!" I heard Brook's unwavering voice call out.

The little boy's coughs reached me then, from inside the room, and I realized the children were still in there. With an armed man. A cornered man.

I stepped closer, unable to stop myself, no matter how strongly I argued that I shouldn't, that I should stay back . . . where it was safe.

I saw him then, the wraith of a man with the sharp features, a gun held to the side of Phoenix's head. Still coughing on the thick smoke, the little boy's eyes lifted when I peered through the doorway, and I wondered how I must look to him, to the children hiding there. Like a ghost. An apparition.

"Get away from me," the man sneered at Brooklynn, lifting the child higher, holding him in front of his face and using his small body as a shield, leaving only his shins and his feet exposed, and giving Brook no kill shot. Still, I watched as Brook took another step closer.

"Move away from the door." The man was no longer speaking in Termani but rather in Parshon as he tried to bargain with her. I'd never heard someone switch between the two languages before and it was disorienting. *"Let me go, and I'll release the kid."*

Brook's eyebrow ticked up as she took a step sideways. I wondered what she was doing, what her plan was, because I was certain she must have one. Brook always had a plan. "Put the boy down and I'll let you escape with your life," she answered in Englaise.

He matched her pace. Each time she moved closer, he moved away. But every step seemed to lead him nearer to the doorway. Wasn't that what the man wanted? Didn't he just ask for her to let him go?

"I don't believe you," he hissed, foregoing Parshon now in favor of Englaise. "Your father said you were a liar. He warned us not to trust you."

Brook stiffened, her face becoming a wall of ice. Impenetrable. Arctic.

And that was when I felt it . . . the hand on my shoulder.

Zafir must have been standing there for several seconds, watching as Brook herded the man closer and closer. Inching him nearer to the royal guard's position.

He pushed me aside, and on feet so stealthy they made no sound at all, he slipped into the classroom.

Behind the wraithlike man.

And in one graceful motion, he wrapped his arm around the man's throat while he buried his blade in the base of the man's neck.

"Why didn't you just shoot him?" I asked as I clutched the coughing boy to my chest. Zafir and Brook and I were moving as quickly as we could through the hallways, the other two children in tow. I worried about the boy in my arms. Carrying him was like carrying a bird; he was tiny and fragile, as if his very bones were hollow. His frail body spasmed each time he hacked and choked. I was sure the smoke had been too much for him.

It wasn't just rubble that blocked our path now; there were bodies, too. It was hard to tell whether they were victims of the blasts or of Delta and her cohorts, but either way, they were a lethal reminder that we weren't safe yet.

Zafir remained at my side. "I couldn't risk harming the boy," he answered.

As if on cue, the boy coughed into my neck, and I tightened my grip on him—a silent reassurance.

I thought about the fragments of skull and flesh I had yet to wipe from my face. "I was right behind Delta when you shot her. Weren't you worried about me?"

On each side of her, Brook held a child's hand—a girl and a boy. Unlike the boy in my arms, they were able to keep up easily, and I could see both sets of curious eyes shoot up to watch her.

"No," she answered.

"*No*? Why not?"

"I guess I'm just better with my weapon," she said, grinning at Zafir.

Zafir ignored her as he dragged me to a stop. Brook followed his lead, hauling the children into a nook at the end of the storage lockers. He lifted his hand, and we all understood what he meant: Be silent.

It was several seconds before we heard what he had, and I felt the boy's fingers tangle into the hair at the base of my neck. I could hear his breathing—tiny, wheezing gasps—and I worried that he might cough again, might inadvertently give away our location. I steadied my own breathing, hoping his lungs might follow my lead, hoping my calm might somehow filter into him.

Rubble crunched coming from behind the heavy screen of smoke. It sounded like a thousand boots pulverizing the broken ceiling tiles beneath them.

Zafir gazed down at me, and I knew what he was looking at. With my skin the way it was, there was no way we could remain hidden. . . . Even if the boy didn't cough. Even if we remained completely silent.

He stripped off his jacket then and draped it around me, covering as much of me as possible. . . . My arms and my hands. He buttoned it around the boy, too, closing it all the way to my neck. Then he took off his shirt and wrapped it around my head, concealing my hair and part of my face, until only my eyes were still visible.

He was camouflaging me.

And then he stood in front of me, using his body to barricade mine.

We waited like that, listening for more screams or shouts. For gunfire or another round of explosives. But instead we heard only the sound of approaching feet. Inside the fabric that swathed my face, it grew harder and harder to breathe, but I didn't complain. I didn't even shuffle my feet. I simply kept my eyes wide and alert, straining to see.

"Commander Maier?" A woman's voice finally cut through the dense smoke, using Brooklynn's formal title. "Are you in here?"

Brook released the children's hands. "I'm here. We're all here."

Behind the woman—one of the guards who'd been in front of the school that morning—there were several more soldiers, all wearing the same uniform. All standing at attention, awaiting word from their leader . . . from Brook.

"The army arrived shortly after the first bomb was detonated," the soldier stated as she stepped forward, her stance formal and stiff. I released a breath and hugged the boy, relief swelling through me as I unraveled Zafir's shirt from my face as I listened. "We lost a lot of civilians in the blasts, even more in the gun battle."

The use of the word "civilians" made my stomach tighten. *Children,* I thought. *She meant children.*

"Once the terrorists realized they were outnumbered, they fled. The ones our forces didn't get, the snipers took care of on their way out of the buildings. Unfortunately, we didn't take a single one of them alive, so we have no way of knowing who, exactly, was responsible for the attack here today."

Brooklynn sighed, and there was nothing rigid about her posture. She looked deflated, defeated. "Yes we do," she said simply, running her hand through her tangled curls. "It was my father."

When we exited the building, the sunlight nearly blinded me and I had to shield my eyes until they'd adjusted.

I heard a woman screaming, but not in the same way the students inside the walls of the Academy had screamed. Her voice, the woman's, was filled with so much relief it nearly undid her. The little boy in my arms wiggled and struggled against me, and I had no choice but to release him the moment his feet hit the ground.

I glanced up in time to see the woman break free from the crowd, still shouting, and I realized she was calling out a name: "Phoenix!" she cried as the boy raced down the steps and jumped into her outstretched arms. She swallowed him up, hugging him ferociously. "Phoenix . . . Phoenix . . . *my sweet baby Phoenix . . .*" Her last words trailed into Parshon, and I wondered if it were simply habit, if she'd even realized she'd done it at all.

It had been easier inside, where the confusion and ugliness of the attacks had been concealed behind a thick veil of smoke. Out here, the destruction was all too clear, far too apparent. We could all see just how much damage had been done. How many lives had been lost.

I gazed down at my feet as I walked, trying not to look at the bodies that littered the wreckage, trying not to remember how I'd once envied those who walked upon these gleaming, polished steps.

It was the halo of golden hair I saw from the corner of my eye that caught my attention, making my steps falter. I froze midstep. My breath caught in my throat as I blinked hard, telling myself it wasn't her. . . . It couldn't be her.

But as I moved closer, something in my gut told me I was wrong.

I stopped in front of the girl lying facedown on the stairs, her limbs at odd, unnatural angles. There was a single bloodstain square between her shoulder blades. She'd been shot while she was trying to escape.

With trembling fingers, I brushed aside her hair, needing to see the truth for myself, needing to be certain.

Beneath the golden curtain, her face, turned to the side, was ashen, and her wide eyes were vacant.

My heart ached as I lifted her hand, clutching her cold fingers. . . . Fingers I'd held not so long ago during a riot in the park, a day that I'd decided to save her life, when we'd gone from being rivals to friends.

And suddenly I wished I'd listened to Brook when she'd warned me about her father. When she'd warned me he'd made threats against me.

Except she got it wrong.

I wasn't the one in danger by being here today. I wasn't the one who'd been injured.

It was everyone else.

Somewhere below me I heard a strange clicking sound, and I set Sydney's hand down reverently, once more brushing my fingertips over her cheek. A final farewell.

Zafir reached for my arm. "We have to go," he insisted, ushering me down the steps.

I heard another click, this time closer, and I glanced up to see a man, just a few steps below me, holding a camera. It wasn't something most people owned, the camera. It had been a luxury item even before the days of Sabara's rule, and seeing it here, in the streets, seemed odd and out of place.

I thought Zafir might take it from the man since he was pointing its lens right at me, snapping photo after photo. Instead, the guard moved to stand in front of me, signaling to one of the soldiers near the top of the steps who rushed down and escorted the man away from us. I didn't know if they'd let the man keep his images, or his photography equipment. It wasn't my concern at the moment.

When we reached the bottom of the steps, the woman who'd been screaming the boy's name—Phoenix—stopped us.

"Thank you, Your Majesty," she said weepily, still forgetting to speak in Englaise as she clutched her small boy to her heart. *"Thank you for saving my son."*

I smiled, but guilt coursed through me as Zafir shepherded me into the awaiting vehicle, a different one from the one we'd driven to the school this morning, and I wondered if the other had been destroyed. I wondered, too, where this one had come from. I said nothing, though. I just waited until the door was closed behind me before letting myself cry.

I saw Max running toward our vehicle long before the palace had come into view.

"Stop!" I shouted at the driver as I was climbing over Brooklynn to reach the door.

I stumbled only a few feet over the pitted road before I fell into his arms, which came around me and lifted my feet off the ground as he hauled me against him. "You're safe. . . . You're safe. . . . You're safe. . . ." he whispered over and over again.

I was shaking all over but I somehow managed to find my voice. "It's okay, Max. I'm okay."

I inhaled the scent of his skin—wondering when I'd stopped smelling the smoke, when it had stopped filling every part of me—while I ran my fingers roughly through his hair. I could taste his worry as his lips moved restlessly over mine, not settling in any one place, just pressing to mine and then moving on to my cheek, my nose, my chin, as if he were trying to memorize my every feature with them.

Then at last, his kisses slowed, and his agitation became something gentler, something far more distracting. My pulse raced as his mouth traced my jawline and he whispered against my ear, his breath hot and teasing and filled with yearning, yet I couldn't understand a single word he'd said.

It didn't matter, though. I understood his meaning well enough.

We were together.

"Brook's father is already claiming responsibility," Xander announced over breakfast. "He's spreading the word that he plans to hit the queen where it hurts."

My stomach knotted. I stared down the table to where Brooklynn sat, wondering if she felt half the responsibility I did. If she'd lain awake last night replaying yesterday's events over and over in her head.

"We have to get you out of here, Charlie," Xander went on. "All of you—your entire family."

My father pushed a loaf of hot bread toward Xander. "Are you sure that's necessary? We're safe here, aren't we?"

"Look," I tried, hoping to stop all this talk about fleeing before it got out of hand, before my family had to be displaced. "I know Brook's dad. I grew up with him. Maybe I could just talk to him."

"You realize what he did yesterday, don't you?" Max's

voice was subdued, his dark eyes serious. "He killed innocent people, Charlie. I think we're past talking now."

"Besides, you didn't see him," Brook said sorrowfully from her side of the table. "He can't be reasoned with. I warned him what would happen if he tried anything—"

Xander's fist pounded against the table and the room went silent. He glowered at Brooklynn. "You saw him? Tell me you didn't know about this."

All eyes turned to Brook.

"It was before the attacks, before her tour. I told Charlie we should tell you, that we should postpone her trip into the city," she explained. "But I had no idea he would actually make good on his threats. . . . Especially not like this. I thought . . ." She shrugged. "I thought he was harmless."

"Brook's right," I tried to intercede. "This isn't her fault. It's mine. If I'd have listened, none of this would've happened in the first place."

Max's hand found mine beneath the table, and without meaning to, I blushed. "It's not your fault either," he said. "He's a madman. Someone like that can't be reasoned with. You need to listen to Xander. We'll get your parents and Angelina to safety, and you'll leave a few days early for the summit."

My eyes went wide as I turned to him. "What about you? You're still going, aren't you?"

Xander's voice drew my attention. "He can't. Not now. Ludania needs someone who can rule in your absence, and Max is the most qualified. He was raised in the palace and he was in the military. He can keep the palace—and the country—running while we concentrate on keeping you safe. Eden and I will go with your family, to my grandmother's private estate in the southern region. They'll be safe there, no one knows where it is."

I glanced down at my mom and then my dad, and finally to Angelina. "They could go with us. To the summit, I mean."

Xander shook his head. "No, Your Majesty. Ludania is nothing without a queen. As second in line to the throne, Angelina's safety is as important as your own. Separating the two of you is the only way." His expression softened. "As her sister, surely you understand that."

I did. Of course I did, but it didn't make it any easier to accept, and despite being the leader of an entire nation, at the moment, I was powerless. Less than powerless.

They were leaving me with no options.

"There's more. These are already starting to circulate." It was Aron, who'd been quiet up until now. He slid a piece of paper down the length of the table.

I stared at it. On it was a picture, one that the photographer had snapped of me kneeling over Sydney's body on the steps of the Academy. My skin looked as if it were reflecting the light from the camera's flash, creating sparks of light all over the image. My expression looked dazed.

Below the image, the caption read: "New Equality Brings Death to School Children!"

"What is this?" I asked, blinking hard as I tried to focus, my eyes stinging.

"It's a periodical. They're like the underground missives we used to read, only now they're no longer secretive. It's how news is being spread throughout the city and beyond," Aron answered.

"The irony is," Xander added, "the person responsible for this periodical is only able to distribute it *because* of the New Equality he or she is condemning."

I folded the paper and slipped it into my pocket. Not because of the message it delivered or because I was proud of the changes I'd made that allowed for such a publication to exist. Instead I kept it because it was the only photograph I had to remind me of Sydney.

PART II

BROOKLYNN

Brooklynn stared out in the general direction of the Capitol. Not that she could see it anymore. The concrete wall that surrounded it and its jagged-toothed buildings hadn't been visible for hours. Instead she watched passing shadows of a countryside shrouded by the cover of night, images that blurred into unfocused smudges, making one impossible to distinguish from the next.

The floor beneath her feet rocked, and she reached for a handrail to steady herself. She waited until her stomach caught up with the lurching motion of the train; something she kept telling herself she would grow accustomed to with time. Train travel wasn't nearly as exhilarating as she'd thought it would be. For her, it was the opposite, in fact. She felt endlessly queasy, and she longed to stand on solid unmoving ground once more.

Unfortunately, fate had different plans for her and her queen.

Everything had happened so quickly after the attack on the Academy. Yet it wasn't until they'd left the school that day that they'd realized the assaults hadn't been confined to only their location, but that nearly an entire section of the city—just barely rebuilt from the rebellions that Brook herself had been a part of—was on fire. Buildings had crumbled like oily black pyres that burned angrily and then collapsed into piles of charred rubble.

Now Brooklynn, Charlie, and Aron were on a train headed north, along with Zafir and fifty of Brook's best soldiers. They'd be arriving at the summit several days early, but at least they'd be arriving intact.

It was now Max's job to find those responsible for the attacks on the Capitol, those who'd dared to kill innocent children and threaten the life of their queen, those who included Brooklynn's own father.

She wished it were her instead of Max.

She'd rather be anywhere but here, she thought, letting her forehead fall against the glass and trying to ignore the stomach acid burning the back of her throat.

"Here," Aron's voice interrupted her, his hand finding the crook of her elbow and leading her away from the window. "Sit down and drink this."

She lifted her gaze to his, frowning as she took the steaming mug from him. Wrapping her hands around it, she inhaled deeply, expecting to breathe in something delightful, an elixir meant to soothe her stomach. Instead, she winced. "What are you trying to do, poison me?"

Aron dropped down beside her, pushing her out of his way so he had room on the bench. "Don't be so grouchy, it's not my fault you can't sleep."

"No," Brook reluctantly relented. "I suppose it's not." She lifted the cup to her lips and blew on it before taking a sip. The bitter liquid scalded her tongue. "Where'd you get this, anyway?"

Aron watched her closely, his warm eyes crinkling when she grimaced. "That bad, huh? The old lady in the galley swears it's a cure-all for motion sickness."

She took another swallow, a more generous one this time. "I'm not motion sick, I just . . . I just don't like trains is all."

"How would you know? This is the first train you've ever been on."

Brook's scowl deepened. "Well, I don't like *this* train."

"Because it makes you sick."

Brook nodded. "Right." And then she frowned at him. "No," she countered. "I mean, that's not what I meant. I don't trust it. It doesn't feel . . . stable." She glowered at Aron over the top of the earthenware mug, but she continued to sip the foul liquid inside. "What do you want, anyway, Midget?" He leaned back, and Brook had to duck to get out of his way. She wondered when his shoulders had widened, and she suddenly realized that the nickname sounded odd rolling off her tongue. "I mean, why are you even here?"

He closed his eyes, and Brooklynn could've sworn he looked relaxed, that he actually liked the rocking of the locomotive beneath them. She narrowed her eyes, trying to decide if she saw the hint of a smile on his lips, or if fatigue was finally getting the best of her and her eyes were playing tricks on her. "On the train? Or here now, with you?"

Brook weighed the difference before answering. "Either."

Aron opened one eye and squinted down at her, forcing her

to admit that he'd grown taller too. "I'm here because Charlie needs us. I'm here because I don't really have anywhere else to go." He sighed, leaning his head back once more. "And I'm here because you're my friend, Brook, despite how hard you try to pretend I'm not."

Silence filled the gap between them, and Brooklynn let the mug settle on top of her lap, her fingers clenching it a little too tightly as she turned to look out the window to avoid looking at him altogether.

He was right, of course, even though it annoyed her to admit it. He *was* her friend; he always had been. Even when they'd been small and she'd competed with him for Charlie's attention, trying to shut him out, to make Charlie choose which friend she liked best, Aron or Brook. But Charlie had never chosen, and Aron had always been there, doggedly pursuing the two girls, never complaining when he was the third wheel. He never worried that his friendship wasn't as valuable as Brook's, or that he wasn't as important.

Brook wished she'd been half as sure of herself back then. Her stomach burned as she thought of all the times she'd convinced Charlie to ditch Aron, to go out without him, or to lie to him about where they were going.

Especially now, as he sat with her, his silent presence assuring her that he'd always be there for her.

The train shuddered, rocking violently, and the liquid sloshed over the sides of the mug, spilling onto Brooklynn's lap.

"Damn," she cursed, jumping up.

"Here." Aron took the mug from her and set it on the other side of the bench. "Are you okay?"

She looked at the mess on her pants, splotchy and wet. "It's fine. It's not really that hot. Just . . . wet."

Aron grinned. "Do you want me to get you some more?"

She shook her head, her eyes lifting hesitantly to his. "No. But thank you"—a small smile drifted over her lips as she tried out his name . . . his real name—"Aron."

He smiled back, his head bobbing in rhythm with the uneven motion of the train. "I like that. Does that mean I'm not 'Midget' anymore?"

Brook's eyebrows lifted and she exhaled loudly as she sat back down. "I'm not sure you've been a Midget for a while now. I was probably the last one to notice it."

"Hmm," Aron uttered, his head still nodding thoughtfully. And after a moment, he said. "You know you have to sleep sometime, Brook. You won't do Charlie any good if you're exhausted."

"I will," she finally answered when it felt like too much time had passed. "Eventually, I will."

VIII

I didn't mind the train; I found the pitching and swaying motions comforting, if a little jarring. Besides, there were a thousand other things plaguing my thoughts, seeping into my consciousness and keeping me from sleep.

I wondered where Angelina and my parents were right now, at this very moment. I wondered if they were as bothered by our separation as I was. If their hearts felt sick and hollow at our being forced apart. I hoped with everything I had that they were safe in their remote sanctuary, and that they were being well cared for.

I worried, too, over Ludania. About those who would do her harm, putting their own needs above the safety and welfare of their countrymen. Namely, Brooklynn's father and his followers.

And I thought about the summit. About the queens I would meet, and the lessons that had been cut short by our premature departure from the palace.

I closed my eyes, letting the worry rattle around in my brain as I listened to the metallic rasp of the iron wheels against the rails. My mind drifted and I speculated over whether *he* would be there, at the summit. . . . Niko Bartolo. Niko, and his golden eyes.

I jerked suddenly, blinking hard and startling myself. *Where had a thought like that come from? Why had I even thought of him at all?*

Taking a breath, I rolled onto my side and stared at the wall. I felt as if he'd snuck inside my head while no one was looking.

Only that wasn't entirely true, was it? I sat up then, yanking back the covers and throwing my legs over the side of my mattress. I knew what it was as I glanced down at myself. My skin was a mere glimmer of what it had been just days ago, after Angelina had tried to chase Sabara away once more. It wasn't *my* thought at all; it had come from *someone* else.

Sabara.

But why?

I shook my head. It didn't matter, I could feel her in there, inside me, her Essence moving and shifting. Her grip tightened like a garrote around my neck, crushing my windpipe. Crushing me.

I'm stronger than her, I told myself. *I am a warrior.*

But I wasn't. And Niko Bartolo was still there, anchored in my thoughts.

All because of her.

As soon as I admitted as much, her hold loosened. I waited until my breathing stabilized and my heart rate returned to something close to normal. Eventually, the savage birds that beat their wings wildly in the pit of my stomach subsided, settling once more.

"Who is he?" I finally managed, my throat feeling scored by the talons of a million razor-sharp claws.

The train continued on, lurching at odd intervals, and I joggled with it, letting it rock me as I concentrated on summoning her, concentrated on forcing *her* to listen to *me*, in the same way she'd done to me so many times before.

But there was no response. Just the sound of my tremulous breaths and the increasing darkness as my skin continued to dim.

And a yearning I didn't understand.

Angry black tides came rushing toward me, washing over my lips, my nose, covering my head. They choked me.

"You don't deserve to be here," a voice whispered, undulating like the surf. And, for some reason, I believed the voice, allowing myself to submit to it, giving in to the churning waters. Letting them suck me under. Letting them drown me.

And then I was floating, drifting somewhere beneath the surface. I didn't breathe—I couldn't. But I was still there. Somehow, still alive.

I tried to blink, tried to move my arms, but nothing happened.

I focused my gaze, willing my indolent body to respond, concentrating on lifting a finger, wiggling a toe. Winking an eye.

The water around me pushed me first one way, and then

pulled me the other. I moved in and I moved out, yielding to the force of the tide.

Panic welled inside me as I realized I was a prisoner. Trapped inside a vessel no longer my own.

Buried alive.

I shot upright, gasping and blinking furiously.

Blink. I could blink.

And I could breathe and move and wiggle my toes.

It was only a dream, but my shoulders dropped as I let the terror of the nightmare subside, like the rippling waters of a wave.

I'd never seen the surf before, yet the memory was so real that I knew, in that moment, exactly what it would feel like, exactly how it would smell—the briny tang of salt lingering in the air.

It wasn't my memory, I realized, easing back against my pillow, which was damp with sweat.

She was there, always inside me. Always trying to find a way out.

This had been Sabara's dream. Her nightmare.

And just like before, with the mirror, and with her ability to speak to me during my waking hours, she was evolving. Before, she'd only been able to find her voice while I was sleeping; she'd only been able to speak to me in my dreams.

Now, I was having *her* dreams. Sharing her memories.

She was gone for the moment. I knew because of the silence in my head.

And I needed to find a way to keep it that way.

IX

"What is this place?" I twisted in my seat, my breath steaming the cool glass as the scenery outside changed, morphing into something more savage and bleak than the landscapes we'd left behind.

Across from me, on the other side of the elaborate spread of warm muffins and fresh jams, juices and brewed teas, sliced berries and stewed meats, I saw Brook shake her head, confusion evident as she held a biscuit halfway to her mouth. She turned to stare out too. I knew she hadn't slept, that she'd stayed out of our sleeping car until the early hours of the morning. Even if I hadn't been awake, I would've known from the dark smudges beneath her eyes.

"It's the Scablands." Zafir's voice was flat when he answered.

I stared off into the distance, to where scrubby gray shrubs sprang up from the dry black earth, but only here and there, making them look like a pox on the landscape rather than a part of the scenery. I saw nothing that suggested life out there would be easy—no water, no trees, and no vegetation, save the spare, sticklike bushes. There were no roads in sight. No signs of civilization whatsoever.

As I contemplated the name, the Scablands, I wondered what I'd expected.

The word "wasteland" came to mind, but to me, wasteland conjured images of flat, desertlike barrenness. And this was anything but flat. I took in the jagged peaks, which seemed to force their way up from the ground, like fat, broken tree trunks, black and dead and fossilized. They were tall and packed together, creating a mountainous forest that looked nothing less than intimidating. Deadly, even.

I guess what I really hadn't expected was for the train lines to run so close to this remote area.

"Where are all the people?" My breath fogged the window even more.

"There are settlement camps farther east, but building isn't permitted this close to the railways," Zafir explained patiently. He poured steaming black coffee into his cup and drank without waiting for it to cool.

I glanced at Brook, and was certain she was just as appalled as I was at the idea of living all the way out here, so close to the northern border, segregated from society. "Why not?"

"The purpose of being sent to the Scablands is to live in isolation."

"What about supplies?" I was surprised that I'd never posed these questions before, that I'd never pondered the living conditions of the criminals who were no longer permitted to live in Ludanian society. I wondered what else I'd neglected to consider. What other populations I'd ignored.

Zafir didn't seem to share my concerns. "Being sent to the Scablands is a punishment, not a reward. Everything is meant to be more difficult, including commerce. They trade the same way everyone else does, they just have to travel farther and through more perilous terrain."

I thought about that as I glanced out at the colorless landscape, feeling something sick twist my gut. "What about the children? There *are* children, aren't there? How are their needs met? How are they housed? Schooled? What about medical care? They're not all convicts, Zafir." I looked up at him earnestly, wanting him to allay my worries, but knowing he wouldn't lie simply to appease me.

"Your Majesty," he started, and my stomach sank over what might follow. He sighed, and I could feel his patience slipping. "These are lawbreakers, and if they're not, if they were simply born to the parents of criminals, then it's their choice to remain here. There's no law that states they *have* to stay once they reach the age of consent. Don't feel sorry for them; this is the life they've chosen . . . either by actions or by will."

I didn't like his answer, but I knew he was right. There had to be a place to send those who'd committed crimes. There had to be consequences and punishments, especially in light of the fact that I'd abolished the gallows. Still, I worried about those who lived out here. They were still my people, still citizens of Ludania.

Aron and Sebastian joined us then, and I had to bite my lip over the eager expression on Sebastian's face. His eyes lit up when they fell on Brooklynn, even though, as always, she seemed oblivious to the stable master's attentions.

"The horses are restless," Sebastian announced, managing to force his gaze away from Brook to address Zafir. "Too much time cooped up in the livestock compartments."

Aron scooted in next to Brook and reached for a hot biscuit that had tendrils of steam still rising from it. He tore it open and scooped a hefty portion of peach jam into it before stuffing the entire thing into his mouth.

Beside him, I saw Brook's gaze shift sideways to watch him, her lip curling in disgust, as she picked listlessly at her own food.

"We can't stop here," she stated, turning to Sebastian who stood at attention, his shoulders back as if he were one of her soldiers. It was her call, though. Zafir was there only to protect me. Brook was the one in charge of the army that escorted us. "We're too close to the Scablands," she said, as if she hadn't just learned this bit of information herself. "We can let them off to stretch their legs at the next major depot . . . *after* we leave this territory."

Aron snorted, and Brook's gaze shot to him. "What? I suppose you have a better idea."

"I jus' don' . . . ," Aron started, but crumbs spewed from his mouth, spraying the table in front of him. He reached for Brook's cup and took a swig, ignoring her scathing glare. When he finally swallowed, choking down the rest of the biscuit in a huge gulp, he tried again. "I just don't see how you're going to get that many horses off, and then back on again, during a single stop. Do you really think the engineer is just going to hold the train for you? For Charlie definitely, but not for you, Brook."

Brook smirked at him, her jaw set, her eyes glinting like hard steel. "Is that a challenge? Because I don't need Charlie's help on this. You just watch. I bet I can get him to stop and wait . . . *without* mention of our queen here."

"Oh, you're on." Aron laughed, slapping Brooklynn on the shoulder. "Can I come with you when you ask him? I gotta see this."

Five hours later we were standing on a wooden platform above the rails. It took several moments to regain my land legs, to adjust to the firmness of the motionless ground beneath me, but it felt good. Normal. Steady.

Several cars down from us, I could already see Sebastian supervising as the horses were unloaded, their hooves beating against the makeshift gangway they navigated, and I wondered how long the timbers would bear the animals' weight. Sebastian didn't seem to share my concerns over its sturdiness, he seemed more worried over the horses' well-being as he handed them off to awaiting soldiers two at a time to be walked about the unpaved streets.

I shuddered, pretending my chill was a result of the weather, rather than the horses we'd soon be riding in place of the train. The idea of mounting the beasts shot cold terror straight to my heart.

Still, it was colder out here than I'd anticipated, and although I couldn't actually see my breath, I could feel it crystalizing within my chest, becoming something denser than normal air, harder to expel. I wondered how long until there'd be ice on the ground. Until we saw the first flakes of snow.

"It's only going to get worse," Zafir stated. "The farther north we travel, the closer to winter we'll get."

I frowned at the guard's upside-down logic as I wrapped my arms around myself, understanding his meaning nonetheless. The summit was being held in the mountainous region of Caldera, Queen Neva's land. I'd been warned the climate could be *inhospitable*.

I lifted my already icy fingers to my lips and blew on them.

"Do you want me to send for your coat?" Zafir asked, always attentive.

"I'm fine, Zafir." And when I saw that he didn't look convinced, I added, "Really."

I glanced around at the tiny town nestled in the jagged hills, just inside the northern border of Ludania. Technically, we were still in Scabland territory, and it still had that same sharp-edged feel to it, as if the town itself had been chiseled from the rocky terrain. Everything, other than the sidewalk we stood on, seemed to be crafted from some sort of stone slab or brick. I saw slate and granite and shale.

The overall effect was as chilling as the wind that whipped through the nearly uninhabited streets. The only sign of life came from the chimneys on every roof: Smoke rose from nearly all of them.

I wondered if this was what Brooklynn had in mind when she'd said we would stop at the next major depot, but I knew it wasn't. The next depot was more than three hours away, and Sebastian's complaints for the horses had grown more uncompromising with each minute that had passed.

I turned to see Brook coming out of the lead car, the train's engine, accompanied by a man wearing a black wool suit with polished brass buttons. Golden fringe hung from his shoulders. The engineer, I assumed. He wiped the sweat from his brow as he gazed adoringly at Brooklynn on the step above him. She gingerly laid her hand in his, allowing him help her down the steel steps.

Aron rolled his eyes as he stood on the walkway, watching them. I could practically read his thoughts, which I was sure must mirror my own: as if Brook needed the man's help. She was about as helpless as a full-grown tigress.

I bit my lip as she led the engineer in our direction, making it look too much like she'd tethered him to a leash. He didn't seem to mind, though. In fact, quite the opposite. If the unflinching grin he wore was any indicator, he seemed to be enjoying himself immensely.

"Are you sure it's no inconvenience?" I heard Brooklynn coo in a voice that sounded nothing like her usual commanding tone. "I wouldn't want to put you too far behind schedule." Her hand, which was on his forearm now, slid lower, until her fingertips brushed the bare skin at his wrist.

His white moustache was stark against his cheeks as they grew redder than the flowers in the palace gardens. His stout chest puffed up as he drew in his belly and held it there. "No bother at all, young lady," he purred, although not nearly as demurely as Brooklynn had. "You just let me know when your party's set to go. I don't mind waitin' a bit."

Aron's eyes rolled so hard I thought they might actually pop out of his head.

Brook flashed a meaningful grin at him as the engineer strolled away, a boyish skip in his step.

"I don't believe it. Are you sure you didn't drug him or something?" Aron scoffed at her.

"I can be pretty persuasive when I want to be." She didn't need to remind any of them that part of her work with the underground rebellion had been to convince the men of Sabara's army to give up information. And she'd rarely had to use force.

Aron shook his head, and I wondered if he was really so unaware of Brook's appeal. If growing up with her, the way I had, had somehow made him immune. "I'm gonna see if Sebastian needs help. He looks like he has his hands full."

I glanced over again and saw fleeting glimpses of Sebastian's red bandana between hindquarters and muzzles and the long, muscled legs of the horses. He looked harried and frustrated, and shouted orders to the men who barely paid him any attention. He'd clearly not mastered the commanding presence of his position.

I felt like that sometimes. Like I hadn't quite found my voice.

Or rather, like a queen with two voices . . . neither of us strong enough to rule.

As if listening to my thoughts, I heard her—Sabara—unfurling within me. *Together we can do it. Together, we're invincible.*

I squeezed my fists, searching for that inner quiet that seemed harder and harder to find. I didn't want to hear her. I didn't want to listen to her toxic oaths.

"Your Majesty?"

I jolted, turning to face Zafir. The unease in his expression told me I'd missed something. "What?"

"Do you—?"

I blinked. "Do I what?"

"Do you want me to get that coat now?"

I looked down at myself, shivering and clutching my arms. I couldn't tell him the truth. I couldn't tell him it wasn't the chill that had gotten to me.

It was her.

Instead, I nodded, and he signaled to someone I couldn't see. "Stay close to me," he instructed as he pushed me to start walking. "Let's see what there is out here."

BROOKLYNN

The hairs on the back of Brook's neck prickled and she glanced once more over her shoulder.

Beneath her, the horse continued to thrash, tossing his head up and down, fighting the metal bit stretched between his lips. But Brook didn't think it was the bit that was bothering him.

She felt exactly the way her way horse did. Spooked.

She tugged the reins, cautioning the animal to settle down. He stomped his feet in reply, prancing anxiously and setting her teeth on edge.

"Quit it," she hissed as she reached down to swat at his neck. She didn't need his alarm contributing to her uneasiness.

Finally he settled, but she couldn't say the same about herself as her heart quickened. She suddenly wished that she'd followed her own orders and stayed closer to town, that she hadn't wandered so far from the train station . . . and from the safety of her men. She'd only meant to be a few minutes, half an hour at the most, as she searched for a better vantage point from which to see how far the Scablands stretched.

She pulled one rein sharply, demanding the horse turn in a full circle, allowing her a 360-degree view of the terrain. There wasn't much to see: some buildings in the valley below her, including the train depot, and at her back, the threshold of a dense, shadowy forest that stretched as far as she could see. On all sides were rocks and stones and black dirt.

The weather up here was even harsher than it had been down at the station, but despite the cutting wind that slashed at her face, a thin layer of sweat prickled Brooklynn's skin. She winced, shielding her eyes from the gusts as she tried to urge her mount forward. She thought she'd get a better view on the other side of the rocky hillside, but the animal dug in, refusing to go any closer.

Finally, she dismounted, dropping the reins and inching closer to the bluff.

She eased forward, balancing carefully as she reached the drop-off. It wasn't too sheer, but the gravel beneath her feet was loose, unstable. She crouched low, surveying everything around her from this new position. Now wasn't the time to second-guess her instincts, and at the moment those instincts were screaming at her, warning that something was off.

She was only planning to take a few tentative steps down the embankment, but the moment her boots hit the gravel, she felt the pebbles beneath them shift and slide. Her stomach lurched as she reached out, trying to stop herself by clawing at the scraggy clumps of grass and shrubbery. All she managed to do was to rip the skin from her palms, abrading them until they were raw and bleeding. As she slid, she leaned as far back as she could, trying to keep from rolling headfirst all the way down. The last thing she needed was to break her neck on a routine scouting mission.

It wasn't until she slammed, feetfirst, into a thick stand of thorned bushes, that she realized that the sounds she'd heard—the grunts and the curses—had been coming from her.

"Damn," she swore again when she glanced down and saw the tear in her pant leg. She collapsed backward on the solid ground with relief. She dug out a ledge for her heels to make sure she didn't slide any farther, then sat up, pulling a twig from her hair. Her hands were killing her. She lifted them so she could examine the dirt-caked scrapes that ran across both palms.

And that was when she heard it. The train . . .

. . . pulling away from the station.

X

Out in the streets, the wind had picked up. Ignoring my protests, Zafir had sent someone back inside the train for my cloak, and even now, as I stood before the stone hearth inside the tavern, warming my cold hands in front of the blazing fire, I was grateful for the shelter it provided. The hood concealed my hair and most of my face, making me feel like I was wearing a disguise, although Zafir's presence still drew unwelcome notice wherever we went.

It was hard to ignore a giant.

He'd left me alone for only a moment, casting cautionary glares at everyone within spitting distance as he went to get me some tea. Under normal circumstances Zafir wouldn't wait on me, but I was still shivering, and my teeth clattered noisily, making it nearly impossible to speak.

Outside in the streets, beyond the tavern's walls, I could no longer hear the rumble of hooves, and I knew Sebastian and the others had headed just outside of town, giving the horses room to run before reloading them back onto the train for the remainder of our journey.

Inside the tavern, however, there were the sounds of dishes being slammed against the long wood-planked tables, mingled with raucous laughter and loud voices. A drunken lot in one far corner warbled a bawdy tune about a farmer's daughter. Not one of the crooners seemed aware of me . . . or my giant.

Along with the smell of burning wood, I inhaled the scents of tobacco and rubbed meats and candle wax as I took in the eclectic furnishings and decor. Black wax dripped onto the tables and floors, creating dark pools beneath the rusty chandeliers overhead. This was the kind of place a girl, one who wasn't a queen, could easily get lost.

Unfortunately, I wasn't so lucky. I spotted the periodicals, first one and then another, and then an entire stack of them, scattered across the nearby tables. When the front door opened, one of them was carried on the breeze that rushed in, and it landed near my feet.

I stooped down, letting my cloak fall around my face as I studied it. I didn't need to, of course. I'd already seen this particular bit of news. I'd already seen this image.

I stepped closer to the fire, crumpling the paper into a tight ball and I tossed it in. I stood there, watching it disintegrate into a thousand pieces of ash, until nothing remained.

And then I heard a sound that seemed compellingly familiar, something I was certain I should recognize. I cocked my head, waiting for it again. It seemed to have vanished, the noise, evaporating into the din of the alehouse around me.

Scanning the room, my eyes fell on a hunched figure

huddled at one of the tables. His black eyes watched me with an intensity that made me retreat within my own skin and I caught myself tugging my hood taut around my throat.

Yet I couldn't tear my gaze away from him. Nor his from me. I saw him, bit by bit, lift one of his fingers to his lips in a gesture that warned me to be silent.

I swallowed hard, telling myself to look away, to search for Zafir within the crowd. To run. To flee from this man. But he held me like that, immobilized, for several long moments while I hoped I was still breathing. While I prayed that my heart was still beating.

The slow, grinding sound came again, that whisper of metal against metal, breaking the spell the man held me under, and this time a shiver of recognition coursed through me.

I knew that sound. This time I recognized it.

It was the train. And it was leaving.

My gaze shot wildly around the tavern, searching for Zafir and coming up empty. *How was that possible? Where had he disappeared to?* He'd never leave me alone like this.

Clumsily, I took a step and felt a voice at my ear, just behind me. I didn't have to see the man's face to guess that it was him. The menacing voice matched the black eyes to perfection.

"Don't move," he warned, his hand clutching my arm through the thick fabric of my cloak.

Again, I searched for Zafir—*my giant*. And again, I couldn't find him.

"What do you want?" I begged. But he shushed me, clamping his fingers more tightly as he pulled me backward, dragging me to someplace I couldn't see.

I thought about screaming, about struggling and calling for help. Surely someone would notice, even among this ribald mob. Surely someone would stop him.

But his next words froze the words in my throat.

"If you so much as peep, your guardian dies. Understood?"

My guardian. *Zafir.*

I nodded. And I was lugged through an almost unnoticeable doorway behind the hearth.

BROOKLYNN

It had taken Brook far too long to scramble back up the hillside she'd just skidded down. She'd lost precious time. Time she could ill afford to waste.

And now she pushed her horse, barreling toward town as fast as the animal would carry her. Beneath her she could see the veins bulging in his withers, sweat lathering his sleek coat.

It didn't matter, though, she needed to get to Charlie. She couldn't miss that train.

But a part of her knew—even though she refused to admit defeat—that she was already too late. She could see the train, too far away now, gaining momentum with each turn of its wheels as the horse beneath her began to lag, ever so slightly.

She dug in her heels harder and slapped his hindquarters. "Yah!" she screamed until her throat was raw. *"Yah!"*

She barely slowed as she approached the empty tracks at the station, even as she raced headlong into the awaiting crowd of her own men, each tethered with horses and looking as confused as she was. The train was long gone, there was no denying that now.

Sebastian raced forward, shoving his way through the throng of soldiers and shouting at Brooklynn as she jumped off of her horse, even before she'd come to a complete stop. She handed him the reins.

"What are you doing? You can't ride him like that!" Sebastian berated her, running his hand along the horse's coat and swiping away layers of thick, frothy sweat.

"Where's Charlie?" Brook demanded, ignoring the stable master's concerns for the animal. When she saw Aron, she repeated herself, calling out to him above the heads of the others, not caring that she should be asking after Queen Di Heyse now, rather than her childhood friend. "Where's Charlie?"

Aron looked frazzled as he threw his arms in the air. "I don't know. I've searched everywhere, but I wasn't here when the train started moving." He ran one hand through his already rumpled hair. "I haven't seen her. I have no idea if she was on the train when it pulled away."

Brook turned to her men then, her voice loud and commanding. "Was anyone here? Did any of you see your queen?"

Heads shook, and among the buzz of voices the consensus seemed to be that no one knew what had happened to her. No one had seen where Charlie had gone.

Brook paced, her shoulders rigid and her boots pounding angrily against the rough-hewn timbers that served as sidewalks. Her hair whipped wildly around her face as she muttered to herself. When Aron tried to interject, tried to ask her what she meant to do, she raised her hand, effectively silencing him.

After a moment, she stopped marching and lifted her chin. "We'll take an hour," she shouted, loud enough to be heard by everyone. "*One* hour. Break into parties of three and search everywhere, and I mean *everywhere*. Homes, businesses, schools, and brothels. I don't care, if it has walls, search it. In one hour we'll meet back here and regroup." She turned to Sebastian. "You take care of the horses." At Sebastian's gaping expression, she added, her expression softening, "You can have five men, but that's all I'll spare." She stepped closer so her soldiers couldn't hear. "Get them ready for travel, Sebastian. Find grain and water, whatever we need. If we don't find Charlie in the next hour, we're heading north."

XI

Zafir looked downright homicidal. He looked like he wanted to wrap his hands around the throat of the man who'd just pushed me through the undersized doorway and throttle him.

Or maybe he would've preferred the use of weapons. To make it a slow and torturous death.

But he was in no position for fighting of any kind. He'd been gagged and restrained, both by ropes and chains. A wise choice on the part of our captors, since surely rope alone wouldn't have held the royal guard.

His eyes blazed with deadly determination as they alit on me, and I could practically read his thoughts: I *will* get you out of this.

I believed him, of course. I'd wager my money on Zafir any day.

I glanced around, taking in our modest surroundings. The cottage was more of a hovel really, built from stacked stones, of course, and sealed with some sort of black ooze that looked—and smelled—like it might have been made from manure. The ceiling was too short, even for me, as was the door, lending the place a confining feel. Filthy straw covered the dirt floor, serving as mats, I supposed, and it was piled thicker against one wall, reminding me of a nest. There were a few chairs that served as the only real furniture I could see, set randomly about the one-roomed structure. Zafir seemed to be bound to the sturdiest of the lot.

"What do you want with us?" I spun to face the man who'd pushed and prodded me along, forcing me through the back alley exit of the tavern. Outside, another man had been waiting for us, and together, the two of them had dragged me into an awaiting horse-drawn cart, where Zafir had already been bound. Like Zafir, I'd been shoved to the cart's floor, forced to keep my head low as we bounced along a potholed road out of town.

Or I assumed that was where we were . . . out of town. Because when I was finally allowed to rise again, there was no train depot or tavern—no buildings at all, in fact—in sight. The ground, which had started out pitted and uneven, had grown nearly perilous over the course of our journey, as we'd climbed higher into the hills. If I'd thought the train had been jarring, it had been nothing compared to the jolting ride in the wagon. My teeth had banged together, causing stars to burst behind my eyes on more than one occasion, and I was still picking straw off my cloak and out of my hair.

Zafir had been gagged the entire time, but I'd asked the same question over and over again, "What do you want from us?" Only to be answered with a curt "Hush now. Be still."

Now, standing within the fetid walls of the cottage, the

black-eyed man finally answered me, his lips parting to reveal teeth that were rotted by decay. "I apologize, but it had to be that way, Your Majesty. We had'ta get you outta there without anyone knowing it."

I took a step backward, staggered by the fact that these men already knew who I was, that I hadn't simply been the casualty of highway robbery.

I was here because of who I was. As was Zafir.

"Wh-wh—" I tried, but my voice seemed to catch in my throat.

"Wh-wh—" The man mimicked, but beneath the short ceiling, his hunched frame seemed somehow smaller . . . more frail than intimidating. His mouth widened into something that was doubtless meant to be a grin, and his brown teeth glistened. He waved his hand dismissively. "Please, let me explain," he said in his strange accent. It was Englaise, but from him, it came out sounding warped. His e's were too long and his a's were too soft, making his sentence sound like "Leet me eexplan." He eyed Zafir suspiciously. "And then I'll let your man there go."

At that, Zafir struggled against the chains that bound his large shoulders, and the chair beneath him wobbled even more. The legs made splintering sounds, and I thought surely they would crack at any moment, shattering beneath his weight. But they managed to hold, and after a moment of useless writhing, he gave up again, falling still.

"Tell me," I said simply. "H-how did you know who I was?"

The man made a clucking sound and rubbed his hands together. "We're Scablanders, Your Majesty, not imbeciles. Well," he corrected, grinning that horrible decaying grin once more as he jerked his head toward the large man guarding the door, the same man who'd been waiting for us out in the alley behind the tavern. His pitch-colored eyes glittered. "Not all of us, anyway. Jeremiah there's about as dumb as they come."

Jeremiah glanced up at the mention of his name, almost on reflex, but didn't seem to register the words—or the insult. He looked at each of them, his expression glazed, his mouth slack as if it were difficult to keep his lips, overfull like stuffed sausages, closed around his crooked teeth. He scratched his head, his thick fingers finding their way beneath the fitted leather hat he wore, the one with goggles like pilots used to wear back when air travel was still possible in Ludania. Back when fuel was plentiful, and transportation wasn't as restricted as it was now. He gave an indifferent shrug when he realized he wasn't actually expected to respond, turning back to his duty.

"News travels out here," the crooked man continued in his odd version of Englaise. "Especially news that our new queen has skin that shines like the sun." His black eyes appraised me and I shrank away. "And like I tried to tell your man there"—he turned his accusatory gaze on Zafir—"someone's looking to snuff out that glow of yours."

At those words, Zafir's entire body went rigid. He flexed again, thrashing violently. The chair splintered beneath him, making a thunderous noise as it cracked, its legs finally giving out. And Zafir, no longer shackled to the flimsy legs, shot to his feet just as quickly as he'd fallen.

Before I could blink, he was charging forward, hurling his entire body weight against the bent man with the festering teeth. The man was too puny by half to fend off a giant like Zafir, even with his arms still bound against his sides. The man's eyes went wide, and I heard him wheeze as he was buried beneath the bulk of the enormous guard. I knew Zafir was crushing—possibly killing—the old man.

"Zafir, stop!" I shouted as Jeremiah hefted his weapon, a wooden club that was no more dangerous than some of the sporting equipment I'd seen used for children's games. Confusion was evident in Jeremiah's bewildered eyes. "You're hurting him. Get off!"

I reached out to push Zafir myself, but he didn't so much as flinch. Instead, he turned toward me, looking just as perplexed as Jeremiah did.

"Let's at least hear what he has to say," I explained, no longer worried about Jeremiah as understanding dawned. Jeremiah was merely a prop. He was harmless.

My hand reached out to the rough burlap tied at Zafir's mouth, but he jerked his head away from me, turning so I could reach the restraints at his back instead. My fingers fumbled with the lock.

Beneath him, the old man groaned.

I dropped to my knees, so my face was even with his. His black eyes were wide and pleading. "The keys," I insisted. "Tell me where to find the keys and I'll have him release you."

He opened his mouth, and then closed it again, like a fish extracted from water. . . . As if he, too, was taking his last gulps of air. "Zafir, ease up a little," I demanded. "Let him breathe so he can speak."

As Zafir shifted, the man's gasp was audible, and nearly

undid me. I wasn't heartless, but I needed my guard to be free. I needed to know what this man knew, and what he meant when he said someone was out to get me.

"M-m-my . . . p-o—" His breath came out more like a whistle, the sound finding its way from between his decayed teeth. I caught a whiff of that breath, which was exactly how I would imagine it would smell, coming from such a foul place.

I winced, shrinking back. "Your *pocket*?" I answered for him.

He nodded, or tried to, and I moved lower, my fingers brushing his trousers, searching. When I felt it, my fingers thrust inside the rough filthy fabric, emerging with the small steel key, no bigger than my pinkie. Hard to imagine that something so delicate looking could imprison someone so . . . so mammoth.

My hands trembled as I rushed around to unlock Zafir, before we were interrupted by someone who was brighter than, say, Jeremiah. Someone with a more effective weapon than a club.

When his wrists were free, and he was wholly unbound, Zafir got up, releasing the man pinned beneath him. The man didn't move at first. He just lay there panting, gasping for breath as his skin changed from a stony shade of gray to a flushed and clammy pink.

When, at last, he regained his composure and sat up, he was facing not just me, but Zafir as well. "We need answers," Zafir demanded, his voice filling the cramped space and making the walls around us quake.

The man held up his hand in surrender. "Fine. Yes, I—I'll tell you everything, just don't sit on me again."

My lips twitched. I didn't blame him, really, I wouldn't want

Zafir to sit on me either. "What's your name?" I asked, my voice infinitely more patient—and less booming—than Zafir's.

"Florence, Your Majesty."

"Florence?" Zafir's eyes narrowed. "You expect us to believe that's your name?"

The man staggered to his feet, using the nearest chair—one that hadn't shattered—to prop himself up. "My mother thought it had a certain . . . flare. Friends just call me Floss, though." His flashed his rotted teeth at me. "You can call me Floss, Your Majesty." He turned to Zafir, his eyes narrowing, becoming tiny, black pellets. "You, call me Florence."

Zafir shook his head. "So you think Queen Charlaina is in danger?"

There was a meaningful pause, and even Jeremiah looked up to see if something important was about to happen. "I didn't say she was in danger. I said she was goin' to be murdered. Big difference." It sounded like "mardeered" when he said it.

Zafir took a threatening step closer and Florence's hands went up again, fending off Zafir as he cowered. "Explain."

"I already tried, back in town, but you didn't want to listen to me then, did you?"

Zafir scowled. "You didn't say anything about someone wanting to harm—"

"Murder," Florence interrupted, and Zafir's jaw clenched.

"Murder her," he corrected himself. "I believe your exact words were: 'We need to get the queen back to my place where we can keep her safe.' That's not the same thing. You sounded like a lunatic."

Florence cackled, making Zafir's point for him. "Lunatic? Could a lunatic knock out a royal guard *and* save the queen from certain death?"

Zafir stiffened. "I think *only* a lunatic would try such a feat," he ground out. "Now tell us what you know before"—his eyes narrowed to slits—"before I sit on you again."

"A'right. A'right. Settle down." Florence blustered, holding his hands up as if to ward Zafir away. "But you should be thankin' us, Jeremiah and me. We did, after all, save Her Majesty's life."

I thought of the way he'd abducted me back at the tavern and forced me to stay hidden in the back of the wagon. "How exactly did you *save* me?"

His grin grew, and this time Jeremiah joined in, whether he understood why he was grinning or not. His smile, though, was infectious, his vast mouth stretching interminably. He was nodding, in the same way Florence was.

"If it hadn't been for us, you'd'a been on that train, and your throat'd been cut before the next stop. That was the plan, sure enough."

Zafir reached for my arm and dropped his voice, glancing suspiciously toward Florence. "Your Majesty, you're not actually listening to this, are you? He's exactly what I thought he was, a lunatic."

I raised my head, pinpricks of curiosity niggling at me. "How could you possibly know that? What makes you think something was going to happen on the train?"

Florence grinned again, and I grimaced inwardly. "As I said, Your Highness, we're not imbeciles out here. We know things. Word travels."

"Your Majesty," Zafir corrected pointedly.

"What?" Florence asked, his brows pinched together.

"It's not Your Highness. The proper way to address your queen is Your Majesty. Maybe you don't know as much as you think you do." The corner of his mouth turned up, and I nudged him with my elbow.

"It's fine," I said, playing arbiter. "Go ahead. You were saying . . . ?"

"I was saying . . ." Florence huffed, turning away from Zafir and addressing only me now. His expression softened. "I was saying that Jeremiah and I were in the next town over when we overheard a girl callin' herself a scout braggin' about how she was part of a new rebellion. She got real loose-lipped the more she drank, and by the time she left the pub, she was telling folks not to get too used to the new queen 'cause she—meaning *you*, Your Majesty," he said, his voice punctuating the *Your Majesty* for Zafir's benefit. "'Cause you wouldn't be around long. Said there was a price on your head and she aimed to collect it."

"So why did you think Her Majesty was in danger on the train? Wasn't that the safest place for her to be?" This time it was Zafir asking.

"Look here." He reached into the back of his waistband and pulled out a scroll of worn parchment. He bent down on the floor and rolled it out, smoothing it with his gnarled hands. "She left this behind. Wasn't hard to figure out it was a map."

Zafir and I leaned down, and my eyes widened. He was right, of course; it was most definitely a map. And despite the fact that it wasn't written in Englaise, or any of the other

Ludanian languages, it also wasn't hard to tell what it was a map of: the train line. More specifically, the train line I had been on.

"See?" Florence said, tracing one filthy finger along the tracks, stopping to tap the spot where two jagged red slash marks crisscrossed them, marking an X. It was just past the train depot where Florence had intercepted us. "This is where it would'a happened, I figure."

I turned to Zafir. Maybe Florence was right. Maybe someone had been sent to kill me.

Zafir continued to glare at the map. "And did she say who'd set the price on the queen's head?"

"Didn't have'ta. After news of the bombings in the city, everyone knew that Jonas Meyers or Mayer, or whatever his name is . . ." He reached into his pocket and pulled out a dirty blade, setting it in the center of the map. "Everyone knows he's out to get the queen. You're just lucky Jeremiah and I convinced that conductor to move along without you, Your Majesty. Otherwise you'd'a lost your head."

BROOKLYNN

Brook shivered, clutching her jacket tighter as she scooted nearer the fire, wishing she'd dressed warmer. Wishing that she'd been more prepared. Instead, not only was she unprepared for the weather, but she had no idea what she was doing. She'd never led a search party before. For all she knew, she was leading her soldiers into some sort of trap.

After that first fruitless hour, Brook had made the tough decision to break her soldiers into three separate groups. She hoped that by splitting up, they might increase their odds of locating Charlie.

She'd sent one group, a traveling party made up of ten of her best riders, back to the palace, with news of what had happened at the depot. It was entirely possible that Charlie had decided to head south, too, and that Brook's riders would intercept the queen on her journey home. Maybe the message to Max would be entirely unnecessary, and her riders would simply become escorts to Her Majesty.

The second group of ten had been ordered to remain in

town, to keep searching. They'd already scoured buildings and questioned everyone they'd come in contact with, never revealing why it was so important that they find the "missing girl" for whom they searched. But they'd come up empty.

The men she'd left behind were to continue hunting, moving outside of town and combing every inch of the Scablands if necessary. Turn every home and shop inside out for signs of their lost queen. For this, Brook had sent ten of her most resilient and well-trained men and women. Survivors. Those whose instincts and skills matched the treacherous lands they'd be searching.

She would keep moving north, the most likely place Charlie was headed. Charlie was nothing if not predictable. Tenacious. She'd made a commitment, and she had a goal in mind, and nothing—not even a little hiccup like losing an entire army to back her up—would stop her.

Brook just hoped that wherever Charlie was, Zafir was as well.

She cupped her hands around her mouth and blew into them, trying to dethaw her frozen fingers.

"You shouldn't be so stubborn. This will warm you," Sebastian promised, sitting beside her and handing her a dented, silver flask.

Across from the fire, Aron nodded. "He's right, you know?" His lips curled, the promise of a smile. "I mean that you're stubborn, of course."

"I don't see you drinking any of it," she shot back to Aron, lifting her hand to ward away the flask. She knew Sebastian was worried, they all were, but she needed some space. Needed to think. "No thanks. That's what the fire's for."

Aron reached for another log and threw it on the already blazing campfire. The red coals beneath the flames flickered, and wayward sparks shot into the chilled air, turning black and then drifting away with the smoke.

Brook worried about that too, the fire. It made them an easy target, pinpointing their location in the yawning blackness that engulfed them. Pointing them out to rogue outlaws who might chance by. But they'd had to stop. They'd ridden hard, her band of thirty-odd soldiers. Well, thirty-odd soldiers plus Sebastian who tended the horses, and Aron who was practically useless. They'd stayed as close as they could to the rail lines, following the tracks as far as possible, until even the moon overhead couldn't provide enough light to let them find their way.

Finally, when they'd realized they couldn't keep going, Brook had ordered the fire, and she'd set up watch shifts, taking the first one herself and giving some of her soldiers a chance to sleep.

They were well into the second watch now, and as far as she could tell, neither Sebastian nor Aron had slept yet either.

"You should turn in," she said vaguely to the both of them. She turned, looking into Sebastian's dark eyes, which reflected the fire's light, and spoke again. "I need you refreshed in the morning. Don't make me order you."

He opened his mouth, as if to argue, but then closed it again when he caught her determined expression. There was no point disputing a command. He leaned closer, and reached for her hand, squeezing it reassuringly. "The same could be said of you, Commander. You need to sleep."

Hadn't Aron said the exact same thing just the night before? Why did it sound so much more sincere coming from Sebastian, Brook wondered. Why, when he spoke, didn't it sound like he was laughing at her? Taunting her?

He pressed the flask into her hand. "Just in case," he said, and then she watched as he gathered his jacket tighter against the chill and went off toward the camp they'd set up just outside the perimeter of the fire, using as many blankets as they'd been able to scavenge from the merchants near the train depot before leaving town. Another reason they'd have to sleep in shifts.

"'Night, Sebastian," she called after him, and he lifted his hand in a wave, not looking back.

"What about me?" Aron asked when it was just the two of them. Somehow he made even that simple statement feel like a joke. "Don't you want me to be *refreshed*?"

Brook pinched the bridge of her nose. "Not unless you've learned to wield a mean sword or shoot like an expert marksman over the past few months. Otherwise, you can water the horses for Sebastian." She peeked up at him, over the top of the fire. "You know, like a stable hand."

Aron laughed then, and Brook caught a glimpse of his scars, captured in the flickering light cast from the flames.

At first, right after Charlie had taken the throne, those same scars had been impossible to miss, a daily reminder of what Aron had done for Brooklynn, of how he'd refused to give Queen Sabara the information she'd wanted. Even when she'd tortured him for it. Of course, he hadn't realized it had been Brook he'd been protecting; he hadn't realized that it was *she* who'd been part of the underground movement Sabara was so desperate to locate. All he'd known was that he had no intention of turning on one of his friends. . . . Traitor or not.

And, for that, Brook had been grateful.

That gratitude had faded, however, as days stretched into weeks, and weeks into months. Aron's scars had blanched, blending into his skin until they were practically imperceptible, unless you knew the right places to look for them. Brook had allowed herself to forget what he'd gone through, allowed herself to believe that nothing had changed between them because of it. In her eyes, they were the same Brook and Aron they'd always been.

But that wasn't the case, she was reminded as she stared at the tiny white fractures marring his otherwise perfect complexion.

Nothing was the same anymore.

"You don't know. I could be the best marksman in Ludania. You wouldn't want to waste a skill like that on horse duty, would you?"

"It wouldn't exactly be wasted, we need the horses as badly as we need another gunman, maybe more. In fact . . ." She shivered, clutching herself tightly, her teeth just starting to chatter. "Until we find Charlie, that's all that matters."

She hadn't realized how loud she'd been speaking until several sets of eyes turned in her direction.

Aron got up and made his way to her side of the fire, lifting both hands in mock surrender. "Fine, I give. I'll be a stable boy, or whatever you need me to be." He settled down beside her, dropping one arm around her shoulder and pulling her close to him.

Despite herself, she found herself leaning into him. He was warmer than he should be, considering the temperature, and she felt like a moth, drawn to that kind of heat.

"We'll find her," he promised, leaning his chin against the top of her head, his voice growing distant and thoughtful. "If it's the last thing we do, we'll find her."

XII

There had to be some sort of mistake.

I repeated those same words to myself over and over again, long after we'd left the confined walls of the rank cottage and Florence had taken us to his main house, a place only somewhat larger, but vastly cleaner and more homelike. It had real floors, real wooden walls, and smelled far less like manure than the other building had.

But no matter how hard I tried to deny it, I'd seen the map with my own two eyes, and even though no one else had been able to read the scribblings in that unfamiliar language, I had. I knew what it said. I knew that whoever had written the notes had inside information, dates and times of each of my stops. Information that only someone from the palace could have known. Information that had been meant to be secret.

Someone had betrayed me.

Florence sat with his elbows on a table made from unfinished lumber. The candle that flickered in front of him was casting strange shadows over his sharp features and making the thin wisps of his hair look like smog rising from his scalp. "Get Her Majesty some soup," he snapped at the woman who'd quietly slipped into the room. She kept her head down, her gaze lowered, in the same way we were once required to do when someone of higher status was speaking in our presence. During Sabara's rule.

I watched the woman for a moment, wondering how she'd come to be here, in this place, with someone like Florence. Was she a criminal, or had she been born out here, in the Scablands, never to leave once she was old enough to make her own decision? I wondered if she could possibly be his wife, although she seemed too young by half.

"It's okay. Really, I'm fine," I said, but Florence waved away my refusal.

"Soup!" Spittle sprayed from his lips, but he wasn't talking to me, his gaze was directed solely on her. "Now!"

She scurried to pull a misshapen bowl from a shelf that hung beside the open hearth, and she wound the stained apron she wore around her hand as she reached for the ladle inside the pot. I didn't know what kind of soup it was, but as soon as she stirred the simmering liquid, the savory aroma filled the room and my stomach growled in response.

Florence shot me a knowing look. "She's not much ta look at, but the girl can cook."

She kept her head bowed as she set the bowl before me. "What's your name?" I asked her quietly.

Florence bit off a chunk of seeded brown bread. "Doesn't have one."

I jerked in response to his words. "What?"

"She doesn't have a name. Doesn't need one," he clarified, as if the explanation made perfect sense. He picked up his own bowl and slurped his soup from the edge of it.

I glanced around, realizing there were no spoons. "Of course she needs a name. Everyone does."

He glanced at me, over the rim of his bowl, which was still poised at his lips. He looked perplexed, confused by my inability to comprehend. "Out here, it's just us. Her, me, and my boy." He flicked his gaze toward Jeremiah, standing silently near the door, just as he'd done in the cottage.

"Jeremiah? Is he . . . is he your *son*?"

Florence nodded, his eyebrows raised. "Little light in the brains department, but he's strong, and tougher'n most soldiers. And ain't no one more willing to break a sweat."

I looked at the woman, at her limp brown hair and her calloused hands, and wondered who she was. She wasn't old enough to be Jeremiah's mother. I wondered if she was Florence's daughter, and the thought made my fingers squeeze into fists beneath the table. How could someone go her entire life without so much as a name? How did a woman, any citizen of the realm of Ludania—Scablander or not—end up here, living with a man who treated her no better than a pet?

"Avonlea," I whispered to no one, my teeth clenched.

"What did you say?" Florence asked, holding his bowl half-way to the table, soup dribbling from the corner of his mouth.

"Her name. It's Avonlea."

"Are you sure, Your Majesty?" Zafir asked as Florence set his bowl all the way down now and wiped his chin on his sleeve.

"Why not? It's a good name. It once belonged to a queen of Ludania." I glanced up at the woman and her eyes lifted to meet mine. They were soft and gray, just a hair away from blue. And for a moment, when I thought she might smile, the skin around them bunched up, crinkling like the gathers of Angelina's pet-tiskirts. I said it to her, then, this time with finality. "Avonlea."

She stood there for a moment, soaking it in. "Avonlea," she finally repeated, with a voice that sounded unaccustomed to use, ragged and untried.

"Thank you for the soup, Avonlea," I said, and then directed my attention to Florence. "Now tell us everything you know."

I was still having a hard time piecing everything together, but I was glad to finally be alone with Zafir.

After dinner, Florence had shown us to a room he called a bedroom. It was barely bigger than a closet, but we could sleep in it nonetheless.

On the floor, there were two worn and musty bedrolls that looked as if they'd seen better days. Tired as I was, it didn't really matter how they smelled. Besides, I'd slept on worse.

I collapsed wearily, my head falling against the lumpy pillow. Even from all the way in here, I could feel the cold night air seeping in from beneath the door—air that had found its way in from a crack in the base of the front door and was filling the entire house. I pulled the covers closer and rolled onto my side to look at Zafir, who was studying the map.

"I've seen that language before, you know?" I thought of the beautiful script work on Zafir's sword—*Danii, a weapon forged of steel and blood*. It was an exact match to the handwriting on the map.

The corners of Zafir's eyes crinkled. "I imagined you would recognize it."

"Can you read it?"

He shrugged. "Some. My father tried to teach it to me when I was a boy. He thought tradition was important."

"You've never told me where your family comes from, Zafir. What's your heritage?"

There was a long pause, and then, "They fled from the eastern region during the Carbon wars. The language is Gaullish, but it was the prevailing language of at least a dozen countries in that region at the time."

I eased myself into sitting position. "And now? How many of those countries still speak it?"

"Four. Maybe five. That leaves several million people who could've made this map."

I chewed on that for moment, and then met his gaze. "Well, somehow that person has found an insider in the palace to work with. We have a traitor in our midst."

Zafir looked at me, his expression grim when he nodded. "I suspected as much," he answered before turning his attention back to the map.

I wasn't sure what to make of that. I supposed I'd wanted Zafir to convince me that everything would be all right. To tell me my suspicions were wrong, because I wanted *so badly* to be wrong in this instance.

"I'm sure we're safe for tonight. You should probably get some rest," I tried, but I knew it was pointless.

"I don't trust him. Not entirely. I'll feel better once we're on our way again."

He was right, of course. Not that I didn't trust Florence, necessarily. Of that, I still couldn't be certain. Yet I didn't care for him, really. He was vulgar, which made no difference to me one way or the other. I could handle vulgar. It was the way he treated the girl, Avonlea, and his son that made my skin itch with resentment.

But he'd made arrangements for us to leave at dawn, providing us with horses and men that he assured us we could trust to take us north, to continue on our way to the summit.

I'd assumed we'd be heading back to the palace, but after hearing Florence out, after the information he'd revealed about a potential assassination attempt, both he and Zafir had come to the conclusion that it made sense for us to keep going, to keep me away until Max cleared things up at home.

And I desperately hoped that would be soon, because I missed my family. And, most of all, I missed Max.

"How long will it take us to get there?" I asked.

"Assuming the other riders don't slow us down and we ride hard enough, we should make it to the ferry in about two days' time."

I grimaced. "And assuming *I'm* one of the riders?"

Zafir smiled, a small, knowing look. "Three days. You can do this; I have faith in you."

I did my best to smile back at him, but the idea of three days on horseback made my stomach knot. "At least one of us does."

There was a soft knock at the door and Zafir stiffened, his hand moving involuntarily to his sword, which he'd insisted be returned to him. Florence had stopped arguing when he realized the guard wasn't messing around, that his very life was at risk.

I raised my hand as I crept closer to investigate. "Who is it?" I called out.

The pause was prolonged, and I thought that maybe whoever had been there had changed their mind and gone. But then I heard a voice, slight and hesitant. "A-Avonlea, Your Majesty," she said at last.

I reached for the door handle and opened it before Zafir could stop me. Avonlea stood there, looking much younger than she had before, and I realized she was probably closer to my age than I'd realized. A timid smile found her lips as she lifted the tray in her hands. "I thought you might want to clean up." I could hear nuances of the same lazy-sounding version of Englaise that Florence had spoken in. Balanced on her tray were a mismatched ceramic bowl and pitcher, along with some washrags that looked as if they'd once been some sort of delicate lace, but were now frayed and threadbare.

"Come inside." I stepped out of her way, watching her tiny frame move deftly, her footing so sure that the tray never even wobbled. "You didn't have to do that."

She nodded, and this time her almost-blue eyes met mine. "I know," she answered, and her smile grew as she set the tray on a battered chest of drawers. "Florence'd kill me if he knew I was wasting water this way."

"Florence?" I asked, wondering at her use of his name. "So he's not your father?" I was even more curious about her than I'd been before.

She shook her head abruptly, limp strands of hair falling against her hollow cheeks. "No."

She poured water from the pitcher to the bowl, and dipped one of the tattered cloths into it, wringing it gently. I took it when she passed it to me.

Avonlea waited eagerly, and I knew she meant for me to use it, so I wiped my face, which was still covered in grime from the wagon's floor, and then my neck and my hands. While I worked, she picked up my cloak and shook it out, oblivious to the way hay and dust swirled in the air around us. When she was finished, her hands brushed over the fabric, and I knew that she was feeling the same thing I had the first time I'd touched it, that the fine wool that was so creamy it felt more like soft velvet.

"Thank you for the water." I said at last, setting the rag aside and staring at the murky water that remained in the bowl. "And thank you for dinner, it was delicious."

Her smile was back, earnest. "Thank *you*, Your Majesty," she whispered, her voice subdued. "For giving me a name."

THE ASSASSIN

He waited until everyone around him had gone still. There were still two soldiers on lookout, but it was easy to steal past them unnoticed. The sentries weren't expecting one of their own to break ranks. Their concern was simply to keep strangers away.

And he was no stranger.

Behind him, the campfire crackled, covering any sound his feet might make against the compacted rock and grit. But it was cold out here, away from the warmth of the flames, and he shivered, steeling himself against the bitter cold of the night.

His eyes were quick to adjust, and soon he could see the path in front of him despite the fact that the moon was virtually nonexistent behind the thick black bank of clouds. He was like a nocturnal predator, he thought slyly, his lips parting into a shrewd grin.

He made his way up to the top of the ridge, so he could look at the encampment below. He wondered if they even realized how exposed they were down there. How obvious and vulnerable they were. He'd have to talk to Brooklynn about that when they stopped again the next night.

Maybe it would earn him some respect in her eyes.

Maybe she'd stop looking at him like some sort of lackey.

The high-pitched whistle that came from behind him, from within a crag in the mountainside, was a dead giveaway. That was sort of the point.

"Keep it down. All that squawking sounds like someone shot a bird or something. Do you not understand subtlety?" It was easy to slip into the cadence of his birth tongue, and he found the rhythm of the familiar speech comforting after speaking Englaise for too long.

The silhouette of a girl emerged, and even without the benefit of light, he knew, from memory, that her cheeks were dirty and that her eyes were hard. *"I wasn't sure you heard me."*

"Everyone heard you. But I had to wait for the right time." He took a step closer, lowering his voice even more and narrowing his eyes curiously. *"You didn't have any trouble finding us?"*

Her shoulders straightened, just as he'd expected they would. She was proud of her skills. *"Don't be stupid. No one can track like me. You might as well have set the forest on fire for as 'subtle' as you are."*

He'd definitely have to warn Brooklynn. His people weren't the only ones looking to find such an easy target, and the last thing he wanted was to end up on the wrong end of a marauder's blade.

A snapping sound behind him made her reach for the dagger at her belt. *"You weren't followed were you?"*

He held out his hand to stop her, straining to see in the

direction he'd just come from. *"No. No. The camp's sound asleep. Just an animal, I'm sure."*

"So? What about the queen? Is she dead yet?"

She may as well have used her knife to stab him in the chest.

He didn't want to answer this question. Wasn't sure how.

"We have a problem. The queen is missing."

She exhaled loudly, not even trying to keep quiet now, and he could feel her disapproval. Why did he even care after all these years?

When her steel eyes found his through the darkness, their intensity hit him like a blast. *"Find her."* Was all she said.

But it was enough.

He nodded, knowing he had to make things right. Knowing he had to convince her she could trust him with this, that it hadn't been a mistake to choose him for this mission.

"There's a party of ten of the commander's men riding for the palace," he told her. *"You need to intercept them. You need to stop them from getting their message to Maxmillian."* He wiped his brow, which was covered with a thin sheen of sweat despite the chill in the air. *"We can't have him sending backup."*

"I'll take care of my part. You just concentrate on yours." She didn't say another word, just turned on the heavy heel of her boot and, without a sound, blended into the shadows once more.

He waited there a moment longer, waited till his heartbeat settled. He hated that she still had the power to make him feel so . . . so weak. So impotent.

He'd prove otherwise if it was the last thing he did.

He was just turning when he heard the sound again, a

snapping, and then a voice. "Who was that?" One of the soldiers asked, revealing himself as he stepped forward.

"I—I . . . what are you talking about? Can't a guy have a few minutes of privacy?" he stammered, not needing to feign surprise. He hadn't expected to rouse suspicions.

"Sure you can, if you were actually alone. But I heard you . . . talking to a girl. Who was she, because I know she wasn't one of ours?" The man just stared at him, waiting for an explanation.

He shook his head, taking an uncertain step forward. "I can explain . . . ," he started, and then he tripped.

Or pretended to trip.

Instead, he moved with the kind of stealth the soldier never could have expected, not from him.

His knife easily pierced the soldier's thin tunic and burrowed into the flesh just beneath his rib cage. He shoved the blade farther, driving it in as far as he could. Even in the pale moonlight that found its way through the clouds, he could see the man's eyes go wide, his mouth opening in shock as he bent forward, his hands reaching for the dagger in his gut. And then he let go of the handle. He lunged at the soldier, throwing one arm around the back of the man's neck, his fingers already slick with blood as he gripped the soldier's stubbled chin. At the same time he reached all the way across the man's chest with his other arm, his fingers digging into the muscular shoulder.

And then he jerked the soldier's chin. Fast and hard.

So hard that a cracking sound filled the night.

For a moment, the only thing he heard was the beating of his own heart and the blood that rushed past his ears.

As the soldier, his eyes unblinking, crumpled to the ground in front of him, he let go of the body, pulling a kerchief from his back pocket and wiping his hands on it.

He wished she'd been there to see how trustworthy he really was. How far he was willing to go to get the job done.

He stayed there a moment longer, waiting to see if anyone else was coming, if anyone had noticed that he'd slipped away. But there was nothing.

Just silence and darkness.

And then he heard it, nearby. The high-pitched whistle—*her* high-pitched whistle.

Just as the first snowflakes of the season began to fall.

XIII

I watched as hands that should've belonged to me reached for a small crystal bottle. My skin was paper thin and covered in brown spots, and even without testing them, I already knew my aged legs were useless. I uncorked the bottle with my crooked fingers and brought it to my nose. The perfume within released a floodgate of memories that I'd thought were long ago suppressed—memories that I knew, even within the confines of this dream, were best forgotten. But it didn't stop my mind from drifting.

A memory within a dream.

The scent brought back images of blue flowers. So fragrant and lovely. So plentiful, floating atop the water along the riverbank. I'd only been a child then, I thought, a little girl. But even now, the memory was lucid and strong.

How long ago had that been? my dream self wondered.

Too long. Another lifetime.

An older girl—who I knew was my sister—had led me to the shore so she could admire the blossoms. It was blistering.

The midday sun had reached its peak in the vast sky, and even children understood the perils of standing too close to the water's edge.

But the flowers were so beautiful. My favorites, I recalled, and I was certain I could reach one—just one—before harm could find me. I'd watched the waters as the scorching sun traced a path along the sky, as I patiently calculated the shifts in the currents, searching for any sign that a predator might be waiting, just below the water's surface. My sister waited, too, indulging her youngest sibling, certain I would never find the courage to try to pluck the flower.

But she underestimated her little sister, and I grew bolder, more confident, and soon I was standing right at the river's edge, water lapping at my bare toes.

"Take care," my sister called in a language I didn't even know I still recognized, still not worried for me.

I took another step, and the slippery sediment below the water squished beneath my feet, pluming outward like smoke and making it impossible to see where I stood. But I liked it, the slick feel, and I took another step, kicking up more of the silt.

The flowers were just ahead of me, their fragrance thick around me, and I leaned forward, the water reaching my knees now. My fingertips grazed one of the petals, sending the flower drifting away from my grasp.

I looked at the still surface, trying to decide. I was already deeper than I wanted to be, deeper than I should have gone. But it was right there, one more step and I'd have it, there was no reason to think I couldn't do it.

I held my breath and lifted my foot out of the muck in the bottom of the river. But when I set it down again, it wasn't on the same slimy surface on which I'd been standing before. It was on something rigid, something scaly . . .

. . . something alive.

I'd tried to stay awake for the rest of the night after I'd been roused by the dream, unwilling to let Sabara infuse me with her memories once more. I hated that she'd found a way to get to me, to try to manipulate me, even if I couldn't be certain it was intentional.

Although with Sabara, everything was intentional.

No matter how hard I'd tried, though, no matter how hard I'd fought it, sleep had eventually claimed me.

We'd awakened that morning to a dusting of snow that coated everything like frost. It didn't stick, and it no longer fell from the sky, but the chill never left the air. And as we climbed higher—moving farther north—I heard my teeth chattering more and more frequently. My fingers felt like icicles as I clutched the reins.

The horses we'd been provided were sturdier and more muscular than the sleek, long-legged ones I'd trained on at the palace. Even their coats felt thicker beneath my fingertips, as if they were bred for this hostile terrain. Everything they were outfitted in was dark and fashioned from iron and leather, making them look as ferocious as the land they traveled.

By the end of the first day of riding, every bone and every muscle in my body ached, my back most of all. I did my best not to complain, or even to wince, since I knew how important it was that we keep moving. My comfort couldn't be a consideration.

When we stopped at a trickling glacial stream to let the horses drink, I thought of the dream I'd had. As the day stretched and my mind wandered, I thought of it often, despite my best efforts to push the dead queen from my mind.

As much as I knew the dream hadn't belonged to me, I couldn't help wondering if it was really hers. If it was truly a memory or if Sabara was simply toying with me.

Somehow she'd managed to make me feel something other than revulsion.

I'd feared for the child in my dream. My heart had stopped and my skin had puckered with dread for her.

I didn't want the little girl in the river to be Sabara.

And I didn't want to waste any more of my time thinking about her.

Zafir kept his gaze on me, almost as often as he watched the new riders who'd joined us. I think he trusted those who accompanied us even less than he trusted Florence and his son, Jeremiah, never turning his back to them.

Avonlea had come along too, although whether it was by her choice or by Florence's order, I didn't know. She hadn't been given her own mount, and was forced to ride with Jeremiah. It was a tight fit in the saddle, but she didn't seem to mind, and whenever Florence wasn't watching the two of them, I caught her turning in her seat so she could talk to Jeremiah. She sang to him, and told him stories. I still didn't know how they were related, if at all.

As we stopped to make camp for the evening, I slid from the mare I'd been loaned and staggered toward a sapling tree, the only solid thing in sight I could cling to for support. I bent over, my back deformed like an old woman's, and I refused to release the tree lest I collapse.

"Are you sure we're going the right way?" I asked Zafir beneath my breath. But when it crystallized, becoming a cloud of fog before my face, I knew the question was unnecessary. We were most definitely heading north.

"We should be at the ferry by nightfall tomorrow," he answered, a wry smile on his lips. "Since the rest of our party was presumably on that train, they'll likely arrive at the summit ahead of us." He didn't voice the part I worried about—the part about a turncoat in their midst.

I still couldn't imagine who that person might be, especially considering that Brooklynn knew each and every one of those we'd traveled with, that she'd hand-chosen each of them specifically for this task because she trusted them. And her instincts were nearly as infallible as Angelina's.

"You two doing a'right?" A voice interrupted us, and I jumped in spite of myself.

"Florence," I gasped, pushing myself to stand straighter.

"Floss," he insisted for the hundredth time that day.

"Floss," I repeated, trying the name out. "You surprised me."

"Just checkin' on you to make sure we're not ridin' too fast." He eyed me suspiciously. "You seem a little . . . How do I put this? *Wobbly* in the saddle."

I nearly choked on his generous description of my riding abilities. I knew how I must look to these men, seasoned riders as they were. Wobbly was putting it kindly. I glanced uneasily at Zafir. "We're managing just fine. Aren't we, Zafir?"

Zafir regarded me apathetically. "If you say so, Your Majesty."

Florence's—or *Floss's,* rather—eyes went wide and he flapped his hands wildly in front of Zafir's face, shushing him insistently. "Stop with the 'Your Majestys' already, and keep your face covered," he insisted, pointing at my hood which had slipped down, leaving my cheeks exposed. "They already suspect she's important. . . ." He tossed his head in the direction of the three riders escorting us—two men and a woman. Each of them looked as if they'd been carved out of the granite hills themselves. "They just don't know why, exactly."

My admiration for Floss just kicked up a notch. I'd been wishing everyone would stop bowing and calling me Your Majesty from day one. I was happy to be plain old Charlie once more.

The corner of my lips ticked up as I turned to Zafir, goading him with this new bit of information. "Hear that, Zafir? *Charlie.* You can call me Charlie."

"Oh, yeah . . ." Floss agreed, his eyes going theatrically wide, and then he winked at me. "I get it. Charlie's a boy's name. No one'll ever suspect."

I frowned at him, surprised he wasn't faster at making the connection between my given name and my childhood nickname. "Really, *Florence*?" I drawled, dragging out *his* name. "I should think you, at least, might be more . . . flexible when it comes to that particular distinction."

Floss's face fell and he frowned back at me. "Fine. Charlie it is. Charlie's a perfectly good girl's name, I suppose." And then he changed the subject. "We got a fire going, and Jeremiah's gone after some rabbit, or whatever else he can snare, so we'll have the girl . . ." He paused as my eyebrows rose in warning, and his jaw clenched at the unspoken reminder. He lifted his fist to his lips and cleared his throat. "I mean, *Avonlea*'ll cook us up some dinner. We'll camp here for the night, and be on our way again at daybreak. If that's a'right with you . . . Charlie."

I smiled, happy to hear my name on the lips of someone other than my closest friends and family. I wanted Zafir to say it, too, although I doubted he'd ever give in. It would be nice to see him loosen up a little.

Instead, I turned to Floss, asking him a question that had been bothering me. "Why are you doing this? Helping us, I mean. Why not just let the plan unfold and let whoever'd planned to kill me . . ." It felt strange saying the words out loud. "Why not let them?"

Floss grinned, his revolting toothy grin. "Could'a, I s'pose." He shrugged. "But I was hopin' there'd be something in it for me if I helped you out. Some sort of re-com-pense for my services."

I frowned, turning to Zafir who didn't seem confused at all. "A reward," he clarified. "He wants a reward for saving your life."

"Oh."

Floss's grin grew. Toothier. More revolting.

"I—I'm sure we can figure something out." Was all I could think of.

But, again, Zafir helped me out. "You'll be compensated. But remember this, if we find out that you're in any way responsible for what's happened out here, if you orchestrated any of this for your own gain—"

Floss lifted a finger, interrupting Zafir, one eyebrow raised knowingly. "From what I hear, the gallows're long gone. What're you gonna do?" he challenged. "Send me to the Scablands?" He barked at his own joke, and then waved off the idea. "Don't worry. I'm clean as a whistle. And I'll be collectin' my reward because I have no intention of lettin' any harm come to"—he dropped his voice—"*Her Majesty* here." He smiled again, and then left us standing there while he whistled an off-key tune.

I started to follow Floss back to where the others were gathering, to where they'd tethered their horses and a blazing fire was starting to swell and dance.

Zafir stopped me, his hand gripping my wrist. "You can't go over there. You need to wrap your cloak as tightly around yourself as you can and stay here, away from everyone."

I glanced down at myself. In the dying light of the day, my glow was finding its way out from between the folds of black fabric. Almost unnoticeable, but not entirely. Not hidden enough.

I knew he was right—we couldn't risk it. But my body was already trembling from the chill.

"We'll build our own fire, and I'll bring you some food once it's ready. I'm sorry, Your Maj—" He stopped himself, and I could see that it was killing him to take Floss's warning to heart. "I'm sorry" was all he managed through gritted teeth.

I watched as he left to gather firewood, and I hunkered down on a boulder, drawing my knees up close to me. I pulled my hood around my face, cocooning myself inside the soft wool. I was grateful for the moment's peace, at least, grateful to be alone, even if I was cold. Sabara's voice had grown quiet over the long day, despite the unnerving dream. She seemed to have withdrawn for the time being, leaving me in relative peace.

Maybe something good had come out of being on the Scablands, after all.

It wasn't until I found myself lying facedown in the dirt that I came fully and completely awake. Until that moment, I'd simply thought I was having another one of Sabara's dreams. The vague buzzing, a blur of voices and shouts, could have easily been coming from inside my own head.

Now, however, I could taste the stringy meat Jeremiah had brought back with him—some sort of scruffy-coated animal I hadn't been able to identify, a meal that hadn't settled well in my stomach in the first place—against the back of my tongue. I gagged on the gamey flavor as I struggled against an immovable weight that pinned me to the ground.

A hand shot out to cover my mouth and my eyes went wide.

"Silence," Zafir's whispered voice warned at my ear.

I nodded, not sure what I was agreeing to, but clear that he wasn't asking for my cooperation. I'd just been issued an order.

When he was sure he'd gained my compliance, he released me, jumping off me and getting to his feet in one nimble motion. He kept me behind him as I struggled to sit upright.

I scanned the area around the embers from our fire, which

had been smaller than the other one. I tried to see past it and into the darkness beyond, where it sounded like there was some sort of struggle taking place.

I thought Zafir would unsheathe his sword, but instead he reached down to his ankle, his hand reappearing with a gun from inside his boot. I hadn't even realize he'd been carrying a firearm.

"What's happening, Zafir? Who's out there?" I asked, getting the rest of the way up and standing behind him.

Even buried within the cloak, I could be seen; there was no point pretending we were hidden where we stood.

He handed me the gun and pulled out his sword.

I considered the weapon in my hand. It was small and light, so much lighter than the steel blade Zafir had been training me with over these past weeks. So much more powerful—a quicker, faster kill—if fired true. I felt safer just holding it.

"I don't know yet, but don't hesitate to use that," he ordered again, and I bobbed my head despite the fact that he was no longer looking at me.

He took a step in the direction of the melee and I moved too, unsure whether that was his intention, but unable to stay behind . . . alone. My hand shook, and I wondered if I'd be capable of shooting straight, or if the others in our traveling party were in danger because of my unsteady grip.

The shouting grew louder and I heard Floss cry out. But his words were muffled and erratic, lost in the chaos of other noises, scuffling and bumping, scraping and clashing. These were the sounds of a battle.

We were under attack.

I froze then, cold dread seizing my heart. Practically right in front of us, someone screamed. It was a deep-down, soul-wrenching scream, followed immediately by the sound of something solid, a reverberating crash that sounded sickeningly like metal striking bone. Iron against skull. My stomach revolted, and I rushed to keep up with Zafir.

Before I could reach him, a figure shot out of the darkness, like an animal—fast and feral. It tackled Zafir from the side, knocking him to the ground. I tried to decide what I should do now, how to help him, as his attacker's form, darkened by night, took shape. My initial assessment had been wrong.

The assailant was indistinct but massive . . . and most definitely human.

My fingers tightened around the firearm as I took an uncertain step back, trying to distinguish one body from the other, worrying that I might have to fire upon the attacker—upon both of them. I tried to ignore the fact that my hands shook violently.

The two became tangled in a heap of limbs and fists, as they hurled one way, and then tumbled the other. I knew the others were under attack as well, but Zafir was my only concern now. My throat tightened as I watched them, my spirit sinking each time I thought he might be losing ground.

Finally, Zafir—and the only reason I knew it was Zafir was because I recognized his voice as he cursed the other man—landed a solid blow to his attacker's jaw. It was bone-crunching. I hadn't recognized that both of my hands—even the one holding the gun—were clenched into tight balls, as if I too were fighting some unseen attacker. When I realized that it was Zafir getting slowly to his feet, while the other man remained flat on his back, I loosened my fingers and released the breath I'd been holding.

And then I noticed the second man, coming at us from out of the shadows. I couldn't see his face, as I was equally certain he couldn't see mine, but there we were, separated by mere paces.

I saw him reach for something, and I didn't have time to think, or even to react. My mind didn't process the fact that I was still armed. Yet even if it had, I was already too late. He was faster.

Or at least he would have been, if it not for what happened next.

A whooshing sound split the air, as if someone had lashed a whip through the darkness.

But there was no whip, and the noise was followed immediately by a sharp, defined *thwack*. Then the man staggered forward, falling to his knees as he roared, crying out in a strident combination of shock and pain.

He was closer to me now, and I could see him reaching for the back of his shoulder, clawing at something.

"Get away," Zafir hollered at me, hurrying toward the man, and blocking my line of sight.

It didn't matter, though; the man had been close enough to the coals of our fire that I had seen his outline—and the shadows of his face. Something struck a chord in me, making every nerve in my body fire. I realized that everything about this scenario was wrong.

"Zafir!" I shouted, in an attempt to warn him.

But Zafir was already there, already reaching for the arrow that protruded from the man's back, just below his shoulder. And when he spoke to him, I realized he already knew what I did. That he'd figured it out too. "I'll have to remove it. We can't just leave it."

Niko Bartolo—the golden-eyed emissary from the Third Realm—glanced up at Zafir, his face contorted by pain. He answered, his voice coming out on a hiss. "Don't worry about me. Your men are with me and we've captured the others," he managed between breaths. His eyes darted around apprehensively and he grasped Zafir by the forearm, his voice lowering. "One of them must still be out there." His gaze shot to me now and I realized he'd known *exactly* who I was all along. "Get her out of here, before it's too late."

It wasn't necessary, however, because his assailant revealed herself at that very moment. She stepped out from the cover of darkness, her bow at the ready, a new arrow drawn.

"You *know* this man?" Avonlea asked, not yet lowering her weapon. She spoke to me and not to Zafir. "You *know* the men who attacked us?"

I knelt before the man stretched on a blanket in front of the fire: *Niko Bartolo.*

Every ounce of common sense I had warned me to stay away from him, while every instinct strained to bring me closer.

"How is he?" I kept my voice low, not wanting to disturb him.

Zafir had prepared a poultice for Niko's wound, some sort of thick paste he'd concocted by smashing the root from one of the nearby shrubs and mixing it with a salve he found in one of the saddlebags. The smell of oiled mint reminded me of the ointments my mother used to spread on my scrapes when I was young, making me cry because they stung the abraded flesh.

Whatever it was, though, I doubted Niko could even feel it after drinking from the flask his men had given him. He'd drained the contents right before they'd held him down to yank the arrow from his shoulder. After he'd stopped screaming, when the arrow had been completely extracted, Zafir went to work treating the injury and Niko had passed out.

As I stared upon him now, sweat beaded across his forehead. He stirred as I squatted closer, trying to get a better look. He thrashed as if my very presence disturbed him.

Inside of me, I could feel Sabara awakening, swelling and reaching toward him.

I squeezed my eyes closed, tamping her back down.

"He'll be okay," Zafir answered, leaning down beside me and wiping Niko's forehead with a rag. "He just needs to rest for the night. He'll have to take it easy tomorrow."

"So, we're letting them ride with us? Are you sure he'll be up for that?"

Zafir glanced at me. "He'll be sore, but they're going to the summit too. Besides, there's safety in numbers. And right now, all I care about is getting you there. Alive," he added, his brow raised.

"Thanks," I said with a smirk. "I'm glad to hear you don't want me dead."

A royal guard can scowl like no other, and Zafir was no exception. "It's not amusing, Your Majesty. We don't yet know who we can trust. Having Bartolo and his men with us adds one extra layer of protection around you."

He was right, of course.

But I was worried, too, about what Zafir had meant by "taking it easy." I didn't want Bartolo slowing us down—injured or not. Brooklynn didn't know yet what Zafir and I knew, what Floss had inadvertently revealed to us about a traitor, and I was worried about her and the others making it safely to the summit.

Plus, there was the other matter to contend with. Floss and his riders weren't quick to forgive the men who'd attacked them—Niko's or Brook's—even though they'd explained that they'd believed Zafir and I had been captured and were being held as prisoners.

Niko's men had come across Brook's soldiers after they'd left the train depot, where they'd been ordered to turn the town upside-down if that's what it took to find me. Eventually, that trail had led them to Floss's place.

Apparently, we hadn't been all that hard to track from there.

Also, apparently, that wasn't the first group of Brook's men Niko's riders had come across. The first party had been butchered and left for dead. Every last one of them.

My stomach heaved as I considered the implications of that attack. Those riders weren't the only ones who were vulnerable.

Floss didn't seem to care about any of that. He didn't much appreciate being accused of kidnapping. . . . Although I wasn't sure what, exactly, he would have called it. He *had* snatched me from the tavern, after all.

Still, I couldn't help noticing the glint of pleasure in his eyes when he realized that it was Avonlea who'd struck one of their *attackers* with her arrow. "That's my girl," he claimed boastfully to the others as they threw more wood on the fire.

"So, Floss is your father then?" I whispered as Avonlea came over to join us. I sat on an old log, which had been ossified from exposure to the cold.

Avonlea, who'd been staring at me, at the faint shimmer just beneath the surface of my skin, made a face. "Of course not. I haven't always lived with them." She leaned in closer, her eyes dancing impishly as if sharing a secret with me. "I was brought there to be Jeremiah's bride."

I frowned at that. "Really? So, are you? His bride, I mean?"

"No," she answered, scoffing at the notion. "Jeremiah has no interest in having a wife. He's practically a child still. All he really wants is someone to tell him tales and help him build forts in the caves outside the settlement camps. He doesn't even like living by himself, even though Floss insists that every man needs his own home." She wrinkled her nose. "I don't blame him, though. His place smells like dung." I thought of the one-room cottage I'd first been brought to. If that was where Jeremiah lived, Avonlea was right, it wasn't much of a home. "Mostly, he sleeps in the main house with us."

"So what do you do there, exactly? Why are you still with them?"

She used a stick to trace shapes in the gravel at her feet. Shrugging, she said, "Floss bought me, is why. He owns me fair and square. Wouldn't be much of a bargain if I up and ran just 'cause I didn't marry his boy, would it?"

I tried not to react, but I wondered if she could see it in my cheeks, if my anger glowed as brightly as . . . well, as brightly other emotions did. "What about your parents? Don't they want you back?"

"I don't have parents," she explained. "Never really did, I guess. I had a mom once, sort of, when I was real small. People said I looked liked her, back when I knew people who could tell me so. I don't remember her much anymore. I wish I did." She lifted her shoulders again. "Never knew my dad, not sure my mama did either."

"Floss said you didn't have a name, but surely your mother gave you one."

She shook her head. "She died before I reached namin' age."

I didn't understand, and I hesitated before asking, "She didn't give you a name when you were born?"

One of the riders, the tough-skinned woman who Floss had found to accompany us, was listening and scooted closer. Her build was solid, and she would've reminded me of Eden—the strength she exuded—except that she was bulkier, thicker beneath her heavy layers of winter wear than Angelina's guard. "Things are different out here, Your Majesty. . . ." I was suddenly aware that there was no more pretense about who I was. "Life's hard in the Scablands. People don't bother naming newborns. Too many of them die in their first few years. Disease, mostly. But sometimes undernourishment or even a particularly harsh winter'll take a babe. Children generally start getting names around their fifth year. Earlier if they're tougher'n most." Her Scablander accent was less pronounced than Floss's and Avonlea's.

"What's your name?" I asked the woman, trying to ignore the stab of guilt I felt over the living conditions of the Scablanders and their families. I made a mental note to talk to Max about this place when I returned.

But then I was thinking of Max—about his steel-gray eyes and his soft kisses that tasted like honeyed mint—and a different kind of pain coursed through me. A deeper, more intimate ache that I had to force myself to shove aside.

The woman smiled at me, revealing teeth that were almost too white, and too straight. "Just Zora, Your Majesty, plain and simple. My mama didn't subscribe to none'a that city naming rubbish. Didn't see the need to cause trouble where there was none."

"Were you born out here, Zora?"

"In the Scablands? No," she explained. "I came to it the proper way, because I broke the law." She glanced back toward the other men she'd been riding with. They kept as much to themselves as they could now that the camp was teeming with military men. *"I was a counselwoman's daughter,"* she said quietly, in perfectly enunciated Termani. It surprised me to hear that kind of eloquent articulation coming from her. She was so rough, almost dangerous . . . at least until the moment she'd smiled. *"And I fell in love with a vendor's son."*

One of the men looked up then. He couldn't have heard her, but it was as if he'd sensed her. Their gazes held, the connection between them palpable, like a wire that stretched from one to the other, joining them.

"Is that him?" I asked, and Zora started, as if surprised that I'd understood what she'd just said, and I realized she probably had been. Everyone knew I was the Vendor queen. The girl who'd been raised speaking Parshon.

But not everyone knew the rest of the story: that I could understand everyone.

She didn't answer, just nodded slowly as the man looked away once more. Her cheeks were red now, and I knew it had nothing to do with the fire. It was unlikely she'd meant to reveal so much of her private life to her queen.

I couldn't stop myself from asking my next question. "Do you ever miss it? Ludania, I mean. Have you ever wanted to leave the Scablands?"

"Everyone has regrets, I suppose. You can't choose one path without missing out on another," she said slowly, thoughtfully. "But I can't say I wish I'd done things differently. It's a hard life out here in the Scablands, sure, but it was a matter of trading one form of tyranny for another."

I knew she meant living under Sabara's dictatorial rule.

She smiled then, her eyes wandering to the other rider. "I think I made the right decision."

I looked too, noticing him for the first time. He was younger than the other man. Younger than both of them, but similar to each as well. "What's his name?" I asked.

She stood up, making an attempt to brush the dirt from the front of her pants but it was everywhere, coating everything, and I realized the gesture was more habit than useful. "Jacob. He was the only child we had that ever reached an age where we could name him," she said, and then she left, joining her family.

I watched her go, determined to change things out here. Determined to give these people a better life.

I turned to Avonlea then, my curiosity unending. "How long have you lived with them? Floss and Jeremiah?"

She dug around in the dirt some more with her stick, pondering the question. "Ten years. Maybe more." She shrugged. "Probably more."

I studied her disbelievingly. "How—how old are you?" I asked.

She was silent for so long I thought she wasn't going to answer me. But after what felt like an endless stretch, she glanced up, her eyes locking with mine. "Last I thought about it, I was in my sixteenth year. So not much older than that, I guess."

I was almost as shocked by that information as I had been by how long she'd been in Floss's care. When I'd first met her, she'd looked so much older . . . so tired and worn-down. Knowing the truth, I could see that she'd been robbed of any real childhood.

I tried to imagine Avonlea as a little girl with no name. A child bride taken away from everything she knew and transplanted into a new home, with another family. I thought of the way Floss had treated her. He was demanding and crude and certainly not affectionate. Not what a little girl needed. At best, she was a tolerated servant beneath his roof.

I wanted to wrap my arms around her, to let her start her life all over again. To give her a new story altogether, one complete with parents and a home. One in which she hadn't been sold into servitude as a mere child. One in which she had her own name, rather than the one I'd made up for her.

"Do you like living with them?" I asked, trying to keep the censure from my voice.

"I don't hate it," she answered. "There're worse places I could'a ended up."

She was right, of course. Everyone in Ludania had heard the rumors of life in the work camps. Stories of children worked in the fields until they could no longer stand on their own two feet, and then being tied to the horses and dragged back to the camps. Stories of children who'd been chained to the fences for speaking out of turn, and then charred to death when the generator-power fences were started up. There were stories of intentional starvations and of guards experimenting on children who weren't old enough to work, using all manner of medical, farm, and science equipment.

The camps were a source of childhood nightmares, and every little girl and boy in Ludania feared that if they misbehaved badly enough their parents might send them to the camps.

Orphans were often sent there when there was no other family. And I'd seen more than one household send their children away simply because they could no longer afford to feed them.

"Are you all right, Your Majesty?"

I blinked, frowning at Avonlea who stared back at me. I nodded slowly. "Of course. I'm fine. Why do you ask?"

Avonlea started to reach out to me, but she paused, her hand frozen halfway between us. Her face scrunched up. "I—," she started. "I didn't mean to make you cry."

I glanced away from her, wiping my cheeks. I hadn't realized

I'd been crying. "It's not you," I assured her when I turned back to her. She was still watching me with that same horrified expression. "I swear it wasn't your fault."

It's mine. I winced inwardly, realizing how negligent I'd been. There was still so much I had to do for my country.

MAX

He tried to tell himself a lone rider wasn't a bad sign.

But it was a lie, and he knew it.

It was the middle of the night. A lone rider was *always* a bad sign.

"What do you think it means?" Claude asked from the empty library behind him.

"A message," Max answered.

"From who?"

Both of them should have been in bed at this hour, but Max hadn't been in his bed in days. Not since he'd watched Charlie board the train to the summit.

It had been too soon for her to go and too hard for him to let her. Sleep, ever since, had been damn near impossible.

Instead he spent his nights like this, staring out the palace windows. He was worried and afraid. He wouldn't rest until Charlie was home again. Safe.

He turned to face Claude, who watched him with quiet resignation. Claude, who could have left him alone hours ago, but who stubbornly remained at his side. Just as he had for years. "Only one way to find out."

The doors were already being opened when Max reached the entrance, and the messenger was escorted inside. His clothing was ragged and torn, and he was covered in grime that went far deeper than a day's ride. His cheeks were lean, and dark circles ringed his eyes. He staggered slightly when Claude's shadow passed over him, not an uncommon reaction—royal guards were known to make grown men cower in fear.

"Who sent you?" Max questioned the rider, who seemed to have a hard time keeping his gaze level.

The man glanced up, ever so slightly. Ever so hesitantly. "A-a man named B-Bartolo, Your High—" He stopped himself in time. It was a common mistake, one that was made often since people still assumed he was the crowned prince. But that legacy had died when Charlie—the rightful queen of Ludania—had taken his grandmother's place on the throne. "I was sent with word that a party of ten soldiers was found slaughtered just outside the Scablands, just south of the train line." He lowered his head now, unable to look at anything but the floor. "They were from the palace," he offered nervously, as if he himself were responsible for the soldiers' demise. "That's all I was told. I ran my horse here fast as I could. Barely stopped to piss."

Max looked to Claude, and wondered if his guard's heart was racing nearly as fast as his own, but he knew that it wasn't. Claude liked to tell that he'd been born without a heart.

Max's, however, was trying to beat its way out of his chest.

There were only so many palace soldiers out there right now.

And the only ones anywhere near the Scablands were those sent with Charlie.

"Damn," he heard Claude mutter.

Damn, Max thought as his airway constricted, *was an understatement.*

XIV

The flowers were just out of my reach and I had to lean forward, the water lapping around my knees. My small hands—my fingertips—grazed one of the blue petals, sending the flower shooting away from my grasp.

I stood there for a moment, studying the still surface, trying to decide. I was already in too deep, deeper than I'd ever been before. But it was right there, one more step and I'd have it.

I held my breath and took a step. Only this time I wasn't standing on the same slimy surface I'd been on before. This time I stood on something rigid, something scaly, something alive.

It moved before I could think, and the water around me thrashed before I could react. The scream that reached my throat came seconds after I felt sharp teeth sink into the tender flesh of my leg . . . tugging, tearing, ripping.

I felt myself being dragged beneath the water as I searched for something to reach for. But all I could see were the flowers, too delicate and insubstantial to keep me from going under. I kicked as hard as I could with my other leg, but it was too late. I came up once, gasping for air. Already the water choked me, filling my lungs. And already blood replaced water in the river around me.

My sister's screams must have alerted the others, the guards who'd been standing watch on the hill above us, making sure the queen's daughters weren't disturbed. I saw them advancing even as I was pulled down once more, until water was all that surrounded me, and pain sliced through my leg.

I didn't remember the jaws releasing me, didn't remember being dragged to the shore, but I remembered hearing my sister's voice: "Please, take me. Take me instead. . . ." The words were repeated, whispered against my ear, over and over again as she rocked me, clutching me tightly. "Take me instead. . . ."

She hadn't understood at the time, but her whispered plea had changed everything.

This time I awoke not startled but spent.

A deep-down kind of fatigue kept me from stirring right away. Kept my gaze unfocused and my breathing shallow.

I hated that I couldn't find peace from Sabara when I closed my eyes.

I reached for my neck, rubbing the cramp in it, surprised that I'd managed to sleep at all. I wondered when I'd finally yielded, when I'd finally leaned my back against the scraggly dead log and let my eyes drift closed.

And then a thought ripped through me like a shot, scalding

every crevice, electrifying every fissure and nook of my awareness.

He's here.

Inconspicuously, I searched for him. I didn't want to be caught if he saw me there, awake. I watched as soldiers and Scablanders worked together to break down camp: rolling blankets and picking horse's hooves and tightening saddle straps. The smell of wood and burnt meat filled the crisp air and I pulled the scratchy blanket up to my lips, breathing into it to warm my lips.

Nowhere did I see Niko.

Zafir spotted me then and took two giant strides in my direction before he halted, his gaze focused on someone over my shoulder.

I turned and found him there—Niko, his golden eyes staring back at me. He held a mug out to me, steam drifting upward. "Sleep well, Your Majesty?"

I accepted the ceramic mug and wrapped my cold fingers around its rough surface. "Charlie," I answered.

He smiled crookedly as he squatted beside me. My stomach dipped, a reaction I immediately regretted. These weren't my feelings to feel.

"Charlie, then. Sleep well, Charlie?"

I avoided his gaze by sniffing the coffee in my hands. It wasn't a smell I normally cared for, but this morning my nose tingled from the sharp scent. "I didn't sleep much, but I'm ready to get going." My gaze drifted to his shoulder. "Are you . . . *better* today?"

"Glad the arrow's gone." He rolled his shoulder, as if proving his point, and I grimaced. "Grateful to your man for fixing me up."

I hated the way my insides quivered whenever he was near, and the way my outsides felt wound too tightly, like I might snap from all the tension. I hated it more that I wanted to touch him.

That a part of me could imagine what it felt like to have his hands on my hips. His lips on mine.

Searching for an excuse to get away from him, I lurched to my feet. "I—I . . . have to—"

Then I froze. From somewhere deep within, Sabara's panic unfurled. The same type of panic she'd known as a little girl on the river's edge: gut-wrenching fear.

He rose too, studying me, his eyes finding me as I battled with myself—with her.

No, she begged me. *Stay.* And I was suddenly filled with a sensation so close to tenderness it was hard to imagine it was Sabara's at all.

I can't, I argued back. But I did as she asked, unable to leave.

I glanced back up at him, avoiding his honey-colored eyes. "Did—did you come through the Capitol on your way through Ludania? Did you stop at the palace?" I didn't ask the questions I really wanted to: *How was Max? Does he long for me the way I do for him?*

He shook his head. "We stayed on the train line most of the way. It wasn't until we heard tell of the slaughtered soldiers at one of our stops that we realized there might be trouble. That we realized . . ." His voice trailed off, and he studied me even more closely—too closely—then. His attention was my undoing, and a tremor coursed through my body while Sabara tugged at me, willing me to move closer. "They didn't hurt you?" he asked, his voice husky and low.

This time I shook my head, slowly. Timidly.

His eyes narrowed, but he nodded and leaned away from me, allowing me to breathe once more.

Allowing me to find my voice again. "Where is the rest of your party? Shouldn't Queen Vespaire be joining you for the summit?"

"That's why we're here. She can't make it. I'm to deliver the message personally to Queen Neva, sending my queen's regrets." Zafir joined us then, and Niko took a step back, smiling wryly. "Mostly," he said, looking at me, "she's sorry she won't get the chance to meet you."

He nodded at Zafir and left us.

And Sabara, who had been quiet for more than a day before his arrival, raged, her shrieks echoing hollowly inside my head.

PART III

BROOKLYNN

The air on the docks was filled with the smell of fish and body odor and wet dog and dirty snow, none of which Brook cared for. She also didn't care for the crowds awaiting the incoming ferry or not feeling in control. Mostly, though, she hated being unarmed.

"Stop complaining, Brook. Queen Neva did it for everyone's good." Aron reached for her arm, forcing her to halt as an old woman crossed the path in front of them.

Aron nodded at the stooped woman, and she smiled back at him, a wide, toothless grin.

Brook rolled her eyes, ignoring the geriatric flirtation. "How is it in my best interest to be weaponless? I'm completely defenseless. How is *that* in Charlie's best interest?"

She watched as two stray dogs fought over a scrap of meat on the ground, near a pile of rotting garbage. They were growling at each other, their hackles raised and their teeth bared. If it had been a sword there, lying on the cobbled pavers, rather than a piece of rancid meat, Brooklynn would have joined the fray.

"Defenseless? You?" Aron laughed, drawing the attention

of several people around them. "You're the least defenseless person I know. Besides, you're forgetting that *everyone* at the summit is unarmed, not just you. *That's* why it's in Charlie's best interest."

Brook had to bite back her smile. She liked that Aron didn't consider her helpless.

If only she didn't *feel* helpless at the moment.

It wasn't just that they'd had to forfeit their weapons when they'd arrived at Queen Neva's palace, although that had definitely stung. Brook had complained louder than any of her soldiers, but it hadn't stopped her from surrendering both firearms and blades from her personal arsenal. Despite her grumblings, though, she understood the need for the security precaution: the fewer weapons available, the less likely someone could be harmed.

Namely, one of the monarchs in attendance.

More specifically, at least as far as Brooklynn was concerned, Charlie.

And after what had happened that first night they'd camped, Brook trusted no one. Not even her own men. It was a sickening feeling, and one she wasn't accustomed to.

She had handpicked that soldier—Caden Evans—just as she had all of them. She was responsible for every last woman and man in her army. So to find Evans like that, his throat ripped apart, mauled by an attacker out in the rocky hills of the Scablands, made her blood boil.

The trick hadn't fooled her, of course. She'd seen right through the shoddy attempt to make it look as if an animal had savaged her soldier. She wasn't stupid.

Unarmed, yes. Stupid, never.

The killer had made a grievous mistake. He—or she—had overlooked the other injury, the stab wound in Caden's gut. It was sloppy and amateurish, and made Brook realize that whomever she was up against wasn't as experienced as he or she thought they were.

Yet here they were, two days later and she still didn't know who that person was.

But she was sure of one thing.

That whoever was responsible for her soldier's death was here with them, in Caldera.

And Brook had every intention of finding the killer.

XV

When Vannova, Queen Neva's palace, finally came into view, my breath caught in the back of my throat. Not because Vannova was the storybook palace little girls imagined as they poured tea for their dollies and sang nursery rhymes.

It was the opposite, in fact. Stark and harsh, a daunting fortress of towers and turrets and spires, all dusted in ice and rising above a thick layer of frozen fog that made it appear as if it was the only thing that existed on the entire snowbound isle. As if the palace itself were crafted from the great glacier that rose from the water.

Clearly, we were no longer in the Scablands, no longer in Ludania at all. We hadn't been since midafternoon, shortly after we'd first boarded the ferry, the massive passenger transport that bridged the arctic waters between the mainland and the glistening, frost-covered island. Yet even before leaving my country, the landscape had begun to change dramatically, becoming more and more wintry. Harsher. And infinitely more treacherous.

Snow had started falling continuously sometime late yesterday, while we'd been riding. It had made the footing perilous in spots, and the sound of horse hooves grating against the icy rocks filled the air. I'd almost been relieved when the frozen waters had finally come into view, when we'd bid Floss and his riders good-bye, offering assurances that they would be rewarded for delivering us safely.

Promises we meant to keep.

But as we rode the ferry, we realized that travel by boat was nearly as dangerous. The nose of the barge carved its way through a thick sheet of ice that crusted the water's surface. I worried that we'd reach a point where the vessel could become incapacitated in the frozen waters.

"Will you miss them?" I had asked Avonlea when we'd stood at the back of the ship, watching the shoreline disappear.

Avonlea had clutched the ragged wool throw around her thin shoulders. "No."

I'd tried to imagine what it must be like for her, to live a life without family. "Are you lonely, Avonlea?"

She'd cocked her head, just enough so she could look at me. "How could I be lonely?" she'd asked. "I'm here with you."

"No . . . that's . . ." My voice trailed away. How could I explain it to her? How could I make her miss something she'd never had. "I'm glad you agreed to come with me," I'd said instead.

At that, Avonlea grinned, enthusiasm rippling the skin at the corners of her eyes. "I'm so glad you asked me, Your Majest—Charlie." She'd corrected herself, remembering my insistence that she call me by my first name.

I thought of the way Floss had reacted to my proposition,

like a child who'd just lost his favorite toy. Sadly, I think that's how he felt about me taking the girl, like I'd stolen some piece of personal property from him.

I was determined to give Avonlea a place in this world, to make her feel wanted. Special.

I'd watched her shiver, with only the blanket to ward away the bitter chill. "Please. Take my cloak." I reached for the top button, but her hand had stopped me, her fingers firm and cold over my own.

"N-no . . ." Her teeth had chattered. "I won't take it. And it won't do any good for you to insist. . . . I won't take it. It's one thing to accompany the queen," she maintained, her hand moving back to draw her blanket tighter again. "It's another thing to take the coat off your back."

I shook my head, wishing she'd change her mind, but knowing she wouldn't.

We'd have to get her something more suitable when we arrived. I told myself. Something warmer . . . and cleaner.

Something new.

Despite my initial misgivings about the beauty of the castle's structure, I had to admit it was magnificent in its own intimidating way. It looked solid, fortified by iron-spiked gates and tall, invulnerable walls. At the very least, I felt safe at the idea of being there, in relative isolation, for as long as the summit lasted.

Now I shivered, rubbing my elbows beneath my heavy wool cloak.

"I can't believe we made it," I breathed, puffs of air punctuating my every word.

"We almost didn't. At least not today." Zafir reminded me, and I eyed him suspiciously, wondering how it was that he never seemed to be cold. He wore the same thin jacket he always had, his hands clasped behind his back as he stood with me at the railing, watching the palace come into view.

He was right, though. The ferryman hadn't wanted to make this last run of the day, warning us that a storm was brewing, that it wasn't safe for anyone to be out tonight.

Dubiously, we'd turned our gazes skyward at his prediction.

"It's coming," he'd assured us when I mentioned that the sky looked clear enough. "Just 'cause you can't see trouble, don't mean it ain't there."

Zafir had offered the man five times the normal fares for each of us, and even though he'd balked, grousing that we were all in danger if we didn't make it to land by nightfall, in the end he'd agreed. Money did that to a man—made him willing to take risks he'd otherwise avoid.

In this case, I was relieved. We were freezing, all of us. And the idea of spending another night out in the elements held no appeal. Already, I worried that my toes inside my boots, were succumbing to "the nip." Everyone knew that temperatures could drop so low they'd freeze appendages right off. I wasn't sure how much more any of us could take.

"Do you think Brook's already here?" I asked, forcing my teeth not to clatter together when I spoke. "Do you think she's worried?"

"You heard the ferry operator, people have been coming and going for weeks in preparation for the summit. Three large parties arrived yesterday alone. We can't be sure any of them were ours." And then he glanced down at me, his expression softening. "Be patient. We'll find out soon enough." His gaze shot back to the looming form of Vannova palace.

"I'm glad we're not the first to arrive."

Zafir didn't say anything; it was third time I'd made that same statement. I couldn't help being nervous; it was my first summit, my first encounter with other queens. Already, I could feel my resolve slipping. I bounced up and down, trying to keep warm. "You should check on Avonlea again. See if she's okay."

Zafir sighed. "She's fine, Your Majesty. She was fine when I checked on her an hour ago, and she's still fine. Besides, I doubt she'd complain even if she weren't."

"I suppose you're right," I admitted, turning my attention toward the darkening sky, although it didn't change the fact that I was concerned about her.

Ahead of us, the docks seemed to materialize from out of nowhere as the boat parted the dense fog. There were far-off shouts coming from people we still couldn't see, as preparations were being made for our arrival.

Somewhere out there, a horn sounded. It was a deep noise that managed to cut through all the other commotion. Mere seconds had passed before an answering blast sounded from our own vessel.

The ferry came to a sudden stop then, jolting us as it collided with the side of the pier. Since there were no surprised gasps from around us, I guessed that the abrupt landing must be usual.

And then pandemonium erupted, as the men and women

working the piers began throwing thick ropes to the crewmembers onboard. Together they pulled and heaved and fastened until the boat was stabilized and the gangway could be set.

Suddenly I was anxious about getting off the ship.

Nerves seized my innards and I wanted to turn back, to journey back through the Scablands and forget all about the summit. To pretend I had nothing at all to gain from meeting the other queens.

I wanted to go home.

And then I saw them.

Aron and Brooklynn, standing amid the gathered crowds. Brook's impatient glare made it seem as if she might storm the ship at any moment. Aron, on the other hand, looked relaxed and nonplussed, the way he always did, as if this was just any other moment in any other day.

I gripped the railing and leaned forward, hoping they could see me on the deck. "Aron!" I called out above the din of voices and the grinding of winches and the clang of bells. Overhead, the seabirds called out raucously. When neither of them saw me, I tried waving at them, my arms flailing. "Brooklynn! Over here! I'm here!"

Brook glanced up then, just as Zafir's arms wrapped around me. Like unflinching iron bands, they dragged me backward. "Do you constantly have to test me, Your Majesty?" His chastising words were quiet but effective. "Let us at least get you off the ship before you start drawing attention to yourself. I'd like to deliver you safely to Vannova, if at all possible."

I just grinned stupidly. "They're here, Zafir."

It didn't take long for Brook to reach us, for her to shove her way through the horde of impatient onlookers. "I can't believe it!" she cried, gripping me in what should have been a hug but felt more like she was trying to smother me instead. She didn't seem to notice that Zafir was still restraining me. I could only imagine how the three of us must have looked, entangled in an awkward, three-way embrace.

Zafir released me, and I practically collapsed into Brooklynn's arms, my voice bordering on desperation. "You have no idea how glad I am to see you, how worried I was. I was so afraid you wouldn't be here."

Brook squeezed me back until my ribs ached. "Charlie! Where the hell have you been?" she demanded. "Where did you disappear to?"

"I swear I'll tell you everything," I promised, glancing around nervously, suddenly realizing that the assassin could be here as well. That Brook had most likely been traveling with the traitor. My pulse flicked raggedly and I pulled her closer. "We have to talk. Privately."

Beside us, someone cleared her throat, an almost imperceptible sound. I might not even have noticed, except that Brooklynn drew away from me.

Avonlea stood there, on the deck of the ferry, her ragged red blanket wrapped around her shoulders like a tatty shawl. I tried to see her the way Brook would, the way I'd looked at her that first day. She was timid, hesitant.

Not at all like the girl who'd shot Niko Bartolo.

"Yes . . . ?" Brook drew out the word, raising one perfect eyebrow and reminding me that there was nothing timid or hesitant about my best friend.

Avonlea opened her mouth, but seemed to change her mind as she took a step away from us. I reached out to stop her before she could flee. "Brook, this is Avonlea. Avonlea, this is . . ." I thought of the ways I could introduce Brook: the commander of my armed forces, my childhood best friend. "Brooklynn."

Brook smiled, a slow, suspicious smile that told me she was sizing up the other girl. She didn't have to say what she was thinking. She, like Zafir, was cautious with her trust. "Avonlea, huh? That's an . . . interesting name."

I frowned at Brook, but she ignored my cautionary look.

"Char—" Avonlea chomped down on her lower lip, stopping herself from speaking the rest of my name aloud. She ducked her eyes. "Her Majesty gave it to me."

"You gave her a name?" Brook's dark eyes turned to me.

I raised my eyebrows. "I did. And a queen's name at that." A slow smile spread over my lips as I wrapped my arm around Avonlea. I could feel her shivering beneath her impractical blanket, and I led her toward the gangway where Zafir was already waiting. "Better than being named for a city," I suggested, winking at Brooklynn as we passed her.

I wished it was Xander who was escorting me, rather than Zafir, as a hundred etiquette lessons flew right out of my head. I could no more remember my own name than I could recall the proper greeting for the queen of Caldera.

Yet here she was, sitting upon a throne fashioned from black marble. The two ivory barbs that rose from its back looked very much like they were meant to bear the heads of those who blundered in the presence of their queen. A warning to those who didn't know whether to genuflect in submission or to spit at her feet.

As a queen myself, Xander had instructed me not to bow to another queen. But we'd only covered face-to-face greetings. This was different. Queen Neva was on her throne.

My mind reeled as I approached her on unsteady legs, my heart trying to hammer its way out of my chest, and I desperately hoped she couldn't hear its reckless rhythm. I felt like a fraud—like an imposter posing as a queen—and I was sure she'd recognize me as such the moment our eyes met.

I stopped when I reached the base of the platform she sat upon, knowing I had to do something. . . . anything. And spitting wasn't it, I was certain.

I was *almost* certain.

I started to bend at the waist, and then belatedly I changed my mind and awkwardly dropped lower, bending at my knees instead. It turned into a strange half curtsy, half crouch, making me look—and feel—foolish. I tried to sweep my arm in a flourish, a grand gesture I hoped, and then I stood, wobbling gracelessly.

When I glanced up to meet her gaze, sure my head would soon be speared atop one of the spikes of her throne, she giggled. "I'd heard you were lovely. . . ." Her voice was deep and lyrical and more regal than I could ever hope to be. "But I hadn't realized you were quite so . . . *inexperienced.*"

I gaped at her—again, not my queenliest move. Second only to the bizarre greeting I'd just offered her. "I—I'm so sorry," I stammered, wishing Zafir would say something, offer some sort of defense for my behavior. Maybe explain that I was tired from travel, or that I'd just been abducted and my life was in peril.

Or maybe say that I was slow-witted.

Anything.

Instead he just stood there, looking stoic and guardly. I wanted to pinch him.

Looking at Queen Neva was like gazing at a snowflake. She was draped, from neck to toe, in a fabric so delicate it was virtually sheer, and her skin beneath was nearly as diaphanous. She was almost as pale as the frost that coated nearly every surface of her queendom, including the snow. Her limbs were long, and even while she was sitting, I could see that she was tall and willowy. She reminded me of the dancers in the clubs Brook and I used to frequent. Elegant and sparkling and lithe.

But it was her eyes that held me, practically as light as her skin. Not in the way Sabara's had been—milky and hazed with age. Queen Neva's were like staring into clouds of spun silver. It was as if tiny filaments of metal had coiled together to create something both soft and hard, impenetrable yet vulnerable.

She rose, looking the way I wished I looked: simultaneously graceful, commanding, and feminine. Like a true queen.

"Don't be sorry," she said in her throaty voice as she took a step closer. Her lips pursed into what could have passed for a smile. "And don't worry. You'll be fine, my dear." She tipped her head closer, as if telling me a secret meant for just the two of us, even though—aside from our guards—it *was* only the two of us in the oversize throne room. "A simple kiss will do," she explained, not lowering her voice at all. "On each cheek. And it's entirely unnecessary." She looped one arm through mine like we were old friends, and her touch, too, had that same duality. That same double-edge of dominance and fragility. She led me with a feather touch, walking me across the massive room. "If anyone should curtsy, it should be me bowing to you."

I glanced up at her, my eyes wide. "Why ever would you do that?" It was the most intelligible thing I'd spoken since my arrival, which was pathetic at best.

"Because you," she answered, without glancing down at me, "have taken Sabara's throne, something no one else has been able to do. You're stronger than you give yourself credit for."

I smiled at that. "What makes you think I don't give myself credit?"

Her lips parted into a cool grin, and I felt as if she were looking into my soul . . . reading my thoughts. "You deserve this. You, Charlaina, belong here."

We reached the door and I glanced over my shoulder, only to find Zafir mutely at our heels. Unlike at the entrance, where it took two men to open the enormous, two-story doors, there was only one girl holding the door for us. As we passed, she stepped aside, dropping one leg behind her and tipping into a perfectly executed curtsy.

I silently memorized the girl's form, grateful Xander hadn't been there to witness my disastrous greeting.

We stopped at the base of a curving staircase with serpentine balusters forged from black iron that stretched as far as I could see, disappearing into the upper floors. Its black marble steps matched that of Queen Neva's throne, as did the flooring we stood on. Ebony crystals dripped from the chandeliers overhead.

For all that Queen Neva was light, the interior of her palace was dark and foreboding. Everything about her was a contrast of sorts.

"Your rooms have been readied, and your wardrobe has been"—she paused thoughtfully—"replenished."

"How did you—"

She held up her hand and wispy fabric revealed wrists so slender they should have been skeletal. Instead I could see lean muscles flexing beneath her skin. "Communication here is better than that in Ludania. We got word of your *detour* almost immediately. Preparations have been made ever since." She smiled then, a real smile. "There's much we can teach you. Much we have to offer. You and I will be great allies, I think."

I tried to imagine the level of communication that could work at that speed, and could only guess at how it might benefit my people. Suddenly it didn't matter that I'd made a fool of myself, or that I was nervous. I remembered exactly why I'd come. "I appreciate that, Your Majesty."

"Neva. Just call me Neva," she said, releasing my arm and waving over a footman who was dressed in all black. I wondered how Brooklynn had felt, seeing that her uniform matched those of the palace staff. "Show Queen Charlaina to her rooms." She turned to me then, her expression brightening. "I'll have dinner sent up to your room. Get some rest, dear. The other delegations will be eager to meet you tomorrow."

❧ ❧ ❧

Neva hadn't lied when she'd said she'd sent up clothing, and not just for me, but for Brook, too. Even Zafir had something to change into.

I had no idea how she'd guessed our sizes, or whose clothes we actually wore, but it felt like heaven to strip out of my dirty riding gear and slip into something clean and soft. Something that didn't smell like horses and sweat.

The only thing better would have been a bath, but I knew there'd be time for that after we filled our stomachs.

We ate in almost total silence, just the three of us: Brook, Zafir, and me.

I didn't eat slowly, as a queen probably should. Instead I couldn't chew fast enough, and I practically shoveled the food into my mouth. Food that hadn't just been hunted and skinned. The meat—whatever it was—was perfectly sauced and seasoned and was probably the best dish I'd ever eaten. It had only been a few days, but it felt more like a lifetime since I hadn't had to choke down something scavenged or moldering.

Brook was still mad about having to share my sleeping quarters, about not being housed in the gatehouse just outside of the palace with her soldiers. It was where all the visiting queens' soldiers were bunking.

Soldiers, especially off-duty ones, could be loud and raucous and lewd, and Brooklynn worried she was missing out on the party they were surely having without her. I think she was even more upset that Aron had been allowed to stay with them, bunking with *her* men, while she was stuck here. With me.

Still, I hadn't changed my mind. I didn't want to be alone, and Zafir wasn't exactly the kind of company I had in mind.

Besides, there were things we needed to discuss.

Things I couldn't keep putting off, despite her irascible mood.

I stilled at the thought, my breath gathering in the base of my throat. "Brook," I whispered. "We need to figure this thing out. We need to find out who was responsible for killing your soldier, because whoever he is . . ." My voice drifted away as the rest of my words got caught. I couldn't say them: *Whoever he is also wants to kill me.*

Zafir glanced up then, too, momentarily forgetting the food in front of him. "She's right. Until we know who the traitor is, Queen Charlaina's not safe. No one is."

Brook swallowed what was left in her mouth, and her expression changed. She no longer glared at me across the table. Now she looked determined. "I know," she answered gravely. "And when I find him, we won't need the gallows. I'll kill him myself."

I didn't recognize the language right away—it was one I hadn't heard in ages. But I knew, even from the depths of my dream, it was long dead.

Just like the girl I saw reflected back at me from the looking glass.

Now she was gone.

Not that I'd minded her body, I realized, gazing into her shining green eyes, so unlike the ones I'd been born with.

Even if the copper-haired beauty hadn't been next in line for the throne, men would've fallen at her feet.

At my feet, *I corrected, a small smile tracing my lips.*

But there was only one man I cared about. Only one who made my heart race and my skin tingle.

I turned my attention to the girls who attended me, their voices buzzing all around me as they fussed and fastened and pinned and smoothed, preparing me for the feast.

"Out!" *I insisted in that strange foreign tongue, and felt a twinge of satisfaction at their skittishness as they jumped away from me, scattering like a flock of startled birds. When I saw their gazes flitting nervously to one another as if to question my command, I raised my voice.* "Now!" *I barked the thick, guttural word, making certain they knew I was serious.*

I waited until the door clicked behind every last one of them, until I was sure I was alone at last, and then I turned back to the mirror once more.

I was flawless. Right down to the fresh flowers woven into my long, copper tresses. I would make the perfect attendant to my eldest sister on her wedding day, the day she'd take a king to rule at her side. The day she'd start trying for an heir to take her place upon the throne.

To displace me in line.

If only she'd been the one to say the words instead of the girl in whose body I now resided. If only I'd been able to trick the new queen into taking my Essence instead of her younger sister.

Then I wouldn't be in this predicament.

Then the queen wouldn't have to die today.

I took a breath and turned toward my bedchamber, not even the second-best quarters in the palace. Definitely not fit for a princess who was second in line.

But I'd requested these rooms for a reason.

I moved aside a heavy table, and beneath that, a thick, cumbersome rug. When I finished, I was winded, but I was staring down at the small, planked door cut into the very floor itself.

I lifted the iron rung and pulled, and then vanished down into the black stairwell.

When I reached the chamber door at the other end of the passageway—my destination—I tapped softy, a sound so faint it could easily have been made by rats scratching against the floorboards.

When I heard the answering knock, I smiled to myself. All was clear.

I slid the door open and stepped out from the shadows into a corridor. Yet even before I was out from behind the heavy door, I heard his voice—just as rough and grating as my own had been. "You look beautiful," *he said in that same long-dead dialect, and even though I'd just thought that very thing while looking at myself in the mirror, I almost couldn't breathe when he told me so.*

Shyly, I stepped forward, just as he held out the gleaming silver blade to me.

It was heavier than I'd expected, and sharper, too. I turned it over in my hand, watching as light reflected from the edge, glinting back at me. "I won't need it," *I said.*

"Take it anyway," *he insisted, his fingers reaching up to*

caress my cheek, making fire lick through my veins. "Just in case."

And then I lifted my eyes to his . . .

. . . and gasped.

For too long, I couldn't find my breath. The air was trapped somewhere between my lungs and my throat, stuck on a lump I couldn't manage to swallow. I blinked hard in the darkness, my skin barely lit at all, and I guessed that was the reason Sabara's hold on me had grown.

And now I was too far away from Angelina to ask for her help.

Instead I waited, my fist clutched against my chest, wondering why this was happening, wondering if Sabara knew what I'd just witnessed.

I wondered, too, if any of it was real at all.

When, finally, I inhaled sharply, my gaze shot over to Brooklynn. I was relieved to find she was still asleep beside me, her breathing even. She, at least, wasn't gasping or suffocating within the confines of her own body.

She wasn't terrorized by dreams that didn't belong to her.

I wished I could sleep half as soundly.

I sat up slowly, carefully, quietly. It was strange to be in this room now, knowing what I knew. Seeing what I'd seen.

It was definitely the same place, the same room from my dream. And unless Sabara was playing some sort of trick on me, she'd unwittingly revealed a part of her past she'd probably hoped would have remained long dead and buried.

Yet here we were, the two of us, under the roof of the

palace where she'd taken the body of one girl, and violently killed another.

All in an effort to remain on a throne—any throne—forever.

I moved to the place I'd seen in my dream, to where the opening in the floor should be. Unlike in the dream, where a table blocked the way, there was only the rug there now.

I reached for a corner and tugged.

It barely moved, and I tugged it again, this time harder.

The rug scraped across the floor, and I cringed, looking again at Brooklynn. She was still asleep. I pulled again and again, and it moved in increments. It was heavier than it looked, and I made slow progress. My heart was pounding when the corner of the trapdoor finally came into view.

I collapsed onto my knees, peeling back the corner of the rug to reveal the rest of the opening.

I reached for it.

My chest ached with hope as I lifted the recessed rung. It squeaked, and I wondered how long it had been since someone had used this passage.

But despite the rusty handle, the door pulled open with a sigh.

Cold air rushed up from the duct below, hostile and unwelcoming. I shivered but took a step inside anyway.

The first few steps were easy; I found my footing by the light coming from the bedchamber behind me. But as I left the stairs and entered the tunnel beyond, my steps grew more hesitant.

The only light remaining came from me, and it was barely enough to see in. There was only the cold, and a vague recollection that I'd been there before. . . . A memory that wasn't my own.

I counted my steps, not knowing how far it was, but finding that focusing on such a mundane task made the notion of being down here—alone—less unnerving. When I stopped, it was almost on instinct. I wasn't sure why, exactly, but I felt like this was the place. That I'd gone as far as I needed to go.

I reached out blindly and felt the walls around me.

It was there: the door.

My chest wall could barely contain my beating heart as I pressed my ear up against it. There wasn't a single noise coming from the other side as I reached for the handle. My breath caught in my chest for an entirely different reason now.

Nothing happened. The door was locked.

I wasn't sure what to do next, so I did what Sabara had done, I tapped on it and waited.

After a moment, I started to feel foolish, realizing that I was chasing ghosts. That what I'd seen couldn't have been possible, despite finding the hatch. Despite navigating through the passageway.

It had been yet another illusion, something Sabara had meant for me to see.

I wrapped my arms around myself, wondering if I should simply go back.

That was when I heard it, the whisper-soft knocking that came from the other side. Just like in the dream. Only this time, I wasn't the one opening the door.

Inside of me, Sabara awakened, and I could feel that this

was what she'd wanted all along. I was a pawn in a children's game, manipulated by a master.

But when I saw him, the reaction was my own. I gasped for the second time.

It was him.

He wore the same face he had in my dream.

The same face he wore in this very moment—decades, maybe centuries later—as if nothing had changed.

Niko Bartolo.

We stood there for moment, and then several more, just staring at each other. I panted, the cold air making my chest ache. His eyes conquered me.

I wanted to say something, to tell him that I knew who he was . . . and what he'd done. What *they'd* done.

But when I opened my mouth, there was nothing. Just silent longing that I couldn't explain.

"It's you," he said, finally breaking the spell. "Isn't it?"

I knew what he meant.

Sabara. He meant that *I* was Sabara.

"No." But I was nodding my head, my actions at odds with my denial. "I mean, sort of." I fumbled over an explanation, but there was no time.

He closed the distance between us, and in the light that came from behind him, I could see that his eyes glittered from something other than the cold and his hands closed around mine as he fell to his knees before me. His voice, when it found its way out, was barely a breath. "I knew you were in there."

My heart nearly broke. This time I was shaking my head.

"She's here," I tried again, even as my hands clutched his harder than they should have. "But *I'm* not her."

His head fell forward, over our shared grip, as if he was praying. To whom, I had no idea. And then his shoulders started to shake, and my stomach fell, plummeting in a way that made me feel choked.

I tried to untangle my hands from his, to pull away so I could breathe again. His pain was almost more than I could bear.

He threw his head back then and laughed, so loud I swore the ground beneath me rumbled. Or maybe it was my own heart. "I knew you were in there. I knew you weren't dead!"

"Shh!" I admonished, glancing around to make certain we were still alone. Being discovered in my nightgown would probably be frowned upon in any land, but I'd have an even harder time explaining my knowledge of a hidden passage. "That kind of talk will get us both in trouble. Besides, even though she's in here, doesn't mean I'm not still me."

He rose, then, lifting my icy fingers to his lips. His golden eyes held mine. "It doesn't matter, it means she's not gone either. Not really."

I frowned, pulling my hands away. "Who are you? I saw you in my . . . in her dreams. But who are you really?"

A chill ran through me, colder than any warning, and I realized that chill was Sabara. *He's no one,* she argued, even though I recognized her lie. *You were confused. You saw nothing.*

Her denials only made me more certain. "Tell me how you've known her for so long." My eyes narrowed as I watched him. I could see that he was trying to decide how much I knew, and how much to reveal to me. And then I said the name I'd heard when I'd been sleeping, the name Sabara had called him. "Thaddeus."

He closed his eyes, inhaling sorrowfully as if I'd just said the sweetest word ever spoken. I was glad he could no longer see me, because just saying the name—*his name*—made my throat ache like it had been dragged from the very pit of my soul.

When he looked at me again, his gaze was clearer, his golden eyes—the same as ever as far as I could tell—were filled with resolve. *"I shouldn't have to tell you. You should know everything,"* he said in a language that was even more ancient than the one I'd heard in my dream. Its mysterious cadence embraced me, filling every crevice of my being, making Sabara ease out of the shadows and strain toward the surface.

I struggled to keep her at bay.

"I-I only remember some of it." I answered truthfully in Englaise, the only language—other than Parshon—that *I* could speak. "Only bits and parts." I looked at him. "But I remember you. And what you meant to her. I saw what the two of you did, to her queen—*her sister*—in this very palace," The words were bitter on my tongue. "So she could sit on the throne." I closed my eyes against the images of the knife. Of Sabara trying to force the older girl to say the words: *Take me instead.*

But there'd been no blood. Sabara hadn't needed the knife, even then. She'd simply lifted her fist, never even laying a finger on the other girl, and squeezed her windpipe closed using only her will.

Sabara hadn't held that girl—that sister—as she'd lain dying. Not the way she had her real sister, the one by the river. She'd simply stepped over her limp form and slipped away, eager to take her place as queen.

Why? I'd silently asked Sabara just as I was awakening after the dream, just as I regained control of my thoughts once more. *Why does it matter? Why couldn't you let her live?*

But she hadn't answered me.

"Why?" I asked Niko now.

His fingertips lifted to stroke my cheek, a feather's touch. Against my will, I leaned in closer, letting his hand cup my face. *"You still don't know?"* he asked, again in that strange, swirling language. *"You still don't get it, do you? It was so we could be together. So I could be with you one more time."*

"Not me," I said, and now I turned away from his touch. But even as I did, I could feel my body resisting. "Her."

"One and the same, it seems."

"No. Not true," I corrected. "So, who are you? *What,*" I amended, "are you?"

His lips curved, but his smile was wistful. *"Does it matter?"*

I nodded. It did. Right now it was all that mattered.

"I'm like you. Like her." He turned away from me, and the part of me that was Sabara followed him.

"That doesn't make sense."

When he turned back, we were face to face. *"I know,"* he said, and behind his back I saw flashes coming from the windows. The storm, I thought. It must be the storm the ferryman had warned us about.

"It's strange to explain this. Again. To you. To her*."* This time

he corrected himself as he switched to Englaise. "There was a time when not all royal heirs were female. It was rare, but there was an occasional male born capable of taking the throne."

"You mean they were born with magic?" I asked breathlessly, my eyes wide.

He nodded at my incredulous expression. "I was one of those anomalies, as was my twin brother, Tobias." His gaze grew distant. "I haven't thought of him in . . ." His voice trailed off. "Well, forever, really."

I waited silently, but something sparked in me. A memory—like déjà vu. I remembered hearing this before. I knew these words and the cadence of this voice.

He'd told Sabara this same story, once upon a time.

"My brother's gift was useless. He could move things just by concentrating on them."

"Like the Canshai masters?" I asked.

A reluctant smile pulled at his lips. "Exactly like them. My guess is that they, too, were some sort of ancient descendants of a male line of royals who were once magic. Now . . ." He shrugged. "Now, they're extinct. Like my brother."

"What about you? What could . . . *can* you do?"

He faced me, his gaze direct and unwavering. "Me?" he asked, his brows raised sardonically. "Haven't you figured it out? I'm immortal."

It was impossible. Even with magic, it couldn't be true. I wanted to say as much, but all I could manage was to shake my head. Yet even that was unconvincing.

Because I remembered him, the way I'd seen him in my dream. The same way he was now.

"Yes," he asserted, stepping closer and scooping my hands up once again. "And you know it. Deep inside, you remember me, and you know it's true. I was with you, not once . . . not twice . . . but we've shared lifetimes, again and again." He moved so close I could feel heat coming off of his body and finding its way beneath my nightgown . . . infusing me with liquid pain.

"So why weren't you with her all along? Why were you with Queen Vespaire?"

He shook his head. "I could never stay anywhere for too long. Look at me, I can't do what you—*she*—can do. I can't change identities. I have only this body, and it never changes. I don't age. People notice that. People start to question why everyone else grows older while I remain youthful.

"Eventually I have to leave. To wait until"—he tipped his head, his brow furrowing as if he wasn't sure how to continue—"until there's a new host. Someone who can *invite* me back. And then we can be together again. For years, usually, before the questions start again. But this time . . ." His voice drifted off. "This time it was too long. There was no word of a new queen. No new host." Pain filled his face as he looked at me with so much longing I wanted to reach out and hold him.

No, I insisted, not me. *She* wanted to reach out and hold him.

"We were apart for too long," he finished sadly. "But now you're here again. I knew I'd find you."

"No." I shook my head, trying to break the spell I was under. "Not me. *Her.*" But this time there was less fight in my voice, and even I wasn't sure what I believed. Every cell in my body responded to him; every nerve bundle, every muscle fiber reacted to his nearness.

"You," he insisted, leaning down and letting his breath graze my ear.

Sabara's voice on the other side of my ear kept repeating, *Just let me have this. Just let me have this. Just let me have this. . . .*

I felt myself close the distance between us, a gap that barely existed in the first place, as I eased myself against him, all the while arguing back with her, *No, no, no!*

His lips brushed my neck just as I felt a tear slip down my cheek. Just as frustration like nothing I'd ever known before welled inside me.

I'd never been so powerless.

"Um, I'm guessing this isn't what it looks like." Brooklynn's voice came from behind me and I jerked away from Niko's touch, from the feel of his lips against my skin, as I spun toward her.

She stood in the open doorway, the one I'd just come through, and she, too, was wearing a nightgown. Yet she still managed to look fierce and unstoppable.

I fumbled for an explanation, my mind reeling with possibilities, none of which explained the open hatch in the floor of our bedroom, or the fact that I'd been about to let Niko kiss me. "I—uh—I—"

"Save it," she interrupted. "All I wanna hear is that we're going back to our room, and that whatever that . . . that *thing* in our floor is will not be used again. Understood?"

I glanced nervously toward the unlit tunnel, wondering if Zafir was somewhere behind her.

Her eyebrows ticked up as she crossed her arms. "No. I didn't tell him," she answered before I could even ask the question. "He still thinks you're asleep." She cocked her head. "In your bed." Then she turned to Niko. "And you . . ." She took a warning step toward him, her arms falling to her side and her hands balling into fists. "I have no idea what's going on here, but I'm warning you: Stay away from her."

"Brook—" I tried to interrupt, to take command of the situation, but she cut me off with a glare so cutting the words slid back down my throat.

Then she grabbed my arm, both of us in nothing but borrowed nightgowns, and she dragged me into the passageway, slamming the door behind us.

"What were you thinking?" Brook asked as I stared out at the flashes of lightning that came again and again, almost without pause.

I wished I could explain it to her, but how could I make her understand? How did I tell her that the ghost of a dead queen was leading me around through underground passageways to rendezvous with her long-lost lover?

Even I thought it sounded like madness.

Instead, I shrugged and kept watching the storm outside.

Brook sighed and joined me at the window. "Did you know the palace doors are barricaded for the night? Because of the storm. No one comes or goes. On Queen Neva's orders."

"Why would she do that?" I wondered aloud.

"Ice storm," Brook explained.

We stood there together, staring out, trying to see past the crystalline blooms of frost that formed on the outside of the glass panes. "It's similar to an electrical storm, with flashes of lightning," she said at last. "Only here, they're far more dangerous. See how the pulses come up from the ground, rather than from the sky? Almost as if they're made from the ice itself? Before you arrived, we were warned about the danger of the ice storm, that those pulses are drawn toward natural heat, making humans and animals easy targets. Basically, the charges search out anything with a pulse." As if on cue, a huge flash sparked in the distance, illuminating the black sky beyond the walls of the palace.

Brook's breath fogged the glass as she leaned closer.

"The lightning strikes have been known to burn an entire person to the ground," she added.

"Impossible." But I wasn't entirely convinced it was an exaggeration. I'd heard the tales too, legends of arctic storms so powerful that entire populations had been blown away on the wind, disintegrated to ash. I'd always thought they were the stuff of fables, though.

After a moment, she spoke again as another blaze ignited the sky. "Apparently, the storms only strike after dark, and this one is unseasonably early. They don't generally come until the dead of winter. From what I hear, Queen Neva's decision to barricade us inside is best for everyone."

I could practically hear her thoughts. She felt the same way about being locked up in here—rather than in the gatehouse with her soldiers—as she did about being asked to surrender her weapons. Miserable.

"Where's the thunder?" I asked, hoping to distract her before she turned the conversation back to me, back to what I'd been doing with Niko. The landscape before us was punctuated by streaks of white-hot light that seemed to be coming from every direction now.

Out of the corner of my eye, I saw Brook shake her head. "There isn't any."

"Never?"

Brook seemed to think about that as she watched. "Hmm," she finally uttered. "Weird, isn't it? We'll have to ask about that tomorrow." She took a breath and turned to me, a wry smile on her lips. "But, for now, we should probably get to bed before Zafir realizes we're up and starts asking questions." She looked pointedly at the chest she'd dragged over and positioned right on top of the hatch in the floor, ensuring, at least in her mind, that I wouldn't be using it again. "You have a long day ahead of you. Lots of 'queen stuff' to do."

XVI

I gripped Zafir's arm as we approached the throne room, where we were convening before breakfast. Through the open doorway, I could already make out several of Queen Neva's guests, and my stomach tightened.

I paused, taking a breath as the footman signaled discreetly to someone inside. And then Neva was standing there, an ethereal vision.

I released a grateful sigh, letting her take me from Zafir as she slipped her cool fingers around mine. "Charlaina, you look"—she grinned, the corner of her lip turning up slyly as she appraised me in the simple yellow dress she'd sent up to my room, more color than I'd ever worn in my life—"like a golden flower. Can you feel every eye in the room on you? There has been much speculation about what you would be like, the girl who conquered a queen."

I kept my attention trained on her for the moment, not yet ready to face the prying eyes of the others. *One queen at a time,* I told myself. *You can do this, Charlie.*

"I can't thank you enough for the dresses. It was far too kind." My gaze swept over her gown, and I was surprised—after seeing what she'd worn the day before—that hers was far more concealing than I'd expected. And by concealing, I simply meant that the material was nontransparent.

Still, she managed to make it revealing all the same, by squeezing herself into a bodice so snug it threatened to push her breasts out of its top.

She didn't seem to notice. Or care.

"You look lovely," I said truthfully. Snug or not, she was quite possibly the most elegant woman I'd ever met. Her ice-blue gown fell into rippling, diaphanous waves that started just at her waist and cascaded all the way to the silver slippers on her feet. Her long, flaxen hair fell in a wild mass of curls around her shoulders, framing her silver eyes.

"The rest of your party is awaiting your arrival. Rather impatiently, I must say. If I didn't know any better, I'd think they don't trust me." She looked toward the place where Brook and Aron were standing, along with Sebastian.

All I could see of my friends through the gathering were their heads, but they didn't look impatient to me. To me, it seemed as if they were enjoying themselves. Making friends, even.

Aron bent to whisper in the ear of a slender girl in a red gown, while Brook watched them, barely noticing that Sebastian was speaking to her.

"Don't take it personally," I offered, hoping to appease our hostess.

She just raised an eyebrow and said, "I never do." Then she waved to a woman who looked as though she might burst if she weren't noticed soon—hopping up and down, trying to get Neva's attention. "Come, dear. It's time for you to meet some of the queens."

The queen in question turned out to be an empress, as I'd been told there would be a few in attendance. Empress Filis was as lively and animated as Queen Neva was graceful and reserved. Surrounding her were three girls dressed in matching white gowns that left their shoulders and backs, and much of their legs bare.

The empress also wore white, but not a gown at all. Instead, her jacket was beaded and covered a gauzy blouse. I envied the fact that she wore pants, yet I heard no one faulting her for her fashion choice. Her hair was cut short and had been smoothed back from her face.

She bent to kiss my hand, and I started, trying to recall if Xander had ever mentioned a greeting like this . . . certain he hadn't.

"It's lovely to meet you." Empress Filis lifted her eyes to mine, and the white-gowned girls tittered behind their hands.

One of them said the word: "concubine," although not in Englaise, or any other language I should have recognized.

Around me, I realized I could hear more than I should have of conversations that were probably meant to be veiled by foreign tongues. One woman was telling her companion, not as quietly as she should have, about a particularly nasty ulcer she'd developed. When I heard the location of the sore—which was in a place I'd probably not reveal to Brooklynn in private, let alone in a roomful of strangers—I couldn't help glancing her way.

"She's lovely . . ." I heard a woman say.

"Unsophisticated," alleged another.

These were words that should have been hidden by language.

I did my best to ignore the things I wasn't meant to hear, to afford others the privacy they sought, but Sabara's name was bandied about more often than I cared to acknowledge.

I turned my gaze back to Filis, who was still holding my hand. "I—I—"

"Let her go," Neva protested.

The empress pouted, but her eyes sparkled playfully. "Can you fault me, really? She's incredibly . . ." She grinned a wicked grin. "She's just plain incredible," she finished at last.

Slowly, understanding infiltrated my awareness as I took a longer moment to study the empress, realizing what it was that I'd missed. Her masculine attire, her flirtatious greeting, the pretty girls who followed her around. I smiled back at her. Under Sabara's rule, those who didn't conform had been forced into hiding, and could only express their preferences in the underground clubs. If caught, they were sent to the Scablands . . . or worse.

I was a different sort of queen. "Thank you, Your Majesty. You're quite"—I raised my brows—"incredible yourself."

Her mouth fell open as her eyes widened in disbelief. My heart stammered and I wondered if I'd misjudged the situation, if I'd just made some grievous blunder. This was a serious matter. I had no business making jokes or light banter in a place like this. Not when I still didn't understand the rules.

A halo of silence enveloped us, ringing painfully in my ears, as it seemed that everyone around us had been listening to our conversation, waiting to see how the new queen reacted to the empress. Maybe she'd been a test of my tolerance.

Maybe I was simply a fool.

I searched the room, looking for Brooklynn and Aron, and instead I found Zafir. I beseeched him with my eyes to save me, but like before, when I'd met Neva, he remained stone-faced.

And then she let out a howl of laughter, Empress Filis, as she reached for me, draping her arm around my neck. "You're going to fit in just fine," she said exuberantly. "Come on, let's see if you're ready for Hestia."

I wasn't, as it turned out, ready for Hestia. Or "Queen Hestia," as would have been proper, if she hadn't been so . . . so odd.

Queen Hestia, as Xander had warned me, preferred not to be addressed by her title, but rather by her country's name. And in turn, she addressed the other royals by their queendoms.

"Lochland," Empress Filis managed to keep her jovial voice dry as she greeted the other queen who carried a small dog in her arms. I remembered, too, what Xander had told me about the Hestia's affinity toward dogs.

"Imperial Brasil," Hestia beamed. "Lovely to see you again! And you," she said, handing the dog to a harried-looking woman who stood at her side. The dog growled at being passed off, and the woman holding him winced, pulling her chin away from it, as if she actually feared the animal might try to bite her. "You must be Ludania!" She reached for my hands and stood back, appraising me. "Oh my, yes, you are as exquisite as I've heard. Just look at that skin. . . . It positively glows!"

I swallowed a lump, wishing I'd listened to Brook and had tried powdering my cheeks. Not that I expected to keep something so conspicuous a secret, exactly—that would be near impossible—but I preferred to draw as little attention as possible.

Except that now everyone seemed to be looking my way.

I tried to smile, but my lips felt stiff. I was worried that I might be sneering instead.

To my right, the crowd parted with a rush of low murmurs, and a woman with soft brown hair and warm eyes appeared. "Astonia," Hestia said, releasing my hands. "Have you met Ludania? Ludania, this is Astonia."

Astonia bordered my country to the east, so I knew who she was immediately: Queen Elena. Like mine—or rather like the borrowed gown I wore—her dress was plain in comparison with some of the other royals in attendance.

Elena stepped forward, a small smile tugging at her pink lips. "It's more than a pleasure, Queen Charlaina." She hesitated, as if she was as unsure how to greet me as I was to greet her. And then she hugged me. "I'm so glad you decided to attend," she whispered in my ear.

I smiled as some of my doubts lifted. "Xander said you might be here," I said loud enough for the others to hear. Xander had told me what she'd done for the resistance, in an effort to help him fight his grandmother. But despite the loyalty she'd shown to Xander, there was still a part of me that bristled at her betrayal of another queen. I dropped my voice as I kissed her cheek. "But cross my borders without permission again, and you and I will have a serious problem."

She didn't so much as flinch from my quiet warning. Instead she drew back, a smile still pasted on her lips. Aware that the others were watching us, she addressed only my original comment. "It was the least I could do." Her voice was earnest as she reached out to squeeze my hands in both of hers. "I count Xander among my dearest of friends. I can only hope to add you to that list as well."

Sabara stirred within me, reminding me that we weren't alone. That I was never alone. *Don't trust her,* she warned on a dark gust that made me shudder. *Don't trust any of them.*

But it was Sabara I didn't trust. Sabara who waited for her opportunity to take my place.

Five queens and eight ambassadors later, I finally found my way to Brooklynn. She'd somehow managed to slip away from Sebastian, losing him among the throng of royal emissaries.

"I'm not sure I can do this," I whispered. "I think some of them might be crazy."

"Who's crazy?" Brook asked, keeping her voice low.

"The queens, Brook. Hestia calls me Ludania. And the way they talk to each other . . . This whole thing is just so . . . They're so . . . *strange.*"

Brook pulled me away from the crowd. "Of course they are," she said, smiling wistfully. "Think about the kind of lives they've had, everyone bowing down to them, doing whatever they wanted, *whenever* they wanted. How weird would that be?"

I raised my eyebrows, reminding her that was *my* life now. "It *is* weird."

"Yeah, but you've only been dealing with it for a few months," Brook countered, waving off my argument with a flit of her hand. She glanced around to make sure no one was listening to us. "Imagine growing up that way. Imagine never having anyone tell you no or never wanting for anything."

"I can't," I admitted. It was hard enough trying to imagine what it would be like to spend the rest of my life this way, let alone never knowing anything different. I suppose it made sense that their views of the world would be somewhat distorted . . . their perceptions warped.

Still, I didn't know how much more I could take.

"Well, trust me, if you were uncomfortable, it didn't show. I've been watching you, and you've charmed the pants off everyone, Charlie." Brook reached out and smoothed a strand of my flyaway hair from my cheek. The sideways grin was back. "It isn't all bad, is it?"

"Honestly?" I asked, biting my lip. "I couldn't remember anything Xander taught me. I'm an utter failure as a queen. I curtsied to Queen Langdon . . . who then spit at my feet. And I'm not even sure *she's* the one who spits. I think she just didn't like me." Brook eyed my shoes warily, but I ignored her. "And then I almost fell on my butt when I tried to do that strange backward bow to Empress Thea. I swear I heard her laugh at me, and not in a good way.

"I don't get it, Brook. Why can't we just . . . ? I don't know, say 'hello' like everyone else? Why do there have to be so many rules?" I chewed my lip. "I did like Queen Elena, though.

I can see why Xander enlisted her help against Sabara."

Aron found us then, slipping out of the buzzing commotion. The girl in the red dress was still on his arm. "So? What do you think of our girl? She cleans up nice."

Heat unfurled in my stomach, reaching all the way up to my cheeks. "Thank you."

"I wasn't talking about you, Charlie." Aron was grinning at me.

I blinked, and realized he meant the girl beside him, the one in the red dress.

It took several moments for my brain to accept that it was Avonlea I was staring at. Avonlea with her almost-blue eyes. Her hair was darker now than I remembered it, with just a hint of fire streaked through it, and shinier than I'd have thought possible. Her bowed lips were painted to match the crimson of her dress.

"You . . . you look . . ." I was at a loss, so I stole a line from Empress Filis. "You look *incredible*."

She blushed, which only made the transformation seem all the more dramatic. "I feel like one of the girls from the stories Floss used to tell us when we were little. The ones about a girl who discovers she's a princess."

I glanced at Brook, whose eyes widened.

"Sometimes fairy tales comes true," a thick voice whispered at my ear.

My pulse stuttered as I turned to find Niko standing there. Niko, whom I'd dreamed about. Niko who'd almost kissed me the night before.

"I don't believe in fairy tales," I answered wryly just as a bell rang, signaling that breakfast was served.

❧ ❧ ❧

I wasn't allowed to sit with Brook and Aron and Avonlea. The queens left their ambassadors and guards so they could dine alone, at a private table.

It was just the seven of us then: Queen Neva, Empress Filis, Queen Hestia, Queen Langdon, Empress Thea, Queen Elena, and myself.

I'd never been more uncomfortable in my entire life and I approached the table on unsteady legs.

Neva sat at the head of the table with Filis at the other end. I was placed directly between Hestia, who had her dog on her lap, and Langdon, who was by far the eldest of all the queens in attendance. Quite possibly the oldest queen alive, although that could easily have been a fact made up entirely in my head.

Let me have one of them, Sabara's voice rang through my head.

I faltered, my feet failing me.

What are you saying? I hated the way my heart pounded, like a sledgehammer against my ribs.

You can be free of me, Charlaina. I could take one of them instead. They simply have to say the words.

She didn't have to explain. I understood what she meant. They were royals, all of them. Any one of them could host Sabara's Essence. Any one of them could give me the freedom I craved.

I shook my head, not caring that everyone in the room was watching me at that moment. I couldn't do it. I couldn't force Sabara onto another person just because I didn't want her. I couldn't take away their life, their free will, just to save myself.

Could I?

Of course not, I argued with myself. *What kind of person—what kind of monster—would I be then? I'd be no better than she is.*

I exhaled and straightened my shoulders, giving Sabara my silent answer.

Neva lifted a glittering crystal goblet, a smile on her lips. "To Charliana, queen of Ludania," she said as I slid into my seat. "It's been a pleasure meeting you. I, for one, can't wait to get to know you better."

Across from me, Elena raised her glass, eagerly showing her support as well. "We've waited so long to have you here. Here's to you, our newest sister."

Empress Thea, who sat next to Elena, watched me through lowered lids. She reached for her own glass and lifted it, but only barely. "Yes, dear. I can't wait to hear more about . . . what you can do."

I paused then, taken aback. I couldn't help wondering if I'd misunderstood the implication behind her words. Had she just asked me about my ability?

I smiled slowly, unsure how, exactly, to respond. "Thank you. It's a pleasure being here." I answered. I hated this feeling of being tested by these women, but I got the sense that was exactly what was happening.

Queens don't discuss their powers, Xander's words rang in my head. He'd been clear and unwavering in that one matter: I was not to discuss what I could do. I was not to tell anyone—ever—that I could understand what was being said around me.

This was still a secret I was meant to keep close.

Empress Filis grinned from her end of the table, and I tried to settle my beating heart as I held my smile, now frozen to my lips. "Ignore Thea. She was born prying."

Thea shot the other empress a glare, but it wasn't her I was listening to now.

It was Sabara I heard.

Thea may be queen, but her power is useless. She only wants to know if you can be useful to her.

I reached for my water, hoping no one could see how badly my hand trembled.

The summit was turning out to be nothing at all like I'd expected it to be—a rigorous schedule of meetings and speeches and negotiations, discussions of how to strengthen our country's economies or trade or military positions. Instead it was unhurried and taut with civility, and seemed to achieve nothing of importance.

There was talk of the night's ice storms, which had been almost blindingly beautiful to watch, and of the absence of Queen Vespaire—who'd sent Niko in her absence. Already, the palace was bustling as decorations and food were being delivered and displayed for a ball that was being held that evening.

"In honor of you, dear," Neva explained, her smile cool, her eyes determined.

"Me?"

"To introduce you, of course. And it will be the grandest introduction this summit has ever seen."

Suddenly it was all too much for me. The frivolity of it. The idea of coming all this way just to attend a party seemed ludicrous, when what I really wanted was to convince the other leaders to extend their technologies, like communication and power resources, to Ludania. I was here to barter, to buy, and to beg if necessary, for the good of my people.

Not to dance. Not to eat and entertain and pretend that those in the Scablands didn't suffer, that the work camps didn't exist. Or that half the Capitol hadn't been razed by a new breed of rebels.

What the hell was I doing here?

I stood abruptly, throwing my napkin down on the table.

The leaders of six nations stared back at me in surprise.

Sit, warned a harsh voice that no one else could hear. And when I didn't immediately obey, she said it again. . . . This time more gently. *Charlaina, don't be foolish. You may not understand the ways of politics, but you need these women. Sit down. Be patient.*

"Is everything not to your liking, Charlaina?" It was Neva who'd asked the question, and I glanced down at my plate, filled with fresh fruits and sliced meats. There were pastries and two kinds of poached eggs, one that looked miniature and the other like it had been stolen from the nest of some sort of monster bird.

My chest tightened.

"It—it's fine." I wavered, struggling against Sabara's words. I did need them, I couldn't deny the truth in that.

How? Was my silent plea back to her, infused with more hope than I'd meant as I wondered if she could even hear me. I didn't want Sabara's help. Or rather, I didn't *want* to want her help.

But, now, standing indecisively at a table surrounded by

women who I didn't understand, who I didn't know how to deal with, I realized I couldn't do this on my own.

At first there was nothing. The kind of void that resonates, buzzing until my head was filled with its nothingness.

I opened my mouth, trying to decide whether I should stay or go, wanting them to stop watching me, as they waited for me to say something. And then I heard her. Quietly at first. Just a whisper of sound that I almost missed, but growing louder, more assured.

I'll show you, she promised. *I'll help you, if you help me.*

I blinked, lowering myself uncertainly into my chair once more.

"Glad we didn't chase you off, Ludania," Hestia said, a wicked smile lifting her lips.

I nodded, smoothing my rumpled napkin over my lap as conversation started again.

I won't give any of them to you, I told Sabara. *I won't let you leave me.* Saying those words, even silently, felt final and filled me with anguish.

That's not what I want, she answered.

Then what? I asked, keeping my eyes on my plate. *What can I possibly give you?*

Heat bloomed up my neck and flooded my cheeks, making me blush so hard I had no doubt the reaction wasn't mine.

You know, her voice rasped, coming from right inside my ear now.

I did know. As much as I wanted to deny it, I knew what Sabara wanted more than anything else in the world.

She wanted *him*.

She wanted Niko Bartolo.

I continued to think about what Sabara had asked of me, even as I bundled in as many layers as I could.

I felt as if I'd struck a bargain with a demon. As if I'd damned myself to a lifetime of captivity. And basically I had. By not agreeing to subject Sabara on one of the other royals, I was acknowledging that I was stuck with her.

My purpose had become clear: to keep Sabara imprisoned within me.

The only hope I had of easing my burden was to come to terms with her, to learn to live—if at all possible—in accord.

I ignored the strange looks Zafir cast my way as I dressed, avoiding his questions about where I was going until the last possible moment. When I finally answered him, I was vague, saying only "Out" and hoping he didn't press me for more.

That had been hoping for too much, of course.

"Out where?" he asked. Then, "Why?"

I smiled at him, trying to look cheerful. I even shrugged nonchalantly. A nice touch, if I did say so myself. "I thought it might be nice to stretch my legs."

Zafir's brows shot up. "Really? You want to go . . . for a walk? Out there? In the cold?"

I couldn't blame him for being skeptical, considering how I'd complained on the ferry. How I'd huddled as far into my heavy cloak as possible and, still, my teeth had chattered so loudly I'd drawn attention from the other passengers. Cold and I weren't exactly on the best of terms.

But I'd heard Niko was out there, in that ice and snow, and I had questions for him. Ones that couldn't wait.

"Yes," I did my best to sound chipper. "The brisk air might do us some good."

There was no point pretending Zafir wasn't coming too. There was no chance I'd lose him and be able to wander the grounds on my own.

Zafir's lips pursed, a sign that he wasn't buying my explanation. But he wasn't arguing, either. He nodded to the two men stationed at the entrance, and they began the arduous task of turning the cranks that would open the immense doors.

Even the small space required to let us pass took several long minutes as the gears shifted and ground together. I ignored the suspicious glances shot my way by my guard.

Outside, the "brisk" air felt like a punch in the gut, and barbs of ice formed in my bloodstream, needling and stabbing every surface of my body from the inside out. Even the tiny hairs inside my nose felt as if they'd turned to ice and might break off should they shift the wrong way.

My chest seized and I had to will myself to keep breathing. My lungs felt powerless against the blast.

I raised my eyes skyward, hoping the rising sun might at least lessen the savage chill.

Walk! A voice insisted, and this time it was my own and not Sabara's.

I took one step and then another, my boots crunching through the snow. My footprints weren't the only ones out there. Several sets of tracks led away from the palace entrance.

I ignored the spasms of pain that came with each shallow

breath I took, and I drew the warm coat closer around me. Neva's clothing was much better suited for the climate, and I adjusted fairly quickly. My fingers were tucked inside the fur-lined gloves and my head was concealed by a hat that protected my forehead and most of my cheeks. I tugged the scarf up so it covered my mouth.

Zafir remained silent, staying behind me.

I moved quickly, making my way down the most traveled trail of prints in the ice-crusted snow. I stopped in front of a large white building that had smoke billowing from several chimneys in its roof. Leaning forward, I brushed at the sparkling crystals that covered its every surface, scraping it away with my glove and revealing the black stones beneath.

I had no idea where I was, or if I was even allowed to be there.

Inside the tall walls, I heard laughter and voices, loud and riotous, and I assumed I'd reached the gatehouse—where Brook wanted to be. The smell of ale and burnt meats reached all the way to the entrance, and I staggered backward, not sure if it was a good idea for *me* to be there at all.

Even if Niko was inside.

I turned away, ignoring Zafir's curious scrutiny.

Ahead, I saw a wonderland of topiaries and statues and fountains, all glittering and covered in that same layer of frost. Everything was white. Ghostly and beautiful, beckoning me.

He's there, Sabara told me. And I doubted she was wrong. She'd been here before. She knew this place.

She knew Niko.

When I found him, standing silently beside a patch of brilliantly flowering shrubs—brilliant red blossoms that stood out sharply against the frozen landscape, as if defying nature by their very presence—I knew he'd been waiting for me.

He looked up, but said nothing.

I turned to Zafir, silently telling him to wait.

My boots crunched loudly through the snow, the only sound now. Even the birds were still.

I stopped before Niko, and we stayed like that for too long. Quiet. Just our breath, visible puffs between us, to fill the void.

A part of me wanted to flee, knowing that I was letting her win just by being here. The other part of me couldn't. I felt as frozen as one of the statues.

All of me wondered what was about to happen.

He moved then, reaching for my gloved hands and clutching them in his. I watched silently, not caring that Zafir could see us, that he was watching my every move.

"I've waited so long," Niko said on a crystalline puff, his eyes holding mine as he leaned toward me. "And I would've waited forever."

I tipped up on my toes then, everything inside me straining to be near him. Needing to feel him.

A sound shattered the air, first one ear-splitting boom, followed immediately by another.

That was when I heard him—Zafir—screaming my name, "Charlie!" just as he collided with me, shoving me into a soft mound of snow.

I blinked so many times I felt like I was having some sort of seizure or fit. For the first few moments it was the snow that blinded me. And then it was something black and oily—something close to rage—as Sabara erupted within me, furious at being interrupted just as she was about to get her way.

Sick shame choked me as I remembered what I'd been so close to doing for the second time. I would have let Sabara take control.

Max's face appeared behind my eyes as I blinked again, rubbing away the ice and trying to blot out my humiliation. *How could I?*

"Your Majesty? Are you hurt?" Zafir asked as he dragged me up, curling his entire body around mine. He hauled me, clutching me like a rag doll, toward a low wall near the edge of the garden.

I tried to focus, but the world tilted sideways. "Hurt? Why would I be hurt?" I noticed the chaos then. The teeming clots of bodies running toward us, filling the space around us. The barking shouts. Soldiers formed around us like a barricade. "Wh-what happened?" I thought of the sound, like an explosion of thunder, and remembered what Brook had said last night: *There's never thunder.*

"Someone tried to shoot you." Zafir answered, scanning the perimeter and nodding to Brooklynn as she raced through the snow in our direction. "The first two missed by a mile. The third one . . ." He glared at the splintered tree trunk I'd been standing in front of. If Zafir hadn't tackled me, I wouldn't be here now.

I didn't even remember hearing a third shot. But I had heard Zafir. "You called me Charlie," I told him, brushing snow from my face.

"I did no such thing," he denied.

I grinned, my concentration shifting elsewhere as I searched for Niko. "You did. I heard you."

I found Niko, standing just inches from the tree, exactly where he'd been when I'd nearly let him kiss me. He stared back at me, concern etched in every feature of his face.

A small part of me, a part of me I didn't want to listen to, couldn't help but wonder if he might have some hand in all this.

But Sabara heard me.

He would never hurt me, she countered.

She wasn't lying, I knew. He loved her. I held that truth somewhere that even I couldn't reach. And even though I didn't understand it—didn't understand him—I knew it in a way that made it more real than anything I could hold in my hands.

Sabara settled down as she sensed my acceptance, and a part of me hated that she could read me so easily.

"What were you thinking, coming out here without an escort?" Brook scolded as she knelt beside me.

"*I* am her escort." Zafir's voice boomed from above us.

"Yeah, well, nice job, escort. How 'bout next time we try not to get her shot?" She reached beneath my shoulder and pulled me up, none too gently. "C'mon, Chuck," she jeered, using the nickname she knew I hated. "Let's get you someplace safe before Round Two starts." She jerked her head around to face Niko then. "You," she shouted. "Meet us inside, I have some questions for you."

Just as we were disappearing beyond the garden's walls, she bellowed to the soldiers who were still behind her. "And someone better find the bastard responsible for this mess!"

Brook was a champion pacer.

I'd never seen anyone pace and mutter, and then pace some more with so much vigor.

I paced too, but less enthusiastically, stopping to warm my hands, my feet, and my face in front of the fire. I was still shivering, even after nearly an hour of being indoors.

Brook stopped only when Avonlea and Aron came into the enormous library.

The library of Vannova was the most incredible place I'd ever seen. Like any library, there were books. But unlike other libraries I'd been in, this collection was vast, seemingly unending. Haphazardly they lined shelves in stacks and double rows that reached all the way to the ceiling and covered every square inch of wall, almost without order or reason.

I'd plucked several free from their spots, and found myself perusing topics from art to war to animal husbandry, and pretty much everything in between. The variety of languages was just as diverse as the topics themselves. I suddenly wished I had time to spend days—maybe years—flipping through the tattered volumes to discover the secrets of the world beyond the borders of Ludania.

When Avonlea burst through the library doors, she practically knocked me to the ground as she thrust herself at me, throwing her arms around my neck. "I heard what happened," she breathed against my cheek. "I'm so glad you're okay." She turned her teary gaze toward Zafir. "Thank you," she whispered, and I thought I saw his chest puff up ever so slightly.

"Oh, brother," Brook said, rolling her eyes. "Don't you dare thank him. If he hadn't let her go out there in the first place, none of this would've happened."

I grinned. I couldn't help it. "Come on, Brook. We all know it's not Zafir's fault. Besides, if he hadn't pushed me out of the way, I'd have been . . . well, you know . . ."

Brook glared at the royal guard, who glared back with equal animosity.

"Avonlea's right," Aron told Brook, dropping onto a chair near the fireplace. He slouched down, looking like he hadn't a care in the world. "Zafir should probably be rewarded for his heroics. . . . Not cursed." His mouth twitched, and he winked at Avonlea. But I saw the way he glanced sidelong at Brooklynn, and I wondered why he was provoking her.

"Look," I intervened. "It was bound to happen eventually. Let's call it like it is: Someone wants to kill me. And clearly they're taking any opportunity they can. Maybe it's better this way. . . ." I wondered if any of the optimism I was shooting for was making its way into my voice. "Who knows, maybe they left a clue behind."

"Yeah, right. And maybe whoever it is'll just step forward and turn themself in. Save us all a lot of trouble." Now Brook was glaring at me. "I highly doubt that, Charlie."

At least I wasn't "Chuck" anymore.

Brook shook her head, more exasperated than I'd seen her in ages, and then she threw her hands up. "Whatever. You guys sit here and pat Zafir on the back." She stormed toward the door. "I've got better things to do."

BROOKLYNN

Brook stalked down the hallway, her boots pounding against the marble and giving away her position. Making her less than stealthy. Not that she was trying particularly hard to be stealthy. If she'd wanted to go unseen—unheard—she could have. She'd have been a ghost. A mere whisper.

Now, however, she didn't care who heard her. She'd convinced herself that her foul mood was because of the conspirator in their ranks, that she was on edge and irritable because she was still no closer to discovering just who had been planted among her soldiers to assassinate Charlie.

She'd gone through the list a dozen times, and then a dozen more: counting the reasons it could be each of her men, and then discarding those reasons one at a time, because she knew these guys. She'd served with them and trusted them with her life. She'd handpicked them for their valor, their superior skills, and, above all, their loyalty.

She'd been unable to come up with so much as a single name.

Her mood darkened, and she clamped down on her lip, assuring herself once more that her temper had nothing at all do with Aron. That it meant nothing to her that he continued to tease and taunt her. That she *felt* nothing at all for him.

Of course she didn't! she insisted, as she caught herself stomping her foot in hallway, the sound echoing sharply.

The low rumble of laughter made her jump and she turned to locate its source.

"I hope I'm not interrupting anything." Ambassador Bartolo's voice drifted from the shadows.

Brook's cheeks flushed when she saw him there, wearing an amused expression as he watched her. "Of course not, Ambassador. I was just trying to sort some things out. I needed a minute alone."

"Call me Niko, Commander," he said smoothly, stepping out from the shadows and into the sunlight. Brook could see the way he wore his easy charm, like a suit or a skin he could shed if necessary, and she wondered what was hidden beneath. What secrets he concealed there.

She decided to play along. It was an easy game for her, a role she'd grown accustomed to during her years with the resistance. "Then call me Brooklynn." She pasted a small, languorous smile to her lips. "What are you doing out here, Niko?"

"Brooklynn," he repeated her name, letting it roll off his tongue, tasting it. Almost absently, he reached out and pushed a curl from her cheek. She didn't pull away, but she could feel him mentally circling her—sizing her up—in the same way she was him. "I came to check on Queen Charlaina. To see how she's holding up."

"She's fine," Brook answered, her smile becoming tighter. "I guess what I should have asked is what, exactly, are you doing here, Niko Bartolo? Not much to do at a summit without your queen, is there?"

He studied her from beneath hooded eyelids. "More than you'd guess," he answered quietly. "There are many things to learn, much news to carry home. And there are other matters to consider, things that have nothing at all to do with my queen and her land."

"Things like . . . *Charlie?*" Brook prodded, remembering the way she'd caught the two of them the night before. "What is it you want with her, anyway?"

"It's"—he closed his eyes—"complicated."

Brook's smile fell away completely as she glowered at him. She was tired of this game. "Well, then *un*complicate it. Leave her alone, Ambassador. She may be my queen, but she's also my friend. And I'm warning you: Back off."

And she left him standing there, false charm and all.

ARON

Aron didn't wait long before following Brooklynn, giving her just enough of a head start to think he didn't care that she'd stormed away. He couldn't stop himself from wondering when he'd started caring at all.

When they were kids, and Brook was always trying to ditch him with Charlie, he'd thought of it as a game, a challenge. To tag along with the two girls—Charlie with her flyaway silver-blond hair and Brook with her untamed mass of tangled black curls. He would follow them as they spent their days wading in the shallow streams formed by the river's runoff, climbing the gnarled trees that grew in the park or along the concrete walls, building fortresses in the sewer passages, or scavenging for "treasures" in the garbage bins that awaited incineration behind the warehouses and shops in the west end of the city.

Most days, they returned home looking like outcasts—orphans who belonged in the work camps—rather than the offspring of respectable vendor families.

It was kind of incredible to imagine that those same kids

had grown up to visit palaces at the invitation of foreign queens.

Vannova was a far cry from sewer drains and waste bins.

Yet here they were, still playing games, he realized, as he turned the corner and stopped short.

She was there, as beautiful as he'd remembered, dressed all in black and clutching the gloves she'd stripped from her hands in a fit of anger. But she wasn't alone. She was with Ambassador Bartolo from the Third Realm. They stood facing each other, their gazes intense. Even from as far as Aron was from them, he could tell that Brook's words came out like a purr.

She was flirting.

Aron clenched his fist, wishing he hadn't bothered coming after her at all. He should have known. Nothing had changed; she was the same old Brooklynn. The same girl she'd always been, still trying to ditch him as she searched for someone better to play with.

He wasn't sure what he'd expected, but it certainly hadn't been this.

He watched as Bartolo reached out and stroked her cheek, and Aron could've sworn he saw Brook's eyes widen, ever so slightly. Ever so provocatively.

He turned then, spinning on his heel, and stomped away.

XVII

I stood before the large mirror, framed in hand-carved ebony, and stared at my reflection.

"Is she kidding? I can't wear this," I repeated for the hundredth time as Brooklynn dug through the gowns spread across our bed, trying to make the perfect selection.

What I lacked in enthusiasm, Brook more than made up for. She plucked up a delicate moss-colored dress and draped it across the front of her uniform. "I don't know what you're complaining about—you look beautiful."

As if she'd even know. She hadn't even glanced my way since the footman—whose uniform was, in fact, almost identical to her own when they were side-by-side—unpacked the multitude of new gowns Queen Neva had had delivered to my room for the gala.

"It's too much." I'd tried to tell him. "I can't possibly accept them all."

"Nonsense," the man said in some form of broken Englaise. "Her Majesty insists. Consider them gifts to the new queen."

Brook hadn't argued. In fact, I got the impression she couldn't wait to strip out of her uniform and start trying on my "gifts."

"It's practically invisible," I complained, turning to face her. I was grateful that Zafir, at least, had noticed and was pretending to be preoccupied by something outside the window. "Look at this," I said, pointing at the sheer fabric across my chest. "You can see right through it."

Brook glanced up then, looking at my breasts, which were indeed covered by the thinnest, sheerest fabric known to humankind, and she covered her mouth. "I think you're wearing it wrong."

I followed her gaze. "I don't think I am, that's the problem. I've seen what Queen Neva wears, Brook, I think this is *normal* for her."

Zafir stifled a chuckle and I glared in his direction. "It's not funny, Zafir. It's not. I'm nervous enough about doing things the right way, without having to do them chest first."

This time it was Brook who giggled.

"Ooh! You two are like children." I turned my back to them as I feverishly dug through the pile, searching for something a little more . . . substantial. "Help me find something suitable. All I need is one."

Brooklynn's hand touched my shoulder. "Charlie. Relax. Stop worrying so much." I lifted my flushed face to hers. "Enjoy the party. There'll be plenty of time tomorrow for business." She held up a gown that fell in cascading scarlet waves and thrust it out to me.

I let my fingers trace the fabric—the nearly transparent

golden threads woven through it gave it a burnished look. Yet it was so delicate. So much softer than it looked, so much more pliable. "You think?" I whispered.

Brook set it aside and reached for the fasteners at my neck. "I know," she insisted with so much conviction that I couldn't help believing her.

She helped me change into a dress that fit like my own skin from just below my neck to the tops of my thighs, hugging my body so closely it was a wonder I could so much as breathe. But I could, almost as if the gown had become a part of me. Strategically placed embellishments woven into the sheer material along the torso sparkled, covering just what needed to be covered, and nothing more. Everywhere else, however, the scarlet fabric was just as translucent as the other gowns had been. Except for the skirt. Shirred silk created a soft, full effect, just a shade darker than the red that followed my waistline, and ended in bold trim that matched the embellishments that covered my chest and wrapped all the way around my hips. My arms were bare, and a simple crimson collar wrapped around my neck, fastening the dress in place.

"Wow." I breathed at my reflection.

Brook grinned from behind me, staring at me over my shoulder. "I told you. Now, let's fix that hair so I can go and make sure Aron and the others will be ready on time. We don't want to keep the queens waitin', do we?"

Brook was waiting for me in the hallway when I stepped out of our shared bedroom, and if it had been my first time seeing her, I would never have believed she was the commander of an army. It would be impossible to imagine she was a soldier at all, that she was capable of killing with her bare hands.

I didn't know when she'd found the time to get herself ready, but she had, and now she looked as polished as any of the women who'd been raised as courtiers. As lovely as any queen.

"Wow, Brook, if I'd've seen *that* gown," I teased as I reached for her gloved hand, leaning on her while I slipped off one of my glittered shoes and massaged my foot. Already my toes felt pinched in the tiny slippers.

"You wouldn't have worn it," she answered with a sideways grin, winking at Zafir. "It's too revealing."

She was right, of course. The black corset-style top barely covered her chest, plunging deeply down the center of her breasts. And of the two of us, she was the one who had a chest in need of being covered. Black beads, which dangled from her neck, fell into the exposed valley of skin.

"You know, for such a tall woman, Queen Neva has impossibly small feet. How she walks in these is anyone's guess," I said, putting the shoe back on.

When we reached the party, I nearly gasped aloud, and I was certain that Brooklynn did.

I'd never been to a circus before, but even children born in Ludania—where circuses had been outlawed years earlier because they were populated by outcasts—knew what they were.

I was aware the moment I stepped through the open doorway to the ballroom: This was no ordinary dance. . . . It was an event.

It was a dark spectacle, complete with glittered jesters and maudlin clowns wearing painted tears. There were ladies riding one-wheeled cycles who wore the snow-white tulle of dancers paired with whimsical striped socks. Overhead, I saw a thick cable extending from one side of the ballroom to the other, on which a woman in a short dress made from inky feathers and carrying a black lace umbrella with fringe that tickled her alabaster shoulders carefully glided. Toe over toe she moved, graceful and unflinching, from one end to the other. All around us there were musicians and animals—some caged and some not—and billowing fabrics that hung from the ceiling to the floor in stripes of gold and ruby and sapphire and silver.

I smiled at a trio of small girls whose faces were painted to match the animals behind bars. Each girl carried a tray with a different candied treat: sugared fruits, iced cakes, and petite chocolate bowls filled with puddings of various colors, each with a miniature silver spoon.

"No. Thank you," I said, feeling a stab of sadness that Angelina couldn't be here to witness the marvel of it all.

"Wow." I breathed as I caught sight of the flags, all hanging side by side on one wall, representing each of the queens in attendance. The white flag of Ludania was at its very center.

Standing beneath the impressive display, I saw Aron, talking with Avonlea and Sebastian.

"Oh, hell," Brooklynn muttered, as I dragged her in their direction.

I saw immediately what she was complaining about, and understood completely. Of all the gowns she could've worn, the one Brook had chosen was so similar to Avonlea's that it was hard to imagine they weren't meant to be part of a matching set. The only difference was, Brooklynn filled hers out in ways Avonlea never would.

"Is this some kind of joke?" she whispered, digging her heels in at the last second.

I tugged harder. "Come on, I think it's kind of cute. You two could be one of the acts; you could be twins who juggle or something." I glanced in the direction of a real juggler who threw daggers in the air and caught each one of them in turn. The handles of his knives were bejeweled and the blades were razor sharp.

"Thanks for that," Brook grumbled just as we reached our friends.

Aron whistled when he saw me, drawing the attention of a sharp-faced woman who stood nearby. Her long, wild hair seemed to blend into the thick fur of her coat, making her look like a shaggy black bear. Her intense brown gaze did nothing to assuage that initial impression. Behind her, perched on a pedestal, a white peacock with its colorless plumes draping all the way to the floor ruffled its feathers uninterestedly.

"You look"—he grinned, his words directed at me, but his gaze finding Brooklynn beside me—"beautiful," he said at last.

I glanced at Brook, and wondered if she'd heard what I had in his voice, but she seemed not to have noticed.

"You do," she agreed. "You made the right call."

I peered down at the gilded red dress, sheer in places that made me feel far too exposed.

"I think he was talking to you," I said quietly, realizing that

Aron wasn't the only one who'd noticed Brooklynn. Sebastian was watching her as well.

Close up, there was almost nothing alike about the two girls—Brook and Avonlea—save the cut of their black gowns. Despite the similarities in their dresses, Brook stood out like no other.

Black curls fell free from the glittering pins that tried to hold her hair up, strategically framing the soft brown of her skin. Her dark eyes alternately reflected electric sparks of enthusiasm, burning embarrassment, and flashes of frustration, since Brooklynn could no more hide her emotions than she could pretend they didn't exist.

Avonlea was plain by comparison. We all were.

Brook elbowed me. "Shut up," she said, the corner of her lip moving upward, and there was no doubt she knew it too. Everyone had noticed her.

Everyone but Niko.

I'd seen him the moment I entered the ballroom. He was impossible to miss, and Sabara had reacted instantaneously, flooding me with hope and anticipation.

I ignored him the best I could. Ignored Sabara too.

But they were persistent, the both of them.

Niko's eyes never left me, and as hard as I told myself I didn't care, I did. Except that now my feelings were jumbled with Sabara's, and even I was having a hard time discerning mine from hers. Fact from fantasy.

I reached out and took a glass of bubbling liquid, so blue it was nearly black, from one of the silver trays as it passed. I had no idea what it was, but I lifted it to my lips and sipped.

I recognized the feel of the refreshment going down, but not the taste. Whatever it was, it certainly wasn't meant for children.

Before I could take another sip, Brook took my glass and downed most of it in several gulps. "Better," she practically hiccupped. Setting the glass down, she signaled for the attendant to bring another.

"Not playing the role of commander tonight, I take it," I said, giggling, surprised at how easy it was to forget about the day's events. At how relaxed I was just being with Brook again, like the old days.

She slipped her arm through mine and pulled me so close I could taste her intoxicating breath. "I'm always the commander," she said with just the hint of a slur, and I wondered what, exactly, had been in that drink. Already, my head was starting to spin, and all I'd had was a sip. When the tray came back around, I waved it away, hoping Brook wouldn't argue. But she never even noticed. "And don't you forget it," she said, her words garbled and unclear.

I glanced up at Niko just as he raised his glass to me, a dark and dangerous smile on his lips.

And then Brook hit the ground.

"Are you sure she'll be okay?"

The "doctor," who I wasn't entirely convinced *was*, in fact, a doctor, looked down at me, perplexed. His beakish nose wrinkled. "Of course she will, my dear. She just needs to rest. To sleep it off, as they say."

"Who?" I asked, leaning over Brook's motionless form, and

relaxing just a little when I felt her breath against my cheek. "Who says that?"

He waved his hands in a flourish of bony knuckles and untrimmed yellow fingernails, both dismissing me and emphasizing his point. "*They*. They say that. She's just had too much Amrita. First-timers should never drink so much. A sip. Two at the most. It's for tasting mostly, not drinking."

I frowned at him, wondering what happened to his other eye—or rather to the place where his other eye should have been. I stared into the withered hole that bored in his skull. "Then why are they serving it in glasses?"

He looked at me like I'd lost my mind. "To drink, of course."

I pinched the bridge of my nose; I was clearly getting nowhere. The important thing, I supposed, was that Brook would recover.

I was marching back and forth after the doctor had gone, chewing on the side of my thumb and listening for the sounds of Brook's breathing, when Aron poked his head inside.

"How is she?" he asked quietly.

I waved him in, and waited till the door was all the way closed behind him. I narrowed my gaze as I assessed the worry on his face, thinking about the way he'd been goading her earlier.

"I knew it!" I exclaimed, snapping my fingers as it all came together. "You *like* her!"

He bit back a crooked grin. "Of course I like her, it's Brooklynn."

"You know exactly what I mean." I poked him in the chest, daring him to argue—*expecting* him to argue.

Instead he just shrugged.

"Don't tell her," he sighed. "It's stupid, really. And she'd laugh if she knew. I've gone from tagging after you, to tagging after her. I'm no better than Sebastian who follows her around with puppy eyes, wagging his tail and practically tripping her with his eagerness to get her attention." He moved to stand beside the bed, his gaze sweeping over her still form. His voice dropped until it was barely above a whisper. "I keep hoping it'll pass. That I can piss her off enough that she'll make *me* mad when she yells at me. Honestly, though," he admitted, "it only makes me like her more."

I grinned. "She has a way of doing that, doesn't she? Getting under your skin?"

He just shook his head, lifting her hand until it was almost to his mouth. He didn't kiss it, though; he just held it there, his lips hovering above her unmoving fingertips, as if he was waiting for something to happen. And then, when nothing did, he brushed his chin across the back of her hand.

It was tender and sweet and intimate, and my cheeks burned from watching them.

"Drunk," I blurted out. "The doctor said she's just drunk and needs to sleep. I'm going back down to the party. You can stay if you want, but she'll probably be out all night."

Aron nodded. "I'll stay . . . if you don't mind." He set her hand down then, placing it gently across her stomach as he pulled a chair up to her side of the bed.

I crept into the hallway, glad to be alone for a moment. Well, alone with Zafir, which shouldn't have surprised me even though it sort of did.

I'd told Zafir to wait downstairs, practically ordering him since I knew I'd be right back. I figured I'd be okay in the company of the palace doctor.

"Do you even care what I want?" I complained when I found him outside my bedroom door.

"Not really."

I did my best to ignore him as I strode ahead, concentrating instead on the music lilting up the wide staircase. It was playful and seductive, the strings and the pipes and the keyboards melding into a symphony of merriment. The circus, it seemed, was in full swing.

Avonlea was waiting for us at the bottom of the stairs. "Is the commander going to be okay?" she asked, biting her lip nervously.

"She will be, after some rest," I told her.

"Oh, good." She brightened. And then she leaned closer, whispering to me, "They're waiting for you."

"They?"

"Everyone," she breathed.

I saw Niko, standing outside the doors.

I didn't have to be told it was me he awaited. That *I* was the reason his yellow eyes lit up—and not Zafir or Avonlea.

I thought about going back, about waiting at Brooklynn's bedside with Aron. But Niko drew me.

Go, Sabara urged.

And I did.

When I reached him, I let my hand fall into his, already outstretched for me. Our fingers seemed to fit together perfectly.

He didn't say anything, just led me toward the ballroom.

And I followed, wordlessly. I kept my gaze fixed on the back of his black jacket, at the way it fit across his shoulders, hugging them just so. I noticed the way the curls of his golden hair fell just over the back of his collar.

We had to pass a pair of fire-eaters who stood on either side of the entrance to the ballroom, and I could feel the heat sweltering from their torches, as they—in tandem—each unhinged their jaws to engulf a mouthful of flames on a stick.

I ducked my head to hide my joy and wished it had more to do with the performers and the party than with the company I kept.

Inside, an ensemble of musicians at the back of the ballroom played enthusiastically for the guests who were dancing in the center of the expansive floor. There were more than a few glasses of Amrita being consumed, and I was acutely aware that there were far more experienced drinkers than Brooklynn and I.

Neva glanced up then and saw me, and without seeing her signal, the music came to a close. Then all the queens lined up, one by one, shoulder to shoulder, as everyone in the room fell silent.

Somewhere behind me, a man's baritone voice rang out, "Introducing Charlaina Di Heyse, Queen of Ludania."

I stood there, uncertain what I was meant to do.

"Go," Niko urged beneath his breath as he released my hand.

People gathered on both sides of me, creating a human corridor, and making it clear which way I was meant to go. Unlike at the Academy that day, there was no chatter coming from them, no hisses or shouts of dissension. Only silence.

I stepped and stepped again, making my way toward the formation of queens.

Neva was the first to greet me, with a cool smile on her lips. "Welcome," she said, kissing each of my cheeks respectfully.

Empress Filis was next in line, also kissing me, although her lips lingered longer than Neva's had. "You're doing great," she told me as she clutched my shoulders.

Empress Thea's kiss was cool against my cheek and she said nothing.

Hestia held her dog in her arms, saying only, "Welcome, Ludania." And I answered, "Thank you, Lochland," with the straightest face I could muster.

Queen Elena and the girl who stood beside her each wore a beautiful gown in different shades of bronze that matched their hair to perfection, as if the very fabric had been spun just for them. The girl's mischievous eyes sparkled as she, too, stepped forward to greet me when Elena did. "This is my sister, Sage," Elena explained, introducing me to the princess of Astonia.

The girl dropped gracefully, making me feel awkward and unwieldy just watching her. I could never execute such a perfect curtsy. "A pleasure, Your Majesty."

"Thank you," I said to Sage, unable to help smiling back at her. She had an impish look about her, as if she were about to laugh at any moment. "I have a sister too," I told them, feeling that there was more that linked us than just a shared border. "I wish she could've come to see all of this. She would've loved it."

"I'm having a wonderful time," Sage said enthusiastically. She picked up the shimmering folds of her gown as if entranced by it. "I feel like"—her nose wrinkled as she glanced back up at me—"like a princess," she finished with a playful shrug.

As I moved past them, I caught the wizened stare of Queen Langdon, the aged queen of Solaris, waiting for me, and I drew to a stop. There was something about her shrewish appraisal that unsettled me, as if she were seeing too much of me. Something that had nothing at all to do with the sheer fabric I wore.

Her lips tightened, so minutely that, at first, I thought I'd only imagined it. But then her eyes followed suit, squeezing to suspicious slits.

Ignore her, Sabara whispered in my ear.

But I was unable to tear my gaze away from the old queen who watched me, and I felt as if she, too, were inside of me now, probing and digging inside my head, searching my thoughts. . . . Even though I knew it wasn't possible. I suddenly wanted to keep Sabara—her very presence inside of me—a secret, and I worried that someone might realize she was with me. That my secret—*our secret*—might be revealed, and we'd be banished. Ostracized.

Then I'd never find the help I wanted for my country.

Keep moving. Sabara's insistence grew. *She doesn't matter.*

I didn't believe Sabara. Something told me she was mistaken, that Langdon did matter. That I was missing something.

She neither spoke nor kissed me. There was no formal greeting at all, and as the music started up, I felt Niko at my side. "What is it?" he asked, drawing me away as the other queens began to rejoin the party. He followed my gaze to Queen Langdon and I felt him stiffen beside me.

She's nothing, Sabara claimed.

Niko didn't lie the way Sabara did, but I felt his hand close around my elbow, and he pulled me away. I followed without question.

"She was reading you," he said when we were alone at last.

"What does that mean, reading me?"

Niko sighed, as if only just remembering that I wasn't her, that I didn't know everything Sabara knew. A tender smile tugged his lips. "She can read your thoughts, but only if you let her in."

"I didn't. I-I don't think I did, anyway," I thought of the way I'd felt exposed and I shuddered.

"You didn't. She didn't have enough time." His smile was meant to be reassuring.

Instead, it was alluring. At least to Sabara. I took an insignificant step closer.

But there was nothing insignificant about it.

Suddenly we were face to face, breath to breath. I wasn't sure my heart was beating, but Sabara's was.

"Dance?" I heard myself say to him, and I nearly gasped, realizing that it wasn't me who'd spoken at all. That I was no longer the one in control. I felt my lips pull into a smile then, unable to make them stop.

Panic seized me, as Sabara's words tried to comfort me. *We had a bargain, Charlaina. This is what I want.*

Niko grinned back, a wild, uncaged grin that matched my own.

He took my hand and led me to the center of the dance floor. Bodies parted out of our way like a tide, until it was only the two of us who existed out there, and a million eyes were on us, like stars, omniscient and watchful.

I placed my other hand on his shoulder and we stepped into the music, letting it envelop us, curl around us, pull us. It was like a force that manipulated and coaxed, controlled and cajoled.

In his arms, my body became supple and pliant, moving in ways I didn't know it could. I followed steps I'd never seen before. I tasted notes and smelled laughter and heard colors all around me.

My world turned upside down, making me dizzy in the most delicious way.

All because of Niko.

All because I was in his arms at long, *long* last.

No! This isn't right. This time it was me arguing with her.

I knew she was ignoring me, and I tried again. I tried harder. My skin tingled, but my head still spun, swirling and whirling, delighting in the sensation of being twirled and held and twirled some more.

Heat flashed through me as I willed Sabara to give my body back to me. To step aside.

I didn't hear the gasps, or the cries. I didn't hear the murmur that erupted around us, spreading like the fire that spread inside of me.

I only knew that when I finally stopped turning, when Niko's hands fell away from me at last, I was no longer helpless and trapped.

I felt whole.

I was me again.

And I was blinding.

❧ ❧ ❧

Bitch, I heard Sabara hiss, but she was quieter now. Distant. Less than a whisper.

"Your Majesty." It was Zafir who tugged at my arm, leading me from the center of the dance floor, forcing my feet to move once more.

I looked up at his face, but there was something wrong with it, it was awash in too much light, emanating a glow that was almost impossible to look upon and I winced, lifting my arm to shield my eyes.

That was when I realized the truth.

It wasn't Zafir who glowed, it was me.

The light beneath my skin shimmered in the way it had before, when Angelina had first brushed her fingertips over me in a last-ditch effort to stop Sabara from taking me over entirely. It was so bright my eyes ached.

I glanced around at the others now, the gathered crowd that had formed around me, queens and emissaries and counselors and ambassadors, along with servants and performers and musicians. The entire party had ground to a stop. The entire party was watching me.

I opened my mouth, wondering what I'd say, wondering how I'd explain my strange transformation. It was one thing to have an unusual pallor, to be so translucent I was luminous. It was another thing altogether to actually, truly, contain sparks beneath my skin.

I worried that I'd somehow revealed too much of myself.

It was Neva who reacted first, despite my best efforts to

come up with something rational. Some logical explanation that didn't betray my secrets.

"Bravo, Queen Charlaina! Bravo!" she exclaimed gleefully, clapping her hands together as she stepped forward, her gossamer gown matched exactly to the shade of her skin, making it seem invisible, as if she were wearing nothing at all. "You've outdone us all!" She clasped my hands in hers, lifting them to her bosom as she beamed down upon me. "You are the loveliest of us all." This time her voice came out husky, and I wondered if I'd heard right, if there was an air of envy hidden there.

She whirled me around to face the rest of the onlookers, lifting my arm as if I'd somehow achieved a triumph and she were declaring me the victor. Doubt moved from face to face, but then I heard one uncertain round of applause, followed by another, and soon the entire room was cheering.

Cheering the fact that my skin was alight.

Cheering because Neva told them to do so.

I pulled my hand from hers as I smiled wanly. Then I fled the ballroom.

I was still shaking when Niko found me.

"Charlaina," he said.

I shook my head. "Go away." I meant it this time. I didn't want to see him. I didn't want to hear his voice. I just wanted things to go back to the way they used to be, when I was me.

The old me.

I huddled as far as I could, trying to find darkness in which I could hide, but there was none. I'd made it all vanish.

Why did I have to ruin everything?

I could scarcely believe what had happened back there—on the dance floor. Could scarcely conceive that Sabara had bested me, had managed to hijack my body and make it her own. Even now, my pulse was racing recklessly.

I bent over, trying to catch my breath. Trying to rein in my reeling thoughts.

How could I stop her? How could I keep her from doing that again?

And then I heard the other voice, not Niko's. And not Sabara's either.

It was a voice I'd been longing to hear for so long, a voice so sweet it nearly undid me as my knees went weak beneath me.

"Charlie," came the ragged whisper.

I shuddered, turning toward the wondrous sound and telling myself that it couldn't be, that something like this could only be a figment of my overtaxed imagination.

I could never be so lucky.

But I was wrong.

Because he was there, staring back at me, looking as weary and broken as I felt.

"Max," I uttered.

"Charlie," he said again, and then I was running toward him. I fell into his arms, not caring that, just minutes before I'd craved another man's touch. Not caring that I'd let Niko and Sabara have their moment on the dance floor.

That was only an illusion.

This was real.

Max was real. And he was here, with me.

Where before, in Niko's arms, I'd felt dizzy and unsteady, like the world was tilting beneath my feet, now I felt solid and secure and stable. Max's grip was strong and sure, and he enfolded me into it like steel. His lips moved over my hair, my forehead, my cheeks.

I looked up, letting his whiskers graze my nose. "When . . . ? How . . . ?" I thought about what Niko had told us, about Brook's soldiers being ambushed and left for dead. "How did you know?"

And then I saw just how weary he really was, and I wondered how hard he'd had to ride to reach me. I wondered if he'd slept at all. I got lost in his gray eyes, so unlike Niko's. So like home.

"Where's Brooklynn?" he asked as I studied him.

"She's . . ." I frowned. "She's not feeling well."

"She's drunk," Zafir answered, apparently dissatisfied by the vagueness of my answer. I'd nearly forgotten about my guard, but it didn't surprise me at all to see Claude standing by his side. And, of course, Niko was still there too.

Max's gaze swept over me, only just now noticing the gown I wore and the way my hair was pinned back from my face. "Am I too late for the party?"

The corner of my lip ticked up. "The best part's just begun," I said quietly. Softly.

His brows squeezed together, almost despondently, as he leaned down and brushed his lips across mine. Not a kiss, but the promise of one. "I wish it were that simple, Charlie. I wish that was why we were here." He squeezed me to him once more, the stubble from his cheeks catching my hair. "I'm so glad you're safe. And I swear I intend to keep it that way." And then over my head, but not releasing me, he said to the others. "Get Aron and meet me in the gatehouse. We need to talk."

"I'm coming too," I protested, wriggling free from his grasp. I was the queen, after all. I was the one in danger. I should be there.

Max just shook his head, as did Zafir and Claude. "You can't go out there with all those men, not until we figure this thing out. It's safer in the palace." He turned to Niko then, and his next words made my heart stop. "Can you stay here with Charlie and Brooklynn?" he asked the ambassador to the Third Realm, the man in whose arms I'd just been. "Make sure no one gets close to them."

I expected Niko to protest, to tell Max that he wasn't a guard, nor was he a babysitter. Yet he did neither. He simply nodded.

I opened my mouth to protest, to tell Max not to leave the two of us alone together.

To tell him not to leave me at all.

But then I saw the dark circles beneath his eyes, and the blisters on his hands—likely from his reins—and I closed it again.

The sooner they resolved this matter to their satisfaction, the sooner Max could get some rest. And the sooner he'd be back . . .

. . . with me.

"Don't touch me," I told Niko, shrugging out of his grip. "In fact, just leave me alone. I can get back to my room on my own; I don't need an escort."

Sabara remained silent, a good thing since I wasn't in the mood to fight with the both of them.

Niko let my arm go but kept up with my brisk pace. "You know I can't do that, Charlaina—"

I stopped short and spun on him, fury and frustration making my vision blur. "I'm the queen of Ludania. I'm not Sabara. And, to you, I'm not even Charlaina. It's 'Your Majesty.' That's all it'll ever be." I wanted to sound firm, resolute, so I spun away from him. I couldn't let him see the way tears stung my eyes, or how my hands shook. "Now, please," I insisted, taking a breath and straightening my shoulders. "Leave me alone."

I wasn't sure how long I waited, but I knew he was gone now, that I was all alone in the hallway.

It would've been dark, except that I was still there, filling the space with too much light.

It would've been peaceful, except that Sabara was still there, filling me with too much darkness.

I climbed the curving staircase up to the second-floor landing. Here, even the sounds from the party were barely noticeable, and with each step I took toward my chambers, the tension in my shoulders eased.

"I wondered if you were coming back," a familiar voice came from ahead, from where the glow from my skin hadn't yet reached.

I recognized the voice, and for a moment, it sounded strangely like the one that should be trapped inside of me.

I was too tired to banter or play politics tonight, all I wanted was my bed. "I couldn't very well stay at the party all night, could I?"

Queen Langdon stepped forward, her skin looking even more like weathered paper in the light I cast. "It didn't look that way from my vantage point. You seemed to be . . . enjoying your company. I thought you might dance forever."

I smiled, but it was small and sad. "No one dances forever," I said, trying to brush past her. "Good night, Your Majesty." But her fingers caught my arm, squeezing me tighter than should have been possible. My eyes shot up to meet hers. "What are you . . . ?" I squinted at her, frowning. "What do you want from me?"

Her lips pulled into a hard line as she appraised me, and I wondered what it was she was dissecting: my skin and its unnatural radiance? My pale hair and eyes? Or just an inexperienced girl playing the role of queen?

She just held me like that, watching me, peeling me apart and, I was certain, finding me lacking.

And then she said them, the words that nearly undid me. "I know who you are."

At first I thought I'd misheard her, and certainly I'd misinterpreted her meaning.

I swallowed, and I tried to draw away from her. But she held me, harder even than before.

That feeling was back, that sick and sinking sensation that she was inside my head, that she knew things she shouldn't—

couldn't. Sabara felt it too, and she unfurled inside me when she should have been hiding.

She knows nothing, she promised me.

Queen Langdon's lips pulled back, nearly resembling a sneer. If it had been dark—if I hadn't illuminated the shadows—I might not even have recognized it.

But I did.

I heard her too. "I knew it." And there was so much triumph, mixed with so much vehemence, in that single phrase that I stumbled backward. Yet still she held on to me.

Her face loomed closer, almost to mine, her teeth bared like an animal's as her fingernails dug into my arms like claws. "I knew it was you. I knew you were in there." But she was no longer talking to me—Charlaina, Queen of Ludania. She was talking to Sabara.

Her breath was bitter, vitriolic, and panic made me struggle to break free. It no longer mattered that she was an old woman and a queen. She terrified me. It didn't even matter that she was hurting me. She knew my secrets, and that was far worse than anything I could imagine.

My heel caught in the hem of my dress and I heard the thin fabric tear, but I stumbled, losing my balance. I fell backward and she fell too. We landed, her on top of me, in a heap, and before I could even think clearly, I was shoving her off of me, trying to break free from her grasp.

It was far easier to free myself from her than from Sabara.

Sabara who came with me as I scrambled backward.

But Queen Langdon was fast for an old woman, and she got to her feet as quickly as I did.

"Leave me alone," I said to her in the same way I had to Niko. "You don't know anything."

Her answering smile made my stomach drop. "Oh, but I do. And I won't be the only one. You," she said, reaching for my wrist and dragging me in the direction of the party. "You will answer to the summit."

I can handle this. I can take care of her, Sabara uttered, making my heart sick. *Let me take care of you, Charlaina.*

I closed my eyes, my resolve faltering.

And that was all it took.

I felt my hand lift. I tried to put it down; I wasn't even sure what I was doing—what *she* was doing—but it remained raised. And then my fingers curled, balling into a fist.

The electricity that shot through my body was like nothing I'd ever felt before, terrifying and exhilarating and humbling all at once.

It was like watching through a pinhole as my body did things I didn't understand, my voice echoing inside my head, as I screamed at Sabara to *Stop! Stop! Please, stop!*

But she didn't, and I saw—not felt—Queen Langdon's fingers uncurl from my wrist as her entire body seized. As her eyes widened with shock.

As her windpipe was crushed from the inside.

And she had no way to stop it. At that moment, she was as helpless in the face of Sabara's whims as I was.

She reached for her neck, trying to undo what was being done to her. She flailed, and would have gasped, if only she could have.

But to gasp there had to be air.

And then I watched helplessly as she fell, her lips turning blue . . . and then white. And she stopped thrashing. Stopped moving at all.

I continued to scream at Sabara, straining against her invisible hold on me as well, yet all the while I heard her . . .

Laughing.

Niko found me there, crouched over Queen Langdon's body.

"Charlai—Your Majesty," he corrected himself, even though the matter of my name seemed foolish now. "What happened?" Unlike me, he was checking the queen, feeling for a heartbeat, putting his cheek above her mouth to find her breath.

But I could have told him: It was too late.

He glanced up at me, understanding reaching his eyes, and he let her limp hand drop to the floor.

"What happened?" he asked again, this time more gently as he spoke to Sabara.

I shook my head, tears clouding my vision. "I . . . she . . . It happened so fast. . . ." I wiped my face, trying to clear my thoughts.

But it was Sabara who cleared them for me. *She had to be stopped, Charlaina. We couldn't let her tell anyone.*

"We?" I uttered out loud, my voice broken. I didn't care that Niko was watching, or that I sounded insane. "*We* didn't do anything. *You* did."

She didn't try to explain, or to convince me she was right. She simply repeated, *She had to be stopped.*

I didn't think she was wrong, but I couldn't agree with her methods. I stared at my hands—hands that had just betrayed me—and wondered how I could possibly agree with her.

She'd just killed a queen.

She'd just *used me* to kill Queen Langdon.

"It's okay," Niko pledged, gripping my shoulders fiercely as he stared into my unblinking eyes. "I'll handle this. I'll take care of things here. The important thing is to get you out of here." He ran his hand through his already rumpled hair and then reached for the top button of his shirt and tore it open. "Go to your room and stay there. Don't come out till morning. By then, I'll have everything under control."

I shook my head. What did he mean, *under control*?

"Go!" he insisted, grabbing my arms and shaking me once. The fire in his eyes left no room for argument, and I wasn't sure whether to be horrified or relieved. "In the morning, we'll make an excuse to get you out of here. We need to get you away from here and back to Ludania. You'll be safer there."

"But . . . what if I'm not?" I thought about everything that had happened, the threats on my life and the soldiers who'd been killed trying to protect me. "What if I'm not safe anywhere?"

I was too keyed up to sleep, but I somehow managed to stay still beneath the covers, mostly because I was afraid. Afraid to move, afraid even to breathe.

I worried that Sabara would come back. Or worse, that someone else would come for me, breaking down the doors to my bedchamber to capture me and drag me away. Take me to the dungeons.

Where monsters like me belonged.

Aron had gone to the soldiers' quarters to meet with the others as soon as I'd come back. If he'd have argued, or even have asked to stay, I would've let him, that's how frightened I was of myself. Instead it was just me and Brook now.

She slept her drunken sleep, never waking. Barely stirring.

Eventually Max came in too, but I remained motionless. I wasn't ready to face him, not after what I'd done. Yet even with him sleeping on the floor, I could sense his presence like my own heartbeat. I could feel each breath he took calling to me.

I'd missed him, and I ached knowing that he was so close. That I could have him if I'd only allow myself.

XVIII

"Charlie." The voice was irritating and I rolled away from it, trying to wrap myself back in the darkness. But it came again, annoying and insistent. "Charlie, wake up!"

I groaned, throwing my arm across my face. "Go away, Brook. Can't you find someone else to bother?"

The bed jostled, and I knew she'd plopped on it beside me. "I could, but I need you. Something's happened."

Alarm shot through me as I realized she could be talking about me. That I could be the *something* she meant.

I turned back toward her, trying to look interested rather than guilty. "What is it?"

She dropped down, so she was right at my face. I didn't tell her that her breath was flammable, that I could still smell the alcohol lingering from the night before. This hardly seemed the time. "Queen Langdon died." She whispered the words, her voice sounding ominous, maybe even accusatory—although I'd probably imagined that last part.

"What happened to her?" I asked, rubbing the grit from my eyes. I glanced down, only mildly aware that I was less . . . *glowy* this morning. "Who do they suspect?"

"Suspect? What are you talking about? She was a million years old." Brook laughed, even though this was hardly a laughing matter. "She died in her sleep. But everyone's talking about it. Some of the other queens are already preparing to leave. Queen Hestia claims it's bad form to continue the summit under the circumstances. Empress Filis just said: 'When a party's over, it's over. And this party's over.'

"They're both planning to be on the next ferry."

I nodded, unsure what she expected me to say. All I could focus on were the words *died in her sleep*. I wondered what Niko had done. I wondered if he'd known a back way into her chamber too, if that was how he'd staged her death.

Shame choked me and I clambered to get upright, where the air felt less offensive, less critical.

"Where's Max?" I asked, only just realizing he wasn't here with us. Brook, too, looked as if she'd been up for a while. She was dressed and her hair was pulled back from her clean-scrubbed face.

"He and Claude are with Aron and Sebastian, making preparations. We're leaving too," she added, her brows raised as if she expected me to challenge the notion.

Again, I nodded. It was the right thing to do, to get back to Ludania. To sort things out at home—and with myself—before trying to negotiate such tricky matters as foreign policies and trade. Clearly I wasn't ready.

Clearly I couldn't yet manage Sabara.

Being on the ferry again stirred up a new kind of discomfort.

I didn't like having Max and Niko together like this. We were too close—the three of us. Four, if you counted Sabara, and she definitely counted herself. She reminded me without words that Niko was still the most important thing to her by forcing my mind to wander, filling my head with all kinds of unwanted thoughts of him. My cheeks burned whenever he glanced my way.

Max, on the other hand, remained by my side and reminded me that I was still me. My reactions to him weren't re-creations of someone else's emotions. They were mine and mine alone.

I leaned into him, watching as tiny snowflakes flitted down from the cold, dead sky above. The flakes were too small to do anything but melt as they landed on our cheeks and eyelashes and hair. But the flurries were lovely, as if we were trapped inside our very own snow globe and someone had shaken up our world.

Shaken. That was an apt description.

"Do you regret coming?" Max asked as I stared absently at the swirling white flakes.

I smiled wearily. "I missed you. I miss my parents and Angelina." It wasn't an answer, but I didn't have a better one yet. I needed time to process all that had happened.

I'd hoped to make a quick—and unnoticeable—escape from Vannova, but Neva had come to see us off.

"Be safe, darling," she'd said as she made a show of watching while my soldiers were rearmed and Brook took inventory of their returned weapons. The elegant queen had leaned closer to me then, the warm skin of her cheek brushing against mine. "I don't know what happened," she whispered against my ear, making my blood run cold and filling me with apprehension so cutting I'd shivered. "I knew she was aged, but I'd expected her to at least survive the summit," she'd said.

I'd relaxed then, releasing my breath in a cloud of steam.

"I wish we had more time to get to know each other," she'd added.

That strange sensation lingered still, the one that warned me that no one, not even the queens—maybe especially not the queens—could be taken at face value. I'd replayed the conversation in my head over and over again, questioning every syllable, every lilt in her speech patterns, every subtle glance she given me as we'd packed to go.

I'd behaved like the epitome of guilt. Yet I was certain she didn't suspect me.

"Perhaps another time," I'd finally managed to say to her, and she'd squeezed me in such a warm and comforting way that I felt as if I were betraying a true friend.

On our way out of the palace walls, we'd passed Queen Langdon's party, also preparing to depart. Her soldiers solemnly surrounded a box covered by a shroud fashioned from their country's flag—green and gold and sapphire blue. There had been no doubt that it was her casket.

I'd turned to Zafir, my brow furrowed. "The writing," I'd said.

Zafir noticed the same thing I did: the flag. "Yes. The language is a form of Gaullish. Solaris is one of the eastern queendoms."

The Eastern Region was a vague thing, defined less by geography and more by the long-dead beliefs that had once allied them. Now, however, the only thing that truly linked them linked them was Gaullish, their shared language—in its various versions. "How many others are there? Of the queens in attendance?" I spoke softly, not wanting to be overheard.

"Astonia and New Rome," Zafir answered, naming Elena's and Thea's nations.

I thought about the map, the one marked with my route to the summit, and I wondered if it could have originated in any one of those countries. If the traitor were Astonian, New Roman, or Solarian.

I wondered if I'd killed the queen of the traitor.

Even now, the thought made me sweat inside my coat.

"I missed you too, Charlie," Max said, bringing me back to the present. "More than I can ever say. When I saw that rider approaching the palace . . . When he told me what he'd seen on the road . . . Brook's men . . ." He'd already said this, or at least tried, half a dozen times. He couldn't seem to finish his thoughts, but I knew.

"Max . . ." I tried to grin, to show him I was okay. "I'm fine. And look, we're together now. We'll be home in no time, and everything'll go back to normal, right?"

He bent down and leaned his chin against the top of my head. "Not really, Charlie. We're not going home. Not yet."

I jerked back. "What are you talking about? Then where are we going?"

His charcoal eyes crinkled. "Relax. We're going south, to the estate where your parents and Angelina have been staying."

He sighed, his voice dropping so no one else could hear us. "We still don't know who the traitor is, and even though I'm sure Brook's father is somehow behind this whole thing, we still haven't managed to capture him. Until we have him in custody, I'd feel better—we'd all feel better—if you stayed away from the palace."

My eyebrows rose. "Just like you all thought I should go to the summit?" I questioned, sounding intentionally dubious of their plans. So far, I wasn't convinced that any of us really knew what we were doing.

Max shrugged. "It wasn't our idea to go south, actually. It was Bartolo's."

Again, conflict roiled through me as I wondered how much faith should be afforded to Niko Bartolo. On the one hand, I knew he'd never let anything happen to Sabara. But could I honestly say that same concern extended to me?

I supposed it had to. At least for as long as she was inside me.

"So, what's his plan, exactly?"

Max shook his head, his fingers threading through mine now, and my pulse picked up. His gaze fell on someone behind me, and I knew immediately that we were no longer alone. "I'll let him explain it to you."

We all sat around a banged-up metal table below deck. The coal furnace filled the room with so much heat it was stifling and hard to breathe. I almost preferred the cold.

I stripped out of my hat and coat, and laid my gloves in front of me, looking around at those who were privy to this information. Since we could only afford to share the details with those we knew—without a doubt—could be trusted, we made for a pathetic assemblage. There were seven of us in all. Aside from me and Max, there were Brook and Aron, Claude and Zafir, and Niko.

"We're going to try to draw the traitor out," said Niko. "Once we reach the palace, we're going to take you, along with a small band, and head south to where your family is staying. We'll slip away so that no one knows we're gone, and hopefully when he tries to make contact with his—"

"Or *her*," Aron interrupted and everyone looked up at him at once. "What? You're talking as if we're certain the traitor is a man, as if it can't possibly be a woman. But Brook could just as easily be an assassin as she could be a soldier."

Brook grinned at Aron, taking his words as a compliment.

"He's right," I admitted. "It could just as easily be a woman."

Niko just shook his head. "When the traitor tries to make contact with his *or her*," he amended, "people, they'll come to the palace looking for you. And when they get there . . ."

Brook's eyes widened. "It'll be a trap!" she exclaimed, slamming her fist enthusiastically on the rusted tabletop. "I love it. So which group do I get to be in? Please say trap, please say trap." She crossed her fingers on both hands, hoping to be part of the ambush.

Max was already shaking his head, but it was Niko who answered. "Sorry, Commander. We need you to be with the queen and her family. Their safety will still be of the utmost importance." I hated that I knew what he really meant: that Sabara's safety was of the utmost importance.

"I don't get it," I said, wondering if I'd missed something. "Won't they know I'm not at the palace? Wouldn't it be obvious that I'm missing?"

"No," Niko said, sounding more sure than I thought he should. "We'll have a stand-in for you. Someone pretending to be you."

"Where are you going to find someone to be me? Who could you get to fool the guards?"

Niko signaled to Claude, who opened the door.

We all watched silently, while the furnace continued to pump out that oppressive heat.

A girl stepped inside, and I frowned. It was Avonlea.

"She can't . . . ," I started to say, realizing that Niko meant for Avonlea to take my place. "She looks nothing like me. No one would ever believe it."

She smiled then, a small slip of a smile that was almost a non-smile, as she reached for her hat. When she pulled it off, her hair fell free. Only it wasn't *her* hair. It was mine. Silver-blond strands that spilled around her face.

"What . . . ? How?" I got up from the table to stand before her. I was amazed. Mesmerized.

I thought of all the nights Brook and I had spent in the clubs, of the rainbows of colors we'd seen people dye their hair for the night. Temporary colors that would never be allowed out in public. But those were *colors*.

This, what Avonlea had done to her auburn-streaked hair, was the exact opposite. This was the absence of color, as if she'd somehow stripped the fiery hues from her hair.

"It's not possible," I said at last.

"It was a gift," Max said, coming to stand behind me. He put his hands on my shoulders. "From Queen Neva."

I reached for Avonlea, fingering a strand of her hair. It felt like mine too. "What did she do to you?"

Avonlea blushed, and even her almost-blue eyes seemed, somehow, bluer.

It was Niko who answered. "Neva knew you were in trouble and she offered to use her gift to protect you. This is what she can do—create illusions."

I stared at Avonlea, and thought about the way Neva had hugged me, about the way she'd told me to be safe. She'd known the plan and had wanted to help.

"Is it permanent?" I asked.

Niko shook his head. "It'll start wearing off in a few days. By the end of the week, she'll be completely back to normal. We'll have to act quickly. For her part, Avonlea will need to keep to herself as much as possible, stay in your rooms and pretend she's not feeling well." Niko turned to Avonlea. "Think you can manage that?"

She looked at Niko like he was simpleminded. "If you're asking if I can lie in bed all day while other people wait on me?" Her Scablander inflection was still firmly in place. "I imagine I can handle it."

"Yeah, well don't get too comfortable," Brook cautioned.

I wrapped my arm around Avonlea. "I don't know, you guys, I think I could get used to this. I kinda like having someone else acting as the queen."

Avonlea pulled away, but she was grinning back at me. "I wouldn't take your job for nothing," she groused. "A few days, sure. But I saw the way those other queens were. Odd bunch, those ones. I'd sooner take my chances with Floss than deal with the lot of them."

We didn't even have to ride an entire day before we reached the train line, and then it was less than two days' travel by rail. Both were heaven compared to the ferry, which was either too cold above board or too hot below. And far better than being at Vannova, where I'd been shackled by the weight of my secrets and burdened by guilt.

At least on the train I could be myself again. There were no rules to abide by. No etiquette I had to follow in order to avoid offending anyone.

The only challenge was sleep, because that was when my defenses were down and Sabara's presence was strongest. I dreamed still. My dreams, and hers, until sometimes I couldn't tell the two apart.

In one, I dreamed of a newborn baby. She didn't cry or kick, didn't breathe at all. She was a beautiful child, so small and fragile. And so very, very still.

I held her, rocking her in my arms as I whispered a lullaby in a broken language I didn't recognize. Yet that didn't stop me from understanding the haunting words.

Close your sweet eyes
Life doesn't last long
You'd better go sleeping
Flying through dreams

Close your sweet eyes
'Cause life is a lie
Find happiness in dreams
And good night, my child. . . .

A knife pierced my chest as I clutched her to me, filling me with so much ache I wanted to open my mouth and shriek, to howl and bawl and pound my fists against everything and everyone. When I opened my mouth again, nothing came out, just a hoarse thread of whimpers that meant nothing, that said nothing.

Then he was there, taking the baby from me, and I knew: She was ours. Mine and his.

I glanced up, into his golden eyes, and back down at the downy patch of golden hair on her tiny, lumpy skull. I wanted to press one more kiss there, to feel that feathery hair against my lips, but he was already wrapping the blanket over her face. Concealing her. Hiding her.

And, soon, he'd bury her, too.

There were other births, and other graves, but never that same sense of loss. Even in the dream, I wondered: *How many babies had Sabara conceived? How many children had she outlived?*

Her life was my worst nightmare, losing those whom I loved. Yet she'd done it for decades, centuries, eons.

All except for Niko.

Niko, who came back to her time and time again . . . in a never-ending migration of leaving her just so they could be together once more.

When I rolled over, I fell into arms that enveloped me, and the scent of soap and leather and musk tempted me from sleep. They were Max's smells.

"You were crying," Max said quietly over the sounds of the train around us. "Bad dream?"

I squeezed my eyes shut, wishing I could tell him everything—about Sabara and Niko, and about Queen Langdon. Instead I whispered back, "Too many to count," and nestled closer.

But I wasn't just nestling, I was reaching for him, pulling him to me. We'd been apart for too long, and I suddenly understood a little of what Sabara must have felt, being away from Niko.

I needed Max to stay with me. I needed him to kiss me. To never let me go again.

I clung to him, my hands moving across his bare chest, gently at first, and then not so gently as my fingers dug insistently into his skin.

Tiny earthquakes started in the pit of my stomach, and then trembled outward, raging until I felt like everything about me might shatter into a million tiny pieces. That was how his lips found mine, trembling . . . quivering with a need I had no control over.

His breath was hot against my mouth, *inside* my mouth, as if he was the only thing keeping me alive. I pressed even closer, letting my tongue find his so I could taste him. I was afraid to open my eyes, not wanting to know if I was as alight on the outside as I was on the inside, but certain I was. Certain I must be.

His hands were as desperate as my own, and his fists balled

impatiently over the thin fabric of my nightgown, tugging and pulling and dragging, until I heard a rip.

I felt his unrepentant smile against my lips, and I sighed. "How many of these are you going to ruin?"

"As many as you put on, I suppose." And then his voice dropped. "Maybe you should stop wearing them," he suggested.

My lips twitched. "And wear what?"

"Nothing," he growled and tossed me on my back, stretching out above me.

I giggled and meant to shove him away from me—a game—but the moment my fingertips grazed his skin, I was reaching for him again, unable to stop myself.

He dropped down, covering my entire body. "I've missed you so much, Charlie. I haven't slept, I've barely eaten. *I* haven't dreamed at all."

"Don't . . ." I whispered. I couldn't hear how he'd been hurting while I'd nearly let Sabara have control, when I'd nearly let Niko kiss me.

"I'm just saying, it's so good to be together again." He rolled onto his side, dragging me with him.

I leaned against him, so I could listen to his heart—my own lullaby, one I didn't need to decipher.

"Tell me what else has happened. Have you gotten any closer to finding Brook's father?"

Max shook his head. "He's been quiet, at least in the Capitol. And Xander hasn't heard anything in the south. I don't think his people know where your family is, though."

I sat up so I could see him. "But they're good? Happy?"

He grinned back at me. "I already told you they were. Angelina's started with her new tutor, and your father has taken over the kitchen. Xander wasn't complaining. I think he prefers your father's cooking over the palace chefs." He stretched, keeping his arm around me.

I settled back down, matching my breaths to his. "It'll be good to see them," I said, wishing we were already there.

If it hadn't been for me, we'd have had no trouble at all sneaking out of the palace.

The plan had been simple enough, to leave under the cover of darkness, while the night would conceal us. But what everyone seemed to have forgotten—or at least underestimated—was that where I was concerned, darkness was relative.

Sneaking out, I draped myself in the thickest, blackest fabric I could find, letting Max and Zafir lead me to where the horses had already been saddled and were waiting for us. I rode with Max so I wouldn't have to uncover my face, which would have given us away in an instant. All we could do was hope that no one had seen us leave.

Inside the cloak, I was suffocated. But I was with Max, and soon I'd be with my family, too.

I had little to complain about.

Avonlea had been given strict instructions to trust only my chambermaid, whom I would have trusted with even Angelina's life.

By dawn, there was enough light in the sky that I was able to come out from beneath the cloak I wore. For much of the ride, we saw no one. We stayed in rural areas or near tree lines whenever possible, following rutted roads overgrown with weeds. We gave a wide berth to villages and more densely populated areas, stopping only at streams and ponds to let the horses drink.

I told Max all about the Scablands, and about the people I'd met there. I explained Avonlea's situation, which I'd already talked about, but which I felt compelled to probe and examine, trying to figure out how things had gotten so out of hand in Ludania. How people had become a commodity.

Max agreed with me, that changes needed to be made. We all did. When talk of reorder and revolutions and homecomings wore thin, I stretched and yawned, and stretched some more as I leaned back against him, closing my eyes.

"Charlie." I heard him whisper against my ear. "Charlie, wake up. We're here."

I was alert in an instant, anxious to see—and hold—my family at long last.

The estate where they'd been living was so much more than I'd expected, almost like a second palace. It was wooded here, surrounded by tall forests with old-growth trees draped with moss and vines. There were ferns and wildflowers and ponds. It was more remote and less manicured than the palace, but no less striking in its splendor.

I guessed that this fell into the category of things I still didn't know, of which there were more than I could count now.

Xander was waiting for us, and behind him I saw my parents. Behind them, Angelina.

Without thinking, I drew my heels against the horse beneath us, spurring Max's horse myself. "Yah," I cried out.

The horse responded, startling Max, who tightened his grip on both me and on the reins. "Dammit, Charlie, a little warning."

I was grinning though, at the same time tears slipped down my cheeks. "She's so beautiful," I breathed in response, unable to tear my gaze away from my little sister. Warmth sprang from my gut, spreading to my weary limbs. I was grateful Angelina was safe. Grateful we'd hidden her from Jonas Maier and his followers.

But I wasn't the only one who was anxious, and my father jumped in front of us, forcing Max to make an abrupt stop. When he grabbed me, I was no longer the queen. I was four again—his little girl. He swung me in a wide circle and then he hugged me to his chest, pressing fat kisses to my wet cheeks.

He was talking, too, but I couldn't hear him over my sobs. Then my mom was there, and we were a tangle of arms and hands and faces and jumbled words. I never wanted to let go. I never wanted to be away from them again.

It wasn't until I realized Angelina was still standing apart from us, that I peeled myself from my parents' grasp. Angelina, who looked so alone there, worry filling her clear blue eyes.

I held my arms open for her, smiling so brightly I was sure I'd blind her.

She took a step away from me.

I looked to my parents, and then back to Angelina. "What is it?" I asked. And when she didn't answer, I turned to Max and Aron and Brooklynn. But all I could see was bewilderment in their faces.

"Angelina . . . ?" I tried again, coming closer but feeling crestfallen. "It's me."

She frowned, and then blinked, then turned and raced away from me, leaving Eden to run after her.

BROOKLYNN

Brook sat on the steps and stared up at the moon. It was a different moon here than the one she'd been watching during their travels through the Scablands, different from the one she'd spied through the icy windows of Vannova.

This was their moon—a Ludanian moon.

She knew she was being fanciful, but she couldn't help herself. It had been a hard journey and it felt good to be home, even if they were still sleeping in strange beds. Something about the warmer climate and the sound of Englaise on every tongue put her at ease once more.

Of course, Charlie's father's cooking hadn't hurt either.

She thought about the old days, and wondered if she was missing out on a normal life because she was the commander of the armed forces.

She smiled to herself at the notion of working in the restaurant once more, of doing homework and chores. Of doing all the things that others had forced on her.

She leaned back, letting the tips of her loose hair brush the concrete step behind her.

"What are you grinning about?" Aron's voice cut through her reverie, bringing her back to reality.

Brook sat up, leaning her elbows on her knees while Aron took a seat beside her. "Just thinking how nice it is to be here." It felt strange opening up to him—just being herself—but she was too tired to banter.

"It is good. Strange, but good."

"Why strange?" Brook wondered, giving Aron a skeptical look.

He shrugged, glancing at her. "I don't know. I kind of liked it when we were out on the Scablands."

"Really? What part did you *kind of like*? The part where we were freezing? Or practically starving? Or was it that we didn't know where Charlie was?" She shook her head, brushing her hands on the hem of her pants. "Oh, wait, I know, it was the part where there was a killer in our midst. That *was* kind of thrilling, wasn't it?"

He chuckled. "You say the weirdest things, Brook."

She laughed, nudging him with her shoulder. "Me? You're the one with the deranged sense of a good time."

She was about to get up when he stopped her.

And all it took was a sentence. "I meant because we were together," he stated, his voice quiet but steady.

Brook froze. Goose bumps dusted her skin. What was he saying? What the hell was that supposed to mean?

"Together?" she repeated, glancing at him out of the corner of her eye, too afraid to face him head-on.

Her heart slammed against her chest as she waited for him to say something. Anything.

He didn't. He touched her instead, brushing his fingertips across her cheek.

She did turn then, her eyes locked with his. She swallowed, if only to convince herself that she could. It was maybe the only thing she was capable of in that single, stationary moment. That, and breathing, which was harder now than it should have been.

She could see it in his eyes, the same thing she'd been feeling for days, maybe even weeks. Hunger, longing . . . conflict. She understood it all too well, and was as uncertain as he seemed to be.

His thumb moved, stroking the skin of her jaw and making her quiver. Unable to resist any longer, she closed her eyes and turned toward his hand, until his thumb reached her lips. She felt a million stars burst inside of her, glittering and spangled and white hot.

When his lips finally touched hers, she thought she might explode as she whimpered softly against the excruciating beauty of it. *How could this be happening?* She wondered. *How could Aron be kissing me?*

Yet she was kissing him back. Her mouth opening slowly, achingly, as she silently begged for him to tell her what to do. She'd never been so inhibited and so frenzied at the same time.

She pulled away suddenly, before the kiss had even taken hold. "What are we doing? We can't do this." But she was lacing her fingers through his. Everything inside of her was conflicted.

"Brook, stop it. We can, and we are." He wrapped his arm around her waist and drew her closer. "Don't tell me you don't want this too, because I've waited months for you to admit it."

"Months?" Brook breathed. Had it really been that long? She shook her head.

Aron just nodded, a stupid grin on his face. "Yes, Brooklynn." He ran the side of his finger from her neck to her chin, and tugged her face up to look at him. And then he said it again. "Yes."

Before she could argue, he leaned down, letting his lips dispute her unspoken words, and showing her, in no uncertain terms, that she was wrong.

XIX

My palms were sweating as I gripped the door handle and slipped inside my sister's bedroom. She knew I was there—they both did, Angelina and Eden—but there were no sounds from either of them to greet me.

"Angelina," I whispered into the silent bedroom.

The only answer was the slight rustling of blankets, but it was answer enough.

I crossed the space to Angelina's bed, glancing up to see her watchful guard appraising me. I could feel the wariness coming off her in waves, and I frowned at her for making me feel like a stranger in my own sister's bedroom.

Kneeling down, I leaned my elbows on the edge of her mattress, pretending I didn't know she was trying to avoid me. "Angelina," I said again, this time not bothering to whisper since we both knew she wasn't asleep. I moved my hand toward hers, meaning to cup it, to beg forgiveness for whatever wrongdoing—real or imagined—she'd thought I committed. But she flinched from me, drawing not just her hand, but her entire body away from me.

If I hadn't known better, I'd have sworn I saw her tremble.

My stomach twisted at the thought that I was responsible for making her feel this way. That I was the source of the disgust on her face.

"What is it? What did I do?"

I waited for an answer, each second my heart breaking just a little more.

And then I heard her, her voice so insubstantial it was barely a breath. "Not you . . ." she said, and I wondered if Eden could even hear her now. "Her."

My eyes widened.

Angelina knew. Angelina who'd always had a sense of who could—and could not—be trusted, knew Sabara was too close to the surface.

I sighed then, understanding her fears, even if I couldn't explain that she was mistaken, that Sabara couldn't hurt us. Not now.

I got up on unsteady legs. I wouldn't—*couldn't*—ask for her help again; it was too much for such a little girl. Besides, I doubted it would matter anyway.

I'd made my decision regarding Sabara. I knew now that she couldn't simply be *healed* away, and I'd resolved to keep her so she couldn't harm anyone else.

That didn't mean I didn't have doubts, though. I'd given Sabara far too much control. So much control that I'd been incapable of stopping her from killing Queen Langdon using my own hand.

I felt Sabara, deep down inside, stirring restlessly.

Her, she whispered, and I could feel her mentally sizing up my little sister, weighing her as a possible host.

I staggered backward, falling over my own feet now as I realized Angelina had been right.

She *should* stay away from me. I was poison to her. I was dangerous.

Maybe deadly.

In the corridor, I crumpled to the floor, ignoring the fact that Zafir was there, as always. He offered no consolation, just stood aside while I clutched my knees to my chest and cried into the hollow space.

"Charlaina," Niko's voice tugged at me, drawing me forth. His hand was at my shoulder, his touch urging me from my misery.

I should have shrugged away from him, the same way Angelina had from me, but I didn't. Instead, I let his fingers move over my back in slow, soothing circles.

"What are you doing here?" I asked, lifting my face to his. "Why are you always around?"

Zafir turned his back to us, affording us all the privacy he could manage.

"I was worried about you, Charlaina. I wanted to make sure you were okay."

"Stop calling me that," I insisted, sounding shakier than I wanted to. I ignored the hand he offered me, and got up on my own. "Why don't you say what you mean?" I kept my voice low so Zafir couldn't hear us. "Stop pretending it's me you're worried about and just say it. Say that it's Sabara you want to protect. Call me Sabara."

He reached for my arm, either to stop me from leaving or to steady me, but I ripped it away from him. "Don't touch me," I hissed.

He lifted his hands in submission. "You don't know what you're talking about. Of course I'm worried about you. None of this is easy. I can't imagine what you're going through, how . . . conflicted you must be. It's hard on me too."

I whirled on him. "Oh, is it? Is it hard for you, Niko? Are you losing yourself? Is your identity being compromised?" I thought of Angelina. "Are you losing the people you love?"

"Yes." His voice broke, and this time I didn't stop him when he closed the gap. Something in his face, something in his eyes, reminded me—or her, I couldn't be sure—of the man who'd held his baby daughter, still and lifeless. His hand closed the distance between us, his fingertips brushing against mine. "Yes, I'm losing the person I love."

"Don't touch me," I said again, but even I could hear the longing in my words. I couldn't blame him for ignoring them.

His hand clamped over mine and he tugged me. He didn't have to tug hard, though. I took the step toward him of my own accord, until our bodies were just a heartbeat apart.

I shook my head, denying him and hoping to keep him at bay. "I'm telling Max. Everything," I whispered.

He stilled, as if turned to stone. "You can't."

Sabara felt it too, the truth in my statement, and I could

feel her panic blooming like a toxic flower. Dread rooted and spread, pricking me with its nettled thorns.

"I have to."

"Sabara," he soothed, his voice as golden as his eyes. "Be reasonable."

My vision blurred and I reached out to steady myself. It was too much, hearing her name on his lips, feeling her tidal wave of sensations, recognizing the sentiment buried in his voice.

I don't know if he mistook my instability for assent, or if he was simply taking advantage of my momentary lapse. But the moment I felt his lips on mine, Sabara broke free, finding the strength to propel me into his arms.

She coaxed and moved my body. She relished every sensation, every caress, stroke, brush, and touch, regardless of whom it belonged to.

I lost myself in the swirl of sensations.

"Charlie?" It was that voice—*Max's voice*, filled with flat accusation—that broke the spell at last. And in that instant, it was just Niko and me. Sabara had retreated.

I was immobilized as I stared into his cool gray eyes, trying to imagine how guilty I must appear.

How guilty I was.

"Max, I—"

But he was already gone.

Together with Zafir, I'd searched the estate grounds long after Zafir had insisted it was too late to be out, that we should call it a night and start again in the morning. But I'd demanded we keep on. I needed to find Max. I needed to explain things to him, so he'd know that it hadn't been me. That it was Sabara he'd seen with Niko.

I'd hoped I could somehow convince him.

I'd tried to tell Zafir instead.

"Sabara's alive," I'd said to him, thinking the words sounded even more absurd out loud than they had when I'd practiced them inside my head.

Zafir hadn't skipped a beat. He hadn't even blinked. "You should get to bed, Your Majesty. It's been a long day."

"I'm serious, Zafir. She's in here . . . with me." I'd signaled that I meant my own body. "She's been here all along."

I wasn't sure he'd even heard me, but I was certain he thought I'd lost my grip on reality. "If it makes you feel better, I'll have someone else stand guard at your room and I'll keep looking for Max," he'd offered, leading me back inside the house. "If I do that, will you go to bed?"

There'd been no point arguing. He had been determined that I needed rest, so I'd let him lead me to my room and position another soldier outside my door as I climbed into bed. I didn't even remember drifting off to sleep, but when I closed my eyes I was falling.

Falling into nothing.

Falling . . .

I awoke with a spasm, clutching my pillow to my chest. It took me several moments, and several long breaths, to assure myself that I was safe. That I was lying in my bed, and not actually falling. I had to wait for my heart to find its normal rhythm once more.

It had only been a dream. There was a time when those words would have been enough to soothe me. But things had changed. Now things that couldn't possibly exist, things that shouldn't be able to hurt me, had found a way out of their world and into mine.

I'd been damaged by them. *By her.*

I settled back down again, telling myself it didn't matter. That in the morning I'd right the things that had been wronged by telling Max, and anyone else who would listen, just exactly what I'd become.

For now, I stayed in my bed, listening to the sounds around me, and trying to acclimate to the noises of this house: the scraping of branches against my window, the night animals that called to one another, the creaks and groans of the foundation and roof. None of the noises were strange in and of themselves; they were just unfamiliar to my ears, making it hard to let them fall into the background of my thoughts.

And then there was a sound that wouldn't have been usual . . . in any household.

I bolted upright once more, my ears pricked as I strained to hear it. It was there again, a muffled shout from somewhere outside. I threw back my covers and climbed out from beneath them, dropping to the wooden floor beneath my bare toes.

My heart stuttered, and I wished my room wasn't so far from my parents. So far from Angelina's.

I moved cautiously, unsure where to step in order to avoid making noises of my own. Yet I continued to tell myself that my worry was for nothing; surely these were only the sounds of a different household.

Still, I couldn't help but recall the reason we were here in the first place: Someone was trying to kill me.

I didn't bother to cover myself as I eased toward the door. Pressing my ear to it, I strained to hear, but there was nothing coming from the other side. I turned the knob and tested the hinges for squeaks. The door slid open noiselessly, and relief swelled in my chest.

Until I saw what was waiting for me on the other side.

The guard, the one Zafir had stationed there, was slumped down on the floor in a heap. But it was the blood that stopped me cold.

Splattered on the floor and on the walls.

Puddled around the guard's body.

I dropped to the ground beside him and leaned over, my cheek hovering above his mouth. There was no breath, not that I'd expected it. His skin was already gray and mottled.

I stood again, clutching the wall to steady myself. This was my fault. I'd brought this upon the guard. I'd brought this into the place where my family was meant to be safe.

I had to find them. I had to warn someone that we were in danger.

I struggled to recall the way to Angelina's room, and in my haste, I stumbled. But I got up again quickly, my feet as silent as my breath was ragged.

I passed another guard, also dead and bloodied, and I wondered if I was heading right toward them—those who wanted me dead. I wondered, too, where Max was. And Xander and Zafir. I hoped I wouldn't find their bodies littered among the rest, casualties of the changes I'd tried to make in my country.

If I were braver—as strong as the warrior I'd always wanted to be—I'd have called out for them. Instead I was a coward and my throat squeezed around the words, trapping them inside me.

I passed two more bodies, one guard and one member of the house staff, and I followed the trail of blood that seemed to lead me toward Angelina's room. Each step was measured by fear as I did my best not to step in the blood, but it was impossible to avoid altogether.

I felt it, more than once, slick between my toes, and I recoiled against the sickening sensation that I was somehow standing in death.

When I finally reached Angelina's room, the door stood open, and my heart skipped several beats.

"Eden," I pled, my voice entirely too quiet. Entirely too shaky.

Eden was nowhere and the room stood quiet.

I stepped inside, terrified of what I might find. Terrified that I was already too late, and that Angelina, too, would be added to the body count that had amassed inside these walls.

I approached the bed with courage I hadn't realized I possessed, silently willing my sister to be there. Silently praying I could simply scoop her sleeping form into my arms, and together we'd escape into the forest to hide.

But my prayers were met by deaf ears.

It would have been impossible to miss the crimson spray that mottled the snow-white sheets, and the blood that splattered my little sister's rag doll, Muffin.

The bed itself was empty.

I reached for the doll and clutched it to my chest. "No," I gasped, and then I was on my knees. "No!" I shouted, rocking forward.

I didn't stay there long, though, because somehow I knew: Angelina wasn't dead.

And that meant she needed me.

It was the strangest thing, I was no longer afraid.

I had feelings, sure. Anger. Outrage. A sudden new sense of boldness. *Did that count as a feeling*?

It didn't matter. Something had broken in me the moment I'd seen Angelina's bed, empty and bloodied. Something inside of me had been liberated, and now I *was* a warrior.

Now I had a mission.

"Angelina!" I shouted. *"Angelina! Eden!"* I didn't care about the others. I didn't care who heard me. Only one thing mattered to me now.

I stepped in pools of blood and left footprints of my own. I no longer grimaced. I barely noticed.

Moving with determination, I followed my instincts.

"Angelina!" I shouted again and again and again, stepping over bodies and daring those responsible to show themselves.

The estate was large, nearly palatial, and they could have been hiding anywhere. I hadn't come across Brook or Aron or anyone else who could have helped me. Instead, I turned corner after corner, and I reached one dead end and then another. I choked on my own frustration until it nearly replaced the fury that spurred me on.

Then I heard it. Just a mewl, really . . . the smallest, palest sound that seemed to materialize from out of nowhere.

But it hadn't. It was my sister.

Hope extinguished all else, and I whirled toward the sound.

"I'm coming," I breathed as my bare feet pounded against the floor in my effort to reach her.

When I saw her, I nearly buckled.

She was tiny and fragile, as any child should be, but her eyes were brimming with the same inner turmoil I felt. She saw me at the same moment I spied her, and reflexively, she lurched in my direction.

It was the knife, though, the one poised at her throat that stopped her from taking a single step toward me. The man holding it—holding *her*—was surrounded by three other men, all of them large, all of them imposing, and none of whom I recognized.

But I would have known Jonas Maier anywhere. I'd seen his face hundreds, maybe thousands of times before. He'd invited me into his home. He'd fed me and given me shelter.

Now he threatened my sister's life.

"Please," I whimpered, feeling the first fracture in my new armor. "Can't we talk, Jonas? Can't we do this peacefully?"

His eyes, so much like Brooklynn's, yet so very, very different, appraised me, making me feel vulnerable and exposed. "Don't you think we're past peaceful here?" His eyes roved from the blood on my feet, to that on my knees and hands. His lips curled into a loathsome sneer. "Besides, you have no intention of listening to my demands, any more than I intend to leave here *peacefully.*" He jerked the knife he held, and its blade burrowed against the soft flesh of my sister's neck.

My jaw tightened and I took another step toward him. "Let her go," I insisted, the words failing to deliver the menace that raged within me as I gazed at Angelina. The look of panic in her clear blue eyes was my undoing.

Blood smeared the front of her nightdress, and I scoured the length of her, searching for signs that it might be her own, that Jonas and the others had hurt her. I held my breath, wondering what had happened to her. I wondered, too, where her guard was. Eden would sooner die than surrender her charge.

Jonas grinned back at me. It was an ugly grin that made my stomach flip. I could scarcely look at the men who stood at his back; their knowing leers and grunts of approval made my vision blur with rage. Each one of them was steeped in the blood of others.

"You've done this," Jonas shook his head, speaking to me in Parshon. *"You brought this on yourself. The Vendor queen . . ."* He let out a derisive laugh, and the other men followed suit, chuckling and mocking me, as if they were in on some secret joke.

But all I could see, all I cared about, was the blade at Angelina's throat.

"Let her go," I repeated, my voice constricted now.

"What did you expect, Charlie?" He spat my name at me. *"Did you think you could just take the throne and change everything at your whim? Did you think no one would care? That there would be no repercussions?"*

Fire shot through me, a sensation both familiar and foreign.

My skin began to tingle and my fingertips itched. "Don't you dare harm her."

One of the men sneered at my words, drawing a knife from the back of his waistband. Another pulled a handgun from inside his jacket, laughing at my attempt to stand firm.

"Let's get out of here," the man with the gun said to one of his cohorts in a language that was neither Parshon or Termani—not Ludanian at all. *"Tell him to stop toying with the child and finish it."*

I couldn't breathe. I couldn't swallow, but somehow I knew what to do. What I *had* to do.

Closing my eyes, my fists followed suit, clenching into angry balls. Energy sizzled through me now, and I was no longer confused about what it meant. "I warned you," I hissed.

"Well, here are your repercussions!" Jonas shouted, still unaware that he was in danger at all. He drew his blade right up against Angelina's throat and I heard her gasp. If I'd had misgivings, they'd have been silenced in that moment.

But I had none.

I didn't need Sabara now. I could do this on my own.

Behind me, in the distance, I heard the sound of footsteps closing in on us. I didn't know who might be coming—if it was my men, or more of Jonas's, but I couldn't take the chance. If I waited any longer I might be overrun, outnumbered by an army I was unable to stop. I had to act fast. I had to save Angelina now, or we could both end up dead.

I lifted both of my hands, raising my fists in front of me. The sensation that ripped through me was welcome, and I had no intention of stopping it. Not this time. In fact, this time, I summoned it.

I targeted Jonas first, concentrating on his airway, imagining it, willing his windpipe to slam shut. Intentionally fueling his death.

Jonas shrieked, but not for long. I didn't blink. I didn't even hesitate. I concentrated instead on Angelina, on the terror I could see in her wide eyes. I concentrated on what these men had done, not just to her, but to the others as well. I thought about what they were willing to do. In my mind, and with my fist, I squeezed, even after he released her, as he tried to tear an opening through his own throat so he could breathe once more.

And when one of the other men, the one with the handgun, reached for Angelina's arm, barely even acknowledging the fact that Jonas was dying right in front of him, I turned my attention to him also. It was easier this time, and he gasped at first, and then dropped to his knees, writhing and clutching his neck, until he stopped. Falling still. And silent.

Angelina blinked, staring back at me, and I wanted to rush to her. To take her in my arms and whisper assurances that everything would be fine. That I was going to make everything okay.

The other man, the one with the knife, moved then, lunging toward her, while the other man stood watching, dumbfounded . . . but no less guilty. No less willing to murder. I took them both at once, ignoring their gasps as I tightened my fists, focusing with my mind. Electricity filled my body, coursing through me until every nerve sang. I held them all like that—all four of them—in my invisible grasp, suffocating them.

Watching them die.

Saving my sister with power I'd stolen from Sabara.

"Angelina," I rasped, not moving from where I stood, not releasing any of them. . . . Even when the footsteps were right at my back.

Even when I heard Brook gasp, "Charlie? What are you doing? What have you done?"

I looked down then, at the men who littered the floor at my sister's feet. None of them moved. None of them breathed—they were all dead. And I was the one who'd killed them.

I turned to Brooklynn, and saw that she wasn't alone. With her were Aron and Niko and Zafir. Max was there too. All of them staring back at me with the same wary expressions, and I couldn't blame them. I knew what they were looking at: a murderer.

"I told you she was in here," I said to Zafir. "I told you Sabara wasn't dead."

But it didn't matter, I told myself. Nothing else mattered except that Angelina was safe.

I spun around again, my eyes raking over the little girl in the bloodied nightgown. She just stood there, looking as dazed as the others. "Angelina," I whispered again, taking a step closer to her.

She ran then . . . but not to me.

She veered as far from me as she could in the confined space of the hallway, running to Brooklynn instead. She wrapped her arms around my best friend's waist, refusing to even glance my way.

Max stepped forward then. Max, who I was sure hated me

after seeing Niko's lips on mine. Max, who I had to find a way to explain things to, to make things right again. He reached for my hands, first one and then the other. I allowed a moment of hope to swell in my chest as relief flooded through me, and then I realized what he was really doing. That I'd still been holding them outstretched, like the weapons they'd become. He pushed my arms down, his eyes finding mine and searching them.

I blinked back tears that stung, not wanting him to see how ravaged I felt inside. "I'm still here too," I offered, hoping he'd believe me. Hoping that might be enough.

His fingers closed over mine, even though they didn't lace through them. "I know." But it didn't sound like an assurance, just a simple statement. *He knew.* Like he knew the sky was blue or the grass was green.

He pulled me then, trying to draw me away from the ghastly scene on the floor before us. But before I'd taken a single step, I froze. "Wait," I said, breaking away from him.

I crept closer to the man with the handgun, the man whose dead gaze stared blankly at the ceiling now. I dropped down, kneeling beside his body. Max was there too, hovering right above my shoulder. "What is it?" he asked.

I frowned as I reached for the slip of red material sticking out from the man's front pocket. I unfolded it, smoothing the edges down until I was looking at a square of fabric.

I glanced to his cohorts, each lying equally motionless. Another of the men had a similar square tied around his upper arm, and the third had one stuffed in his back pocket. I searched Jonas too, digging through his pockets and sliding my hand inside the front of his shirt, feeling his lifeless chest beneath my fingertips. He didn't have the same red fabric the others did, not that I could find.

That same simple fabric. Plain, yet familiar.

Red bandanas.

My stomach dropped as I remembered where I'd seen a bandana like them before. "Sebastian," I breathed, looking from Max to Zafir, from Brook to Aron. "It was Sebastian. He must've overheard us, maybe while he was readying the horses. He must've told them where to find us."

Brook turned away, holding Angelina even closer, and I wondered if it was hard for her to see her father like this. I wondered if, even after everything, she blamed me for killing him.

"Let me see that," Max said, reaching for the fabric I clutched. He ran his finger along the edges, where there was a darker red ink—a pattern, some sort of leaves or ivy. He looked up at me. "Did you hear them say anything?" he asked.

I glanced uncomfortably at Angelina, and I answered quietly, "They said to stop toying with the girl and finish it."

He stepped closer, gripping my hands in his. "But *how* did they say it, Charlie? What language did they speak?"

"I—I don't know," I answered, shaking my head. "I'd never heard it before. Why? What do you know?"

He turned to Zafir, lifting the square of fabric. "This is Queen Elena's insignia—the crimson laurel. It's the basis for her country's flag. These men were Astonian, and Sebastian must be too if he's working with them."

I glanced at the fabric, and recalled the flags I'd seen at Vannova, the night of the ball. I hadn't stopped to study them individually, I'd only taken in the splendor of them as a whole. But now that he said it, there had been a red one . . . one with a crimson laurel.

"They must've been speaking Gaullish, just like the writing on the map. I've never heard it aloud before; I didn't recognize its sound." I tried to imagine why these men, these Astonians, would want me dead. Why they would ally with Jonas Maier against me. And then I remembered that Queen Elena had tried to invade our country once before. "You don't think . . . Elena wouldn't dare. . . ."

Zafir stiffened. But it was Brook, her jaw tightening, who said the words aloud. "If she's behind this, then this is war."

BROOKLYNN

Brooklynn stared into the water at the edge of the pond, watching as the morning sun reflected off the surface and trying to decide what the hell was the matter with her. It wasn't as if she'd miss him, as if he'd been the kind of father who'd commanded love and respect. He'd done nothing but treat her as a servant from the moment her mother had died. And when she'd joined Charlie at the palace, he'd all but disowned her. She should be rejoicing his death.

So why did she ache? Why did she feel a hollow space where her heart had once been?

She squeezed her eyes shut, refusing to shed a single tear. She had no use for tears. Not now. Not over him.

"Brook?"

She spun without thinking, without needing to see who was approaching. She'd recognized the voice clearly enough. It was Charlie—her queen.

"Brook, I'm sorry," Charlie said in a voice filled with sincerity. She still wore the bloodied nightgown, covered only by a thin robe. "I—I didn't want to . . ." She didn't finish her sentence.

"Don't apologize," Brook said, her own voice flat, emotionless. She turned back toward the water that rippled with bursts of orange and pink and gold. "He doesn't deserve your apologies."

She could hear the footsteps behind her, as Charlie came closer, until they were standing shoulder-to-shoulder at the pond's edge. "No," Charlie agreed. "He doesn't. But you do. You're my friend, and I wouldn't hurt you for anything."

Something twisted in Brook's gut. *I'm not hurt,* she tried to convince herself, but she couldn't say the words aloud. She couldn't say anything at all to Charlie.

A long silence filled the space between them, and she wondered how long Charlie would stand there pretending that everything was okay between them. That killing her father was acceptable . . . justified or not.

She wondered too, when Charlie had become a killer. Or if it was even Charlie she stood beside now.

The idea that Sabara was in there—inside the body of her friend—made her skin itch.

Sabara who should have died months ago.

From the corner of her eye, Brooklynn saw Charlie move, her hand closing the gap between them, and she withdrew before the queen could touch her. "Brook . . ." Charlie's voice came out as a plea.

"Don't," Brook answered. "Just . . . don't."

There was a pause. "I'm so, *so* sorry," Charlie said at last.

Brook stayed where she was, forcing her gaze to remain fastened on the water long after the soft, swishing sound of fabric told her that Charlie had left her alone. Long after the sun had risen from its hiding place at the horizon and was climbing the clear blue sky. And long after her tears had dried and her sobs had subsided.

XX

I stripped out of the nightgown I'd been wearing, thinking I should have it burned. I'd had to pass the carnage in the estate hallways on the way back to my room, and it had reminded me, again and again, of why I'd had to do what I'd done . . . to Jacob Maier and to his men.

To Brooklynn.

It didn't matter, though; I couldn't worry that I'd made a mistake, or that I'd misused the power Sabara had afforded me. This wasn't the time for regrets of that sort. They would have killed Angelina.

Still, I couldn't help but wonder just how much of myself had been sacrificed when I'd allowed myself to succumb to Sabara's baser drives. Had I become a little more like her because of what I was capable of?

Or had Sabara simply revealed the darker side of my true nature?

I was no longer certain where Sabara ended and I began.

And then there was the other question, the one that

challenged everything I believed in: Had Sabara been right all along? Could peace in Ludania only be maintained through violence? Through imposed will?

Had the class system kept people in check?

It couldn't be true, I insisted silently as I pulled a simple embroidered top over my head. *The New Equality will work; it just needs time.*

I looked up when I heard the door open, and my heart skipped.

"Max?" I breathed, grateful to see him. Grateful that he, at least, hadn't turned his back on me entirely, the way Brooklynn had seemed to.

"May I come in?"

"Of course. I have so much to tell you, so much I need to explain." My words rushed out as I struggled with where to start. I prayed I could do this. "That thing . . . last night in the hallway with Niko . . . That wasn't me in control. I swear it."

He shook his head, and I wasn't sure if he was telling me that he didn't believe me, or that he didn't want to hear it, but his face crumpled, making him look wounded. I took a breath. "I should have told you," I uttered. "I wanted to tell you, but I didn't know how. I was so . . . so afraid. At first, I thought I could handle it. I thought Angelina could help me get rid of her. And then, after time passed, and I realized she wasn't leaving—that I was stuck with her—I didn't know how to explain it—how to explain her. Not without sounding"—my chin inched up a notch as I took a steadying breath—"*insane.* But you have to believe me, Max; I didn't mean to hurt you. I would never hurt you."

"And what about that other thing . . . that you did to the men who were holding Angelina hostage?" His eyes held mine as he asked me about their murder. "Was that Sabara too?"

I knew what he wanted to hear. He wanted me to tell him that I wasn't responsible then, either, but I couldn't.

I shook my head, trying to feel ashamed for what I'd done. But I wasn't sorry, not for that. "No. That was just me. That was me saving my sister."

Max's gaze drifted over me, and I tried to imagine what it was he was searching for. "I suppose I have to accept that. I even understand it, sort of. The rest of it, I don't know yet. I haven't figured out how I feel. It's strange, the idea of Sabara living inside of you. . . . She was my *grandmother*."

"But that's just it—she wasn't." My words tumbled over one another. I had to make him understand this much, at least. "That woman—the body that was your grandmother—is dead. The woman inside of me, the Essence I carry, is ancient, going back further than either of us can imagine." I pictured the little girl standing ankle-deep in the river's current. I could see the terror in her sister's eyes as the girl was dragged beneath the water's surface, savaged by a creature neither of them could see. "It's not Sabara, not really. I don't even know her true name. . . . Her *original* name."

His brow crumpled as he started to take a step toward me, but he stopped himself. "Why Niko, Charlie? Why him?"

My eyes burned and my throat ached. I wasn't sure Niko's secrets were mine to tell, but I didn't have a choice any more. Sabara had backed me into a corner.

"Niko is ancient too," I admitted. "Sabara has memories of

him that go back as far as I can see. He loves her, the Essence I carry. But it's not me he loves, it's her."

He glanced out the window then, his eyes growing distant. I waited for him to say something more, but he was silent, his shoulders stiff and his hands clasped behind his back. He looked stiff and resolute, and faraway.

He didn't ask any more questions about Niko or Sabara, and he didn't push me for details, the way I'd imagined he would.

He also didn't say what I'd hoped to hear: that he could forgive me. But he was still there, still with me all the same.

For now, that had to be enough.

I stayed where I was, watching him. I could be patient. I could wait until he was ready to talk again.

And then I heard her. . . . Sabara. She'd been silent throughout the night and long into the morning as I'd struggled with what I'd done. But she'd been there. I'd felt her. And now her voice was small but clear. *Layla,* she said. *My name was Layla.*

EPILOGUE

I sat in the gardens, letting the night wrap around me like a shawl, even as I drew my arms around myself to ward away the chill. The first snow had fallen on the palace, leaving a thin layer of crystalline flakes that coated everything. It reminded me of Vannova. Of the days when I still had friends and people who loved me.

Sebastian had been long gone by the time we'd returned to the palace, along with any clues linking him to Queen Elena or Astonia. But that didn't mean he didn't leave evidence of his duplicity behind.

Before he'd vanished, he'd killed one of the stable boys, and the only explanation anyone could come up with was that somehow the boy had learned what Sebastian was up to, or discovered his true identity. The boy had just turned twelve.

Niko and Xander had set out after Sebastian, hoping to catch up with him before he'd gotten too far. They'd wanted answers. We all did. Declaring war was tricky business, and none of us wanted to act too rashly.

As it turned out, we didn't need Sebastian's confirmation that Queen Elena was involved in the conspiracy. Brook had found enough evidence when she'd gone to tend to her father's business. He'd been using his butcher shop as a means to communicate—sending messages hidden inside the meat parcels. Brook had discovered plenty of damning information when she'd torn his place apart.

His extremism had made him careless.

But none of that changed the fact that Brook was still barely talking to me.

I didn't push her, though. Maybe she'd never get over what I'd done. Maybe no one would.

Angelina hadn't.

Max either.

He pretended to. He tried to. But things weren't the same between him and me. Neither of us said as much, but I could feel the difference—in his words, his actions, his touch.

When he was ready, I'd explained as much as I could to him. I told him about Niko, and the connection he and Sabara—who had once been a little girl named Layla—shared. I held nothing back, and maybe that was the problem. It was all too much. It was all too strange.

Could I blame him for pulling away from me, when I wanted to pull away from myself?

Sabara was the only constant in my life. She was the only one who hadn't changed after everything that had happened.

She was still here, inside of me. And still promising to help me.

I wasn't sure how I felt about that. . . . Now more than ever.

She'd let me save my sister; how could I ever repay that?

By letting Niko stay, she'd repeated time and time again. And I hadn't answered her, one way or the other, which was an answer in itself, I supposed.

"Mind if I join you?" It was Avonlea, her thick coat buttoned up to her chin.

I smiled as I scooted over, despite the fact that there was plenty of room on the bench beside me.

She sat, and we were quiet for a long while. Avonlea, like Sabara, had become permanent. She'd taken a liking to my father—or rather he to her—and he'd started mentoring her in the kitchens. I doubted she needed the tutelage, especially since I'd tasted her cooking, but she seemed to enjoy his company. I think, in a peculiar way, a part of her missed Floss. He had been the father she'd never had.

"Everyone'll get over it, you know? Even Angelina," she said at last.

I just shrugged, unconvinced. I'd thought that once too, especially about my sister. I thought, once the dust had settled and we'd found Eden injured but alive, that Angelina would forgive me. Or at least stop looking at me like I was some sort of monster.

But she hadn't.

Yet I didn't fault her, not really. Because I realized, it wasn't *me* she hated. It was that she no longer knew me, that she could no longer trust whether it was even *me* she was looking at. "I don't know. Maybe they shouldn't. You weren't there, Avonlea. Maybe I'm too dangerous to be around."

She snorted and shoved me with her shoulder. "You're

crazy." And I knew that she, at least, didn't mean it in the literal sense. "You," she said, more seriously now, "are the kindest person I've ever known." I glanced up at her, afraid to trust the sincerity in her voice. "You saved me."

"Charlie, wait." Max's voice stopped me just before I slipped inside my bedroom. Zafir wasn't with me tonight as he and Claude met with Brooklynn to coordinate mounting our defenses at home.

My new guard turned away when Max reached me.

"Xander and Niko are back." And before I could ask, he shook his head, reading my thoughts. "No word on Sebastian. They lost his trail near Astonia's border."

"Dammit." I exhaled. "So what now?"

"Xander's leaving in the morning to Astonia. He and Elena were friends once, or at least he thought they were. He wants to ask what her intentions are. He wants to hear it from her directly."

"Why would she tell him the truth?" I asked.

Max shrugged. "She might not. But then again, she doesn't have any reason to lie. If she wants you dead, she might as well just admit as much. We've already discovered the messages, presumably in her hand, to Brooklynn's father. Denying it just makes her a liar."

"And if she doesn't deny it? If she admits she was behind the plot to have me killed?"

Max came closer to me then, and his nearness made my heart lurch. His hand moved up and down my shoulder, almost absently. "Then we have no choice. We have to protect you."

I closed my eyes, not wanting it to be a duty—his allegiance. Wanting it to stem from desire.

"It'll be okay," he said, misreading my hesitation.

I looked at him again. "I know."

I turned, then, to go into my room, needing to be alone so I could sort through my tangled emotions.

"Charlie?" he said, pulling me back to face him. "I do love you." My breath caught on his words . . . words I'd waited so long to hear. His fingertips found mine, just barely. "I just need time. Not much, just enough to get used to . . ." He grinned as he watched the skin beneath his touch ignite. And then he was reaching for me, and his lips were on mine, and we were kissing desperately, and the world faded away around us.

When I finally drew away, just enough so I could breathe again, I glanced up at him, my gaze sheepish. "I thought you needed time," I teased.

Max's grip, when he reached for me the second time, was confident. And final. "I lied."